ME: THE BEGINNING

AKHIL S. VERNAS

I dedicate this book to three people-
My Father- Varun Sharma,
My Mother- Pallavi Sharma,
My Best Friend (My Bro)- Saurav Sharma

Contents

Preface vii

1. The NDJJC 1
2. Capitrolis & Alex 4
3. School & A New Crush? 8
4. Happy Birthday Alex! 22
5. Where Is Everyone? 28
6. Alex Blows Up A Building 31
7. Cyclone In Cheniaros! 36
8. A Non-human Friend? 42
9. Gopiz Goes Into Hibernation 48
10. Alex Surveys The ISROEM Centre 52
11. Visiting Jessica's House 59
12. Study Time? 78
13. First Automated Meal 86
14. Last Day At Home 101
15. Back To SpaceVillage 105
16. Day One At ISROEM 115
17. The Manufacturing Process 122
18. The Pulldown 135
19. Journey To Russia 141
20. From Prisoners To Guests 148
21. A Tour Of Moskva 154
22. Back To India 160
23. Manufacturing Again! 172
24. A Memorable Evening 176
25. The Final Pulldown 188

Outro 197

About the Author 199

Preface

So being just a teenager, it was never easy to write and publish a book on my own. But well, this story hit me different, and is quite close to me, probably due to its history and journey as a story.

I must be proud of myself, of this unique idea of this story, that popped up into my mind when I was just in sixth grade. I do consider myself as quite different. I have less friends than others- probably due to my 'quality' rather than 'quantity' approach, I think everything with a high degree of farsightedness, and I can call myself slightly lazy, but still a person who dares to dream things close to impossible. I'm best known as 'The boy who wants to create his own country- Akstonea', but well, that's a different story. When I got the idea of this story, I was about to finish my sixth grade. But then, this story was in a form of a screenplay rather than a novel or book. I wanted to create a movie. Now obviously I didn't have much budget, so I had called of the sci-fi aspects of the story, while keeping the main plot intact. I invited some of my classmates, who were also as dumb as me back then, and gave different characters to different friends. Someone became William, and the guy I knew as one of my close friends became Alex. Our sixth grade ended, and we even planned the locations, shooting and other stuff.

But well you can give the credit of this story taking the form of a book or novel to a thing we all are familiar with- Coronavirus Pandemic of 2020. Lockdowns were imposed, and our movie plans were called off. I was quite hurt, because this was a story that I wanted the world to see, read or experience. So I opened up a Google Docs document, and started writing some of the story. But then with time, I abandoned it, and got busy in other aspects of my life. Unfortunately, the remaining story remained shut inside my mind for months and some more years. And then, suddenly last year in 2024, a young lady inspired me. She reminded me of my long lost dream, of making ME - The Beginning a reality. Well I cannot dedicate this book to her yet, due to some specific reasons I wouldn't disclose. Anyways, 2024 was the year I got back to writing, and with my consistent efforts and months of determination, I finished this novel the same day my 11th Grade final exams got over.

Now because this book is writter by a non-adult, that is, a kid- many people would treat it as a boring or silly story. To such people, I only want to say one dialogue- "If you don't read this, I have no idea what you'll miss."

Perhaps the best experience of this novel would be to daringly imagine each and every scene that is being described. After reading this book, and its sequels, you'll view not only this world but the universe from an entirely different perspective.

That's my promise!

ONE

THE NDJJC

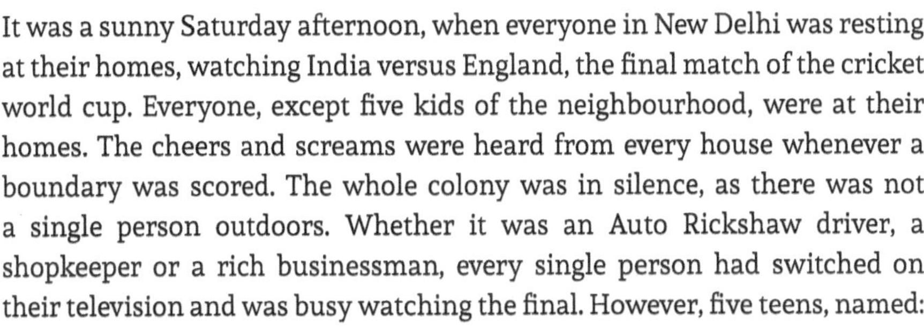

It was a sunny Saturday afternoon, when everyone in New Delhi was resting at their homes, watching India versus England, the final match of the cricket world cup. Everyone, except five kids of the neighbourhood, were at their homes. The cheers and screams were heard from every house whenever a boundary was scored. The whole colony was in silence, as there was not a single person outdoors. Whether it was an Auto Rickshaw driver, a shopkeeper or a rich businessman, every single person had switched on their television and was busy watching the final. However, five teens, named: Aryan, Rhea, Sandeep, Garima and Peter, had different plans.

Aryan, the head of NDJJC or 'New Delhi Junior Journalists Company', an initiative started by Aryan and his four friends Rhea, Sandeep, Garima and Peter, was ordering his friends. "Rhea, turn on all the lights." "Sandeep, set up the camera, mic and the recorder." "Garima, remove unnecessary stuff from the interview table." "Peter, just stop playing video games and help us!" The whole group of five friends, or can be called as the whole crew of NDJJC, was busy setting up their small cabin, for the interview with William Gates, a fifteen-year old teenager, who shifted to India from the United States when he was seven.

"Oh my god, I'm panicking! William will be here any moment now." exclaimed Aryan. "Well don't be anxious, it's his interview, not ours." replied Rhea. "Oh look! I did 17 kills in this match. I have become a real expert in this game–" said Peter. "Oof! I'm really irritated with your playing of video games. Just grow up Peter!" replied Garima angrily. "Ugh... Fine!" said Peter. Suddenly, the doorbell rang. Aryan was horrified. "It must be William. He is coming today for an interview, right?" said Peter, not showing much concern. Garima opened the cabin's door. "Hey, guys! This is NDJJC, right?"

asked William. "Welcome to NDJJC sir! I'm Garima, she's Rhea, this is Peter, here's Sandeep and this is Aryan, our chief journalist." Garima introduced her teammates and herself to William. "Nice to meet you all!" replied William.

"So, it's a nice and cool cabin! And yea... I really like that video game. I play it too. Who amongst you all plays it?" asked William. Everyone pointed towards Peter. "You're Peter? You're American?" asked William again. "Ummm No... I was born in Scotland, but my parents are Indian. So I'm an Indian too." replied Peter. William replied- "Oh! Okay." Then Aryan changed the topic, and started his business talk- "So about this story you were telling about before, you said it's your great great great grandson's story?" Everyone was stunned. The astonished eyes looked at William, waiting for an answer. He was embarrassed a bit because he was too shy, so took a while to reply- "Technically, Yes." "What?! I mean, you can look into the future?" asked Sandeep. "How and why do you know about your great great great grandson?" asked Rhea. "What is your User ID on this game?" asked Peter, the dumbest question. William started saying- "Oof. So many questions at a time! The thing is, let me begin with the time when I was going to bed, one week ago. I was singing a song to myself and went to brush my teeth. When I took my brush and saw myself in the mirror, I didn't see myself! I saw a boy, who looked 2-3 years younger than me, and just said- "Do you know me, great-great-great grandfather?" I was stunned! And suddenly looked back at the mirror, then saw myself. I was horrified that night and really creeped out-" Suddenly Aryan interrupted, "Sorry to interrupt Aryan, but can I switch on the mic and camera? Just for recording the story?" William replied- "No-no-no. You don't need to switch them on now, because this is just a teaser of the real story."

Everyone was now so excited to listen to the whole story, that everyone brought their stools and formed a semi-circle type formation in front of William. "It is really stressful and weird to even think about this story. Because, I saw this whole story in my dreams at night, while sleeping, continuing its series in parts, one after another, starting from the night I saw the boy in the mirror. I saw the whole series of these stories, for 5 continuous nights during the week before last week." William described more. "Okay, so this story is a real or a true story of the future? Like you looked into the future?" asked Rhea. "Well, you can say that." replied William. "But how are you so sure that this story is about the future? Like it can also be an illusion or something?" asked Aryan. "See, I felt the same after seeing the first dream and waking up the next day. But, when I completed the whole series, I understood the continuation of stories one after another, then the same topics of all these dreams in the sleep, and all these hints which were given to me, actually proved that this might be the future. Otherwise where do such big coincidences happen?" said William.

William then said that he would be starting with his story now, so Aryan commanded his team to switch on the camera and mic to record it. The whole cabin was lightened up, and everyone was instantly ready to listen to the story. It was 2:00 in the afternoon when William started with his story...

TWO
CAPITROLIS & ALEX

It was a cloudy evening in Capitrolis, in the year 2162. Flying Drones and vehicles were in a rush. The city was dazzling with lights, and skyscrapers as tall as Mount Everest were touching the sky. Capitrolis was the new name of the city of 'New Delhi'. Since the new century, many Indian cities, places and river names had been changed. The Yamuna river which flowed near New Delhi was renamed as 'Yartrunas river', but the country's name was the same: India. And yes, then too, New Delhi, I mean- Capitrolis was still the capital city of India. New Delhi and Delhi merged to form the newly renamed city, with new and modern architecture and designs, named Capitrolis.

In a green field of football, two teams were playing football professionally and with energy. The yellow team tried to beat the blue team. "Alex! Pass me the ball!" "No Alex! Pass ME the ball!" Everyone was just trying to cooperate with an expert young footballer, who was just 12 years old. Despite his age, he used to play with teenagers of 16-19 years of age, because he played better than those teenagers too. "And GOAL!!!" Everyone screamed as Alex scored a Goal. "Yay Alex! You nailed it again! Kuddos Bro!" All Alex's teammates were so happy that they bought him drinks and munchies. Of course, soft-drinks like Cola.

They happily were talking about their match, the goal misses, the strategies they applied and were having fun, in the park of their society, which was a complex of apartment towers of 80 floors each. Alex, the player of the match, is my great great great grandson, in the story. So, he was having fun with his older friends. Some were telling him to join an academy, some were suggesting him to build up a body, and some told him to try impressing girls with his skills. But Alex was a pure-hearted, emotional and cheerful child. He believed in his own potential and was a motivated young teen.

He finally took leave and entered the glass elevator of his building, to head to his home. "Elevis, take me to Floor 71st," commanded Alex, to the smart elevator. "Roger That." The voice recognition replied. The elevator was pretty fast. But it still took a minute to reach his floor. The doors opened up, Elevis (voice recognition AI voice) said, "Floor 71st." Alex walked up in the corridors, to the main door of his apartment. He clicked a button and a scanner came out of the main door, doing a retina scan. "Retina Scan Successful. Welcome Home Alex!" the doors opened up.

"Hey Alex! How was your match?" Alex's Mom asked him. "I guess he lost." replied Sierra, Alex's elder sister, with sarcasm. "Huh. Yeah it was great. My team won by 6 goals difference." replied Alex. "That's great. Well, the day-after tomorrow is your birthday, so me and your mom are thinking of giving you a SateRadar as a gift." said Alex's dad. Alex's eyes widened up! "A SateRadar! My dream Gift!" Alex exclaimed. A SateRadar was nothing but a computer monitor, simply known as the Radar, which showed all People on Earth's location with signals and all. The radar is linked to a common satellite orbiting the earth which scans the whole world and shows live telecasts of people's location, with the help of thermal energy. However it won't show who a particular person is, just a red dot representing a person.

SateRadars were really in trend in the 2160s and all teens loved to see billions of people at the same screen, on a world map, with zooming, location and everything. Alex wanted it too, so he was really happy when he got to know that he was getting one. He was really happy that night. "What's dinner for tonight?" asked Alex. "Well, Mom was making sandwiches, but now we're thinking of ordering a few Cheese Rolls." replied Alex's dad. "This is perhaps the best day of my life! I love it!" said Alex. Sierra scoffed. Alex rolled his eyes and went to his room. The view of the skyline from his room's window was exactly like the 71st floor of Burj Khalifa. It was just beautiful! Alex switched on the yellow lights of his room, and opened the curtains. "I am really going to miss this view, especially when I go to Educity." Alex mumbled. "Awww... Will you?" Sierra mocked him, standing on his room's door. "Look sis, just because I am gifted in Mathematics and Physics and got a chance to go to Educity from 7th grade onwards, and just because you didn't get that opportunity, doesn't mean you have the right to mock me."

said Alex briefly. "Yeah, yeah, blah-di-blah, Maths and stuff, Physics and stuff, equations, and all those stupid numbers and variables that don't make any sense to me." said Sierra. "Why don't you just go to your room and listen to those stupid Korean songs? Why disturbing me?" taunted Alex. "Sierra! Alex! Stop arguing and take your dinner. The Drone just delivered the cheese rolls. Hurry up!"

Both the kids rushed to the Kitchen. They took their plates and went to their rooms. Alex enjoyed the cheese rolls while watching his favourite Web Series, on his Airtop (a hovering laptop). The series was about saving the world, war on other planets, spaceships, and all that. After he finished his dinner, he switched off his Airtop, and sat on a chair in his balcony, with a sandalwood candle lightened up. The drones, the cityscape, calmed Alex. "The only thing I want is never leaving this place. Capitrolis, the capital of India- the world's current richest and most developed country with over 3 Billion people living in it!" he said to himself. Then he brought a guitar, and sat on the chair in the balcony, and played chords on guitar, while singing a beautiful song.

At 11 'o' clock, the drone traffic used to stop, and the city used to go to sleep. This rule of sleeping at 11 'o' clock was called- 'The 23-Sleep Rule', 23, denoted as eleven 'o' clock in a 24-hour format. This rule was made by the Government of India, for all cities, to conserve electricity and energy for future use. It was not mandatory, but widely accepted and implemented, and the city services used to shut down after 11, and started again at 5 'o' clock in the morning.

So, Alex went to bed, and slept peacefully, remembering that he has to go to school tomorrow. Alex was brilliant in Mathematics and Physics. Thinking of choosing Science as the main subject in future, his parents were sending him to Educity, a kind of city where there were Advanced Education centres or Schools, which were only for gifted and talented students. In the year 2120, many students started to become exceptionally brilliant in many fields. By 2140 these numbers rose so much that in 2146 the Government of India gave a project to some company to make a city with Schools of different subjects, where advanced and gifted students can get better education according to their level, and named this new city for students as Educity. It was constructed in the direction of North-east to Capitrolis, and many residential areas for students and teachers were also constructed. Alex was also going to Educity after completing his 6th grade from his regular school, to live there as an Educity Student. So he was going to miss his home, in Capitrolis.

THREE

SCHOOL & A NEW CRUSH?

The next morning, he woke up and got ready for school. "Bye Mom! Bye Dad!" Alex took a leave from his home and went to the nearest School Metro Station. In 2162, the school bus system ended. Most schools started using the metro transportation system, which consisted of small metro trains for kids, which were compact yet fast. These metros from all over the city went to a common terminal called the- All School Terminal. From here, from the other side of the metro line, other metro trains departed from the terminal, to respective schools. So for students to reach their school, they first used to go to their nearest metro station, climb on the metro train heading to All School Terminal, then boarded the metro train on the other side of the terminal, to their respective schools.

Alex was waiting for the metro to arrive. It was a cloudy and hazy morning, at 7:00 AM. The metro arrived, almost full of kids. "Oh right. Kids want to take the first metro to the terminal, always!" mumbled Alex. He swiped his ID Card and boarded the train. He got a seat in the last coach. The seat arrangement of these metro trains were just like passenger planes' seating. Two seats on left, two on right, and an aisle in between. They were quite like a flight's premium class seats. The rear side of the seats were occupied with a sound jack, a mini computer touchscreen, and a music player, to listen to music. It was a driverless metro, with a few teachers boarded in the first coach, and the rest three coaches of the metro train were for the students. A pretty impressive train, yet the students didn't like the crowd, and so didn't Alex.

He sat on the leather seat, beside which was sitting a girl with headphones, vibing to some song. Alex said- "Ummmm excuse me." No answer. He repeated- "Excuse me." Again, no answer. Then he waved his hand and caught the girl's attention. "Uh yes?" the girl replied. Alex sighed and said- "Could you lower down the volume? I have a test so I gotta revise for it. The music is loud and the sound is literally coming out of the headphones too." "Do you have a problem with music, nerdy kid?" asked the girl, who was senior to him, maybe 1-2 years. Alex just got irritated, and went to another empty seat behind. The 'Fasten Seat Belt' sign showed up and the doors of the train closed.

Alex opened his Physics book and started revising the formulas. He then got tired and looked outside the window. Capitrolis's skyscrapers and buildings were glittering in the morning sunlight, and the beautiful green trees were looking peaceful. The city was literally a futuristic heaven on earth. He then saw the metro television screen, showing how many stations are remaining to stop on before the Terminal arrives. "5 more stations? Oof." mumbled Alex. He got really bored, for the first time in the train, suddenly he saw another girl, who was solving a physics equation, on the metro's window, as well as its inside wall, with a thick black marker. She had straight hair, wore glasses, and was very dedicated to solving the equation. She was sitting in the same row of Alex's but the opposite side of the aisle.

Before the metro stopped at the next station, Alex whispered to the girl- "Psst. What are you doing? That is the metro's window and wall, you might have to pay a huge fine for what you are doing." "Bro just shut up, I am very close to calculating the velocity of this object." the girl replied back. Alex was stunned. For the first time he saw a maniac student writing on the walls and windows of a metro train.

The next station arrived. The doors opened. A small kid of a junior grade sat next to that girl. He was too surprised to see someone write numbers and letters on the metro's wall and window. "Excuse me, are you doodling? It is nice!" said the kid to the girl. The girl was so busy solving that equation, that when she ran out of space, she said to the kid- "Show me your hand." The kid showed his hand, and the girl continued solving the equation on the child's hand! He was trying to withdraw his hand but she was not leaving his arm. Stations came and went, and 2 minutes were left to reach the Terminal. When the girl was finished solving the equation on the window, the entire wall beside the window, both of the child's hands, both her hands and even the seat she was sitting on, she finally said- "Done! Finally! The velocity of the object is 16 kilometres per second." The kid, and Alex, literally clapped after she said this, but also clapped sarcastically for all the metro property that the girl spoiled. "Thank you! Thank you." The girl thanked them for their applause and smiled brainlessly.

When the Terminal Station arrived, Alex couldn't wait more to board the metro to his own school. He boarded out of the metro he came from, leaving the responsibility to tell the authorities that a girl spoiled a lot of metro's property, with a marker. He swiped his ID card again, and entered to the other side of the terminal, where he went to the platform where the metro heading to his school started. He reached the platform, just to see that there was no train, just a crowd of students near vending machines, trying to buy packets of chewing gum. He just sat on a bench he saw, waiting for his school's metro to arrive, when suddenly he heard a familiar voice. "Okay. So if the mass of the object is equal to the mass of another object, then its total acceleration will be x. Find x. Easy question." The voice was of the same girl who spoiled the metro walls and seat in the metro Alex and she came from. Now he got irritated. He tried to avoid being seen by the girl, who immediately identified him. "Aren't you the guy who was stopping me from solving the equation in the Terminal Metro?" said the girl, to Alex. Alex simply acted like he didn't hear her. "I'm Jessica. Jessica Smith. I am from Yartrunas International School." said the girl. "Wait, Yartrunas International School?!" Alex asked. "Yeah, I am a new admission there, starting from today." replied Jessica. "Which grade are you in?" asked Alex. "Grade 6th." Alex panicked now. Jessica was in the same school, as Alex. "Okay, okay." said Alex in a nervous way.

Suddenly he saw his teacher- Mrs Sharma. His teacher came to him and said- "Good Morning Alex! Prepared for the test? Oh look! You met with your new classmate Jessica already?" "Ma'am she's in my class?" "Of course she is! She is starting her session from today, you gotta help her from now on. It seems you are friends already. That's great!" replied Mrs Sharma. Jessica smiled. Alex panicked and said- "Ow. Ma'am I am having a stomach ache, can I go back home?" "Alex, enough of your acting. Our metro's about to come in 2 minutes. You already have the Physics test today. Except that, Jessica can skip the test as she is new." replied Mrs Sharma. "No ma'am, actually I would love to give the test, I am good in Physics so yes I'll be able to take the test." replied Jessica, confidently. "That's great then! Good

Jessica! Alex, learn something from her." replied Mrs Sharma. Alex's face was like an angry ostrich. He was already so irritated by Jessica that the thought of her being in his same class, for another half year until the year is finished, is fearful, and Alex was stunned. To be honest, Alex was irritated with Jessica's doings- ruining a metro's window, wall, seat, and basically almost everything. Her straightforwardness made him feel irritated.

The metro came, and Mrs Sharma, Alex and Jessica boarded the train. Unfortunately for Alex, Mrs Sharma stared and gestured to Alex to sit beside Jessica, to 'welcome and introduce himself to the new student'. So Alex was under pressure because he really didn't want to sit with her. The metro doors closed, and the journey to their school started. After the metro left the All School Terminal Station, Jessica asked- "So, Alex. How's your school? Like can you introduce it to me?" "Oh, yes. It's quite weird. But if you can become the topper here, well you'll like it." replied Alex, without making eye contact. "So, do you like it?" asked Jessica. "I don't know. I will be in Educity next year, so I really don't care." replied Alex, again without making eye contact.

Jessica understood that Alex was not interested in talking. After a pause, she said- "Look Alex, I am a Science freak. Once I start doing something related to it, I can't stop. Sorry about what I did in the metro, but I don't know why, I couldn't resist." said Jessica. Alex was stunned that Jessica was sorry for spoiling the metro. He then thought that she understood that she did something wrong, and was sorry about it, and decided to forgive her. "Well, it's kinda okay. Just, you might have to pay the fine for it. The metro has security cameras." replied Alex. "Oh don't worry about that. I'll do some chores, and babysit a few kids, and earn money for it." replied Jessica. Alex started making eye contact with her now, seeing how unique she is. She could have just said that she'll ask for the money from her parents, but she is independent. Now Alex started to get involved in conversations with Jessica. He told her about his life at school, and about the bullies and all, and told that this School also is hard to be in. And Jessica too talked with Alex. They both talked the whole way to school, and soon started to become good friends.

The Yartrunas International School's station arrived. The metro stopped and all the children and teachers got off the train. They headed to the School campus, Alex and Jessica talking to each other, while walking to their school building. "Wow! It's a big school." said Jessica. "Indeed, it is!" replied Alex. "Don't you ever get lost here? So many corridors, classrooms, pathways?" asked Jessica in surprise. "Well, that's why I asked for a map of the school when I was new, and I got it." replied Alex. They both headed to their classrooms. They entered the hexagon shaped large classroom, with benches, teacher's table and the E-Board, a futuristic white board in which writing and drawing things, and explaining topics was easy.

They sat on two classroom benches placed beside each other. After some time, Mrs Sharma entered the class and said- "Good Morning Class!" "Good Morning Ma'am!" replied the students. "I hope you prepared for the test, but before starting with it, I would like to announce that we have a new student in our class- Jessica Smith. Jessica, please introduce yourself." said Mrs Sharma. "Hello class, I am Jessica Smith, from Nexionsia, shifted to Capitrolis a few days back. I have a huge interest in Mathematics and Science, and I love dancing too. Thank You." Jessica introduced herself to the class.

"Thank you Jessica! Now, everyone open up your notetabs, and start writing your test with the stylus. No need to write the test questions, just see them on the E-Board and write your own answers. And no-cheating!" said Mrs Sharma. Notetabs were notebook-like tablets, with large screens, which had features like touch-screen, and storing notes of all subjects in a single notetab. "All the best, Alex." said Jessica. Alex wished her back too. They both started their test, and finished it before-time. "Ma'am I am finished with the test!" both of them said together, with maybe a one-second break. Surprised, Mrs Sharma checked their notetabs. When everyone's tests were checked, the results were- Alex got 94% on his test, while Jessica made the highest score in the class of 98.5%. Alex got a new competitor. But he was happy for her.

Later, in the 2nd period, during the history class, both of them were giggling and laughing at silly things. Like about the history of the War of East Asia in 2076, when the whole world was ready to fight China because of a funny meme Chinese Government created about global warming of that time, made them laugh like monsters. Yes, that chapter was funny, because it showed the power of a silly joke. All the revolts in China, how the world united against China, just because of a meme or joke, fascinated them. Further, in the Snack Break One, they both went to the terrace garden of the school, from where from one side, a part of the Capitrolis city's skyline was visible and on the other side, Educity's campus buildings and residential zones were visible, and Yartrunas River flowing in between. Few other kids and teachers were also in the terrace garden, sitting on benches, playing tag and talking to each other.

"So, after all you're really good at Physics." said Alex, to Jessica, before taking a bite of an apple. "Ummm... I practise physics in all my free time, so yeah, I kind of try my best in the subject." replied Jessica. "Tell me more about yourself. Do you have any friends in this city?" asked Alex. "My situation is kinda weird. You see, I am pretty much an introvert, and stay away from people. But when I am confident or busy in my hobbies, I have the ability to become an extrovert, and my behaviour changes. Due to this weird combination, many kids and people try to avoid talking to me. You're the first kid in this city, who took interest in talking with me." replied Jessica, with a sigh. Alex felt bad for her. So to charm her, he took her to the Virtual Reality Room, so she could enjoy and cheer up a bit. They both enter the dark room, with its walls, ceiling and floors, everything made of smartphone like screen, huge in size, with black background and tiny white dots just like stars in the night sky. "Whoa, what's this?" asked Jessica. "Welcome to the Virtual Reality Room! A technology nobody cared about after 2050, and left it as it is. But our school since the last 10 years has focused on its development. With the help of brilliant students and teachers, we were able to create amazing illusions! You just stand on this room's floor, and you will feel like you are in some place you want to be!" said Alex, while describing the room. "So, where do you wanna go?" asked Alex, while starting the software of the Virtual Reality Controller. "I want to see myself in the centre of Paris, my dream place." said Jessica. "Hmmm... Sure... Welcome to Paris!" said Alex, while clicking a button. Suddenly the whole room's screens started to create illusions on the screen, and the machine switched on, and created a sphere like illusion around Alex and Jessica, just so lifelike that they felt like they were in Paris. The crowd's background sound was also so realistic that Jessica literally felt that she was standing right in Paris city's streets. "This is amazing!" said Jessica. "I know right? I always come here during breaks." replied Alex. Suddenly, there was a warning message all over the walls, floor and ceiling of the room- "Warning: Machine is overheated. Please Shut Down in 15 seconds, to avoid any machinery fire." and a beeping sound started. "Alex! Shut it down right now!" said Jessica. Alex ran to the controller and shutted the machine down. The room turned back to the dark, and starry background. "This is the only problem. This machine doesn't run for more than a minute or two." said Alex, frustrated. "It's okay, let's head back to the class. The break is almost over. But even for a minute, I loved it!" replied Jessica.

Alex and Jessica exited the room and went back to their class. They reached their classroom and sat on their respective benches. The Astronomy teacher entered the classroom. "Good Morning Sir!" all the students wished the teacher. "Good morning class. I hope you had a great snack break. Sit down." replied the teacher. After clicking an option on the E-Board, the digital windows of the room turned opaque and dark, making the classroom dark as well. "So today let's study about the nearby celestial objects in our universe, through holograms." said the teacher, after making the classroom dark and switching off the lights. Then he clicked another option on the E-Board, by which a 3-Dimensional Hologram like illusion was made where the teacher was standing, with blue celestial object illusions with labels, and their orbits. Even the Earth, Sun and all planets were visible in the hologram. Jessica was amazed, after seeing another branch of illusions. She was pretty much impressed with the school's technology and infrastructure. The period passed, and the students were studying astronomical observations. The next period, while the English lecture was going on, someone drew a cartoon doodle of a boy and a girl holding hands, on the E-Board through their Notetab, and labelling them Alex and Jessica. The whole class bursted into laughter. "Okay. Silence please! Who the heck is doing this rubbish on the E-Board using their Notetab? The doodling feature is for doubts and edits. Not for this nonsense! Let me just check the recent edits." said the English teacher. He checked the last edit on the E-Board and said- "Charles, please stand up and get out of my class." the teacher said and punished the child who did this.

After the snack break two, and several more periods, finally it was the lunch break of 1 hour. Alex and Jessica were quiet and didn't talk to each other until lunch break, after what happened in English class. In the school dining area, after getting their meals, Alex said- "Hey Jessica... Sorry about my classmate Charles. He is kind of my enemy and friend as well, and keeps irritating me." "You don't need to feel sorry for it. It's fine. I am habitual of this stuff. Nexionsia's students were worse. They humiliated me more than this. So yeah, I don't care about all this now." replied Jessica with ease. During their lunch, when they were sitting opposite to each other, on the table, in the school's large dining area, a senior boy from Grade 9th or 10th said to Alex- "Hey Alex the nerd! I see you have a new friend. Do you only talk to newcomers or something? Idiot fellow." Jessica was full of anger with what that boy who was sitting at a table a few metres away from Alex and Jessica's table, with his friends, said to Alex. "Alex, hold my plate and watch this." said Jessica. "Wait, what are you doing?!" Alex asked in curiosity and panic. Jessica takes out a metal electronic magnet-like device, with springs and buttons attached. "What's this?" asked Alex. "I present you- My first ever invention- Metal Electro-magnetic Polar Attraction Metal Attacher, or simply MEPAMA." said Jessica. "I request you, don't use this." said Alex. "As if I'll listen to you. Just wait and see what this Mepama can do." replied Jessica. Alex was in shock to see Jessica so aggressive towards that senior bully. Just sitting on her chair, Jessica clicked a button on the 2-inch sized Mepama, and first signalled the Mepama radar, to the metal badges on the senior's school bag that he was wearing, and then threw the Mepama at the big metal banner of the canteen's menu display. The Mepama got attached to the metal menu display. In just a few seconds, the Mepama's light blinked, and the senior grader literally was dragged towards the menu display's banner, and everyone saw him struggling to stay on the ground, but then Jessica clicked a button on her remote, and the senior grader started hovering over the ground, slowly and steadily moving towards the exact place where the Mepama was stuck. All the teachers, and students came to him and tried to bring him down. After the Mepama stopped working, the boy fell from the small height, but reacted like he fell from a mountain. Alex was speechless after seeing what Jessica did. Jessica just smiled at him, and after everyone went from the place, she picked up her Mepama.

Both of them, while walking back to their class, were again- silent. Alex started to get scared of her now, and she felt a little awkward. "This is one of the most dangerous inventions I've ever witnessed," said Alex. "Well, dangerous inventions shall be used on evil people." replied Jessica. "How did you make this? And how did this 2-inch metal magnet pull that 70 kg guy?! And why did you bring this Mepa- whatever to school?" Alex asked so many questions. "First of all, it's Mepama. Second, I took your revenge. Third, the electro-magnetic radiation and a few special secret features of this Mepama creates a very strong magnetic field, which could pull any object upto 100 kg to itself, after sticking to another metal object. Fourth, I made this Mepama in my previous school's physics lab, when everyone started to tease me so much. There too, I troubled many bullies like this. Lastly, why do you bring pens and pencils to school? They can also be used as weapons, can't they?" replied Jessica, with confidence. Alex was stunned, and just replied- "Ohkay..."

They finally reached their classroom, and got ready for their next two lectures, which were the last ones. The gossip of the senior hovering near the menu display in the canteen reached the classroom students in no time. Everyone was whispering and talking to each other about the funny tragedy. "I don't understand. How could he be flying and hovering to the menu display? Ugh." the Sports teacher- Mr Gupta, entered the class whispering and talking to himself. "Good Morning Sir!" The whole classroom stood up. "Uh, yeah. Yeah. Sit down, class." Alex loved sports because he loved football. So he was the first one to ask. "Sir, can we go and play football today? Look, the weather is perfect for it." asked Alex. "Unfortunately today we will be playing indoor games, because the outdoors are reserved for some special ceremony of the seniors of the school so yeah." announced Mr Gupta. Alex's face frowned. "Okay so class, let's head to the indoor games building, and whatever you wanna play, go ahead and play with your friends or classmates." said Mr Gupta.

Nevertheless, now Alex somewhat was not very sad, because he thought to himself, "Jessica is perfect in everything, but I don't think she knows chess. I'll challenge her in chess and win against her, and show that even I can do something!" So the whole class boarded the corridor van, which was a kind of a van without a roof, like a train of multiple seats attached like a train, which hovered above the floor, and had 36 seats in one van, and dropped the whole class from one classroom or building to another. This corridor van, a futuristic indoor transport, had no roofs or windows. Just doors for boarding in. Alex and Jessica, sat in the last row. "Uh so… Any indoor games you are good at?" asked Alex to Jessica. "Not really. I am really good at volleyball and lawn tennis, but in indoor games, I don't play any games. However, recently I started to learn chess. But I am not very good at it." replied Jessica. Alex was satisfied. Now he could show Jessica what he is capable of. So he already got a proud feeling and started acting like he is the boss. "You know, I am a pro-chess player. I have won more than 56 online tournaments and 8 city tournaments in chess, in the last 2 years. Would you like to play a chess game with me?" asked Alex. "I know that I am losing for sure, but sure! I don't see why not." replied Jessica. She became nervous about the game, on the other hand, Alex became proud of himself. The van was passing through the corridor van road, in the central lane of the corridor, and the other lanes for students and teachers to walk through. Then the van exited the corridors and entered a tunnel with blue lights. "Whoa! This looks scary!" said Jessica. "Don't worry. This is a shortcut tunnel to the indoor sports building. Instead of going on the ground floor, then through the garden, then another building and then the indoor sports building, this tunnel is the connection between all the three buildings. It's a bit dark, but nothing to worry about." replied Alex. Suddenly the van stopped, because of the red light in front. Children from the rest of the class chatted and talked in the front rows of the van. Mr Gupta calmed them down. Suddenly two more corridor vans passed through the front tunnel, heading towards the other tunnels. That was basically an intersection of two tunnels. After they passed, the green light switched on and the van continued its journey.

Finally, the corridor van reached outside the indoor sports building and children boarded off. It was a large building with the statues of all the past sports masters. Children went inside it, and Jessica was shocked to see the touchless chess, Drone-minton, Swimming, Basketball and so many more zones in the indoor sports building. "Whoa! Touchless Chess? I've never seen them in my life!" said Jessica. "It's a very recent invention, like touchless chess was invented in 2155 year, 7 years ago. And the inventor of this technology is the very parent of a smart student from our school." said Mr Gupta, after seeing how amazed Jessica was. "Woww! Who invented it?" asked Jessica. Alex gave a nervous smile. "The inventor of the first worldwide Touchless Chess who made it in 2155 is- Joseph Gates, who is Alex's father." replied Mr Gupta. Jessica was literally astonished. "Your dad made this?! It's amazing! Then you must know a lot about it!" replied Jessica in surprise. "Actually, no. I mean of course almost everyone knows how to use it including me, but I really never understood the technology behind it. It's a big secret. Maybe some magnetic field and some external force acting upon the chess game pieces, but I am not sure." replied Alex. "So you both want to play together? Go grab that table, that is the last table left." Mr Gupta pointed towards the table with two chairs at the centre, with the whole Touchless chess on it. Alex and Jessica grabbed the chairs and the table.

"So, can you teach me how to use it?" asked Jessica. "It's easy. Simply say the chess piece name like- Pawn, Knight or Queen and say the coordinate or notation of the chess block you want to move on. It has a microphone, and will automatically move the chess piece to that block." replied Alex. Alex then clicked on the start option on the monitor of the Touchless chess, placed beside the chess set or chess board. "Welcome to Touchless Chess, version 6.5. To proceed, one of the players, please select your colour." said the automated voice system of the Touchless Chess. Jessica said for the option White. "Player with White colour, please tell your name." replied the voice system. "Jessica Smith." "Player with Black colour, please tell your name."

"Alex Gates." "Great! So let's begin. White colour player starts the match, and now I'll be on mute till the end of the game." said the voice system.

"Knight, f3." said Jessica. The piece moves after an immediate beep from the system. "Whoa! This is really amazing!" exclaimed Jessica. "I know right? Pawn, d5." Alex said. His piece too moved after the beep sound. The game continued like that. Alex was confident that Jessica would lose, thus after a few minutes, he got distracted towards the vending machines with Potato Chips packets in it. He thought, "Maybe, I'll take one." Alex stood up and said- "Be right back." and went towards the vending machines, a few metres away from the chess table. Jessica was still thinking about what piece to play. She thought for a while, but then she saw that Alex's Queen would be gone using her bishop piece. "Well, I'll just wait for him." she said and smiled. Alex came back with a cyan colour chips packet. "You didn't play your chance?" asked Alex. "Well, I was waiting for you." replied Jessica. "Oh, okay. Go on." Alex replied back, not even knowing that his queen was in danger. "Bishop, c6." said Jessica, and immediately after the beep, boom! Alex's queen was eliminated. He was shocked and Jessica became more confident. "How the heck did this happen? You did some cheating, didn't you?!" exclaimed Alex. "Well, this is a computerised touchless chess. There is no way I can cheat." replied Jessica.

Alex realised his mistake of getting distracted towards those salted potato chips. Now he didn't eat them because he was angry and frustrated. And Jessica checked Alex's king so many times, that eventually, it was checkmate. Jessica won! "Whoa! Tournament champion? What happened now, huh?" Jessica exclaimed and teased Alex. Alex was as red as a tomato. The bell rang, period got over. Now it was the last period of the day, and Alex stopped talking to Jessica. She understood that he became jealous and frustrated. All students walked out of the indoor sports building. "Uh, there is a problem kids. All corridor van's are occupied and busy right now. So we gotta walk to the class. Don't worry, it's just 800 metres away." Mr Gupta announced. "Oh great! Now we also have to walk to class!" exclaimed Alex with frustration. On the way back, the main hall of the school, where other students used to hang out in their free periods and by making excuses of going to the washroom, a lot of students were sitting there on the main hall's stairs, which surrounded a small circular green garden. Alex's class passed through the garden, and other students always used to bully or tease the junior kids. "Oh! So Alex has a new girlfriend? How nice is that, huh?" a tenth-grader started teasing Alex and Jessica. Alex was offended but both

Alex and Jessica ignored the bully. Then the same bully started teasing more and more. Eventually, Alex lost his temper. He went to that kid, and said- "Excuse me sir. Can you repeat-" and suddenly punched the bully on his face. The bully was shocked. Then there came a few more punches, on the face, on the stomach and then a fight started. Alex's class students and his friends joined Alex and tried to beat the 2-3 tenth graders and other kids tried to stop both the groups from fighting. His whole class's line stopped to see the fight going on, and Jessica was shocked to see Alex so angry.

Mr Gupta eventually took all the kids involved in the fight and Jessica to the principal's office. Her office was huge, and she was so busy that half of the last period passed until she was ready to talk to the students. 11 students standing in front of his desk. The large window from which the school's metro station and the whole city of Capitrolis with drones, Helicars (which were basically driverless and self-flying vehicles), and everything. "So, 6th and 10th graders. I know and heard everything, and Mr Gupta told me. Do you have anything to say?" said Mrs Jones, the principal. "Ma'am I think the 10th graders were bullying him and he went and started a fight." a kid from the group spoke of 6th grade. "As I said, I know everything. Jessica, you're new here, am I right?" said Mrs Jones. "Uh, yes ma'am." replied Jessica. "We're really sorry for this kind of behaviour from our students. We never want them to become such brats." continued Mrs Jones- " And, Alex, I understand your concern that you wanted them to stop teasing you and Jessica with those ill mannered words, but that doesn't mean you go and engage in a physical fight. You're a future Educity Student, and you must not become like this. On the basis of my ideology, I allow Alex, Jessica and these 6th graders to go back to their classes, and you three 10th graders are going to detention. We're calling your parents to tell them to pick you up at 6PM in the evening." Jessica, Alex and the students headed back to their classes, and the last period was almost over. The dispersal time for their home was about to start.

Alex quietly went to the class and sat on his bench, without saying a single word. Everyone did the same. The bell rang, and the dispersal started. All students of the school rushed to the metro station. Alex and a few students waited, and were still sitting on their classroom benches, because they knew how to avoid the dispersal metro crowd. They take the last few metros. Jessica too, kept sitting on her bench, and waited for Alex to depart. She was emotionally thankful and sorry for Alex, that he went to thrash the bullies, and sorry because he got lectured by the principal.

After ten minutes of scrolling about the school news on his notetab, and seeing his own picture clicked and posted as news headlines titled- "10th graders mock 6th graders, Alex - the Educity student thrashes the bullies." Alex stood up and took his bag and notetab, and exited the class. Jessica followed him and met him at the platform of the metro station. Alex was waiting for the metro. His notetab rang. "Hey mom! Yes, the metro is slightly late, I will reach in an hour or so. Yeah Bye." and Alex hung up the call. A lot of students were standing on the platform waiting for the next metro to the Terminal Station. Jessica was slightly nervous to talk to Alex, so she waited for a minute then said- "Uh, hey Alex. Are you still sad that you lost? Duh, it's just a game. Come on, leave it." Alex replied- "What do you know about why I am sad? This school is full of bullies. And now they are just simply shipping me with you—" "Hey, hey. Just don't care about them! Their idiotic mentalities believe that a boy and a girl can't be friends. Just ignore them!" interrupted Jessica.

Alex finally calmed down. The metro arrived, and all teachers instructed children to board the train. Alex and Jessica, again, got seats beside one another. This time, this metro had gaming consoles too. All kids were surprised to see the new version of school metros. "Shall we try to play this game together?" asked Jessica. "Sure! Let's see who wins this time." replied Alex. A lifelike and 3D car racing game attracted both of them, and they began to play. After a few minutes, the game ended and Alex finally won. "Finally, at least I won something!" exclaimed Alex. The gaming consoles were white and futuristic. However, the Terminal Station was about to arrive in a few minutes, so they both shutted down their Gaming consoles and screens, which were attached to the backside of the seats in front of them.

The Terminal arrived, and both of them rushed to take the last metro to their route. They both ran together, went to the departure schedule. "New Southern Capitrolis, last metro, in 2 minutes. Run!" said Alex. They both ran to the respective platform, and their metro's yellow lights were on and beeping for doors closing was being heard. As soon as they entered the partially empty metro, the doors closed. "Whew! That was close. I am scared of being stuck between metro doors." said Jessica. "Eh, it's no problem. The metro is smart, and the emergency beeping will start, and the train will not move if someone is really stuck." informed Alex. Jessica was further relieved. Then they sat beside each other, and Jessica began to tell Alex- "You know, Alex? You're the first person who ever became such a nice friend to me just within a few hours. Usually people judge me on the basis of my craziness and because I am a nerd, but you, on the other hand, understood me. Thank you so much for your support and friendship. You're a nice kid. Just practise more in Chess." and then she laughed mockingly.

"Well, you're the first girl I became such good friends with. You're smart, and a competitor for me too, but you're too, a nice kid." replied Alex. Both liked the way their friendship started, in just a bunch of hours, from drawing on metro's interior walls till school, the Mepama event, chess and so much more! Finally, Alex's station came. Alex stood up and started to head towards the closed door as the metro slowed down. Suddenly, Jessica interrupted- "Uh, Alex! Here's my Call 'n' Chat number. If you would like to communicate online too, and it's my own phone number." said Jessica. Call 'n' Chat was an app which allowed users to call and chat informally and formally with each other. It was made in 2152, ten years from that time. Alex smiled, and took the small paper slip, with the number. "Bye Alex!" Jessica waved her hand. "Yeah, see you tomorrow!" Alex replied. Alex left the metro, and the metro left the platform. Jessica waved from the window. He smiled and waved his hand back.

He exited his school metro station, and went to the electric taxi stand. He scanned his ID card of his school, and the taxi opened. The taxis and all kinds of cars were made electric and hovering cars, as well as self driving. In these hovering cars, there were no tyres, just large magnets placed in the place of tyres, to hover the car. Plus, the taxi service for students of any school was free nationwide. So Alex sat inside the futuristic hovering taxi, and entered his home's address as the destination. "Journey is Starting!" the taxi automated voice announced. There was a lot of traffic, and it was 3:20 PM, and the ETA was 17 minutes. So he decided to listen to some songs. He connected his school notetab to the taxi's speaker and played his favourite songs, and relaxed in the AC. Truly, life of every person in the future, especially in the 2160s became peaceful and wonderful!

FOUR

HAPPY BIRTHDAY ALEX!

Anyways, Alex reached his society and entered the gate, still holding the paper slip that Jessica gave to him. He greeted the security personnel, and entered his building. Many children were coming back to their home from school. Alex went to his elevator, Elevis greeted and asked: "Good afternoon! Which floor?" "71st." replied Alex. The smart-elevator began to take him to his floor. Alex felt somewhat different today. He was usually frustrated or bored when he came home from school. Today, he felt like he had a great day.

He kept looking and smiling at the paper slip with Jessica's phone number. "Ding!" his floor came. Alex went to his apartment door, did the retina scan, and entered his apartment. "Hey, Mom, Dad!" Alex greeted. "I'm here, if you didn't see me. Mom and Dad went to the superstore to buy groceries." said Sierra, Alex's elder sister. "Oh great! So now I have to greet you as well? Why don't you go to your room, which is full of stupid and fancy Korean and American singers and celebrities posters?" replied Alex. "Do you have any idea how popular they are?" said Sierra. "Yeah, so go ahead! Don't start with your university, and go marry them!" back answered Alex. "What?!" said Sierra sarcastically. "Oh wait, then what about James? Your boyfriend? Huh? He will be left broken–" Alex said and ran away to his room and locked his door, knowing that Sierra would hit him badly after he said that. "Shut up you worm!" shouted Sierra, banging on his locked door. "Hey, AlexRoom!" Alex said, and all his room lights switched on, curtains got closed, and the futuristic lights at the ceiling started glowing. "Good afternoon, Alex!" the AI voice echoed. Alex loved his room. He went to his study table's softboard, and pinned the paper slip which Jessica gave him, on which was written: "Jessica: Ph Number- 928.7391.824" "I'll text her this evening." he said to himself. He lied on the bed, and took a nap.

He woke up at 5:20 PM, when his mom was knocking on his room door. "Alex! Open the door, beta!" He opened the door and had his mom and dad scolding him for locking the door for almost 2 hours. "Uh mom! Dad! Sierra was about to beat me up! That's why I locked the door. To escape." answered Alex. "Beta we came an hour ago, and were worried about you. Don't do it next time, okay? Plus, we got your birthday gift, and you'll get it tonight at 12." said Alex's dad. "Yay! Okie!" said Alex. Sierra was heading to her piano classes, she said bye to everyone and left.

"So you're not gonna go play football today?" asked his Mom. "Uh, not football. Today, I'm just gonna hang out with Manish, my best friend and other friends." said Alex. He got ready and went downstairs to the park bench area, near the big fountain in the lake, and waited for his friends to join him. He called Manish with his phone. "Hey Manish! Are you gonna come today? I am at the fountain benches." asked Alex. "Alex bro, let's hang out at my building's terrace garden, it's cool. We'll see the sunset as well." replied Manish. Alex hung up and went to Manish's house to pick him up. He asked Manish to come with him, and they both went to the terrace garden at the top of the 80 floors building. Clouds seemed near, and the sun was red, and the whole city of Capitrolis was visible.

Manish was in 11th class, but a good friend of Alex, as he also plays football with Alex. Both of them were sitting at a white bench in the terrace garden, facing the sunset. "Hey dude! You seem more happy today. Anything special?" asked Manish mockingly. "Uh nah bro. Just a new friend at school. She's kind and nice!" replied Alex. "Ohoooo! So you like her or something?" asked Manish. "I don't know. But I really saw something different in her. I mean she is supportive, caring and kinda beautiful too." said Alex. "That's great. At least you have your first crush on someone, in your life!" replied Manish. Alex smiled and blushed. Suddenly, his phone vibrated. "Whoa! I got her message right now." said Alex. "What?! You have her number?!" asked Manish surprisingly. "Uh, she gave it to me herself." replied Alex. He continued- "She's texting and asking when is my birthday." Alex replied that it is tomorrow. He got her message: "Whoa! That's great! Can we meet after school at the Metro Terminal Cafe, tomorrow?" He texted back: "Sure! But we would need to catch the first metro to the terminal to spend time at the Terminal Cafe, so we don't get late going home ."

Manish was enjoying reading the chats. "Dude, that's great. Does she like you back?" asked Manish. "Bro I don't know! Anyways today was the first day so let me take it slow." replied Alex. Manish agreed. The sun went below the horizon, and the city of Capitrolis shone with yellow, blue and white lights. The drones were the busiest right now. Alex and Manish were heading back downstairs to see the beautiful evening rainbow fountain show. It happens every Thursday evening. Alex saw it with friends, talked with his friends and Manish, and finally came home at 8:45 PM. "So late today? Dinner is in the kitchen. It's not exciting but for now eat healthy to eat junk tomorrow." said Alex's Mom. There was Cucumber and Onion Salad for dinner. Alex didn't hate it, but it seemed boring to eat it. Sierra went to the bathroom around 5 times to vomit after eating the salad, because she hated it. Alex peacefully went to his room, watched his favourite web series, and finished his dinner. He was too lazy to keep the bowl of his finished salad in the kitchen, so he simply kept it on the side table, and slept on his bed.

Soon at 11:10 PM, he started to sleep deeply, and was sound asleep. "Mai kazhodekontika." "Kudioschatorisica. Mi! Mi! Torakaporica!" Alex heard some sounds of some people talking in a weird language, but thinking it was a dream, he continued to sleep. He also heard some vibrations, and then, a small tremor occurred, which made the whole city of Capitrolis shake for 2-3 seconds. Alex suddenly woke up with that, and said "Whoa!" However, seeing the city buildings in a normal shape and nothing disastrous, he slept again, relaxed.

Now, he slept till the morning, and didn't get the chance to cut the cake at midnight. But thinking it's his birthday, he woke up with excitement. "Finally the day came, for which I kept waiting for months! Yay!" But then he saw the time, it was only 5:35 AM. "Oh well, let's start the day early with a nice early morning walk!" Alex said, and hurriedly rushed to his apartment's door, with the thought that his parents and his sister were still asleep. He closed the door soundlessly, and went to the elevator. "Elevis, take me to the walking park floor." Alex gave the command to the Elevator. "Sorry. Elevis is currently out of service due to an unknown issue. Please enter the floor you want to go to, manually. Here is the list of floors." Elevis' automated voice replied, and a steel tray came out of the elevator walls, with a lot of buttons to press, each one representing a floor. Alex pressed the walking park floor button, and the elevator started to move with an unusual thrust.

"Something is wrong today. What the heck is happening?" Alex murmured to himself. But it was taking very long to reach the floor. It had been five minutes and the elevator was still going down really slowly, and was on the 46th floor. Alex decided to switch on his phone and check the notifications. He was also excited to see his new and first-ever crush today- Jessica. However, when he suddenly switched on his shiny, as thin as a compact-disk smartphone, the screen didn't turn on properly. There were lots of glitches. The display was dislocating again and again to different corners of the screen. Alex got frustrated. But suddenly, when the elevator reached the 43rd floor, the elevator suddenly speeded up to its normal speed, the smartphone switched on and started working properly, and the Elevis AI came back online.

"Well, prolly it's a technical glitch city-wide. After all, it's just 5:50 AM." Alex said to himself and became normal now. In no time the elevator now reached the walking park floor. Alex got out of the elevator, and entered the walking park, which was a large botanical garden-like park, especially for walking, jogging and recreation. Its wonderful fragrance attracted anyone who was attached to nature, like Alex. Alex enjoyed walking there. He stepped down the few stairs and came on the pathway of the park. The park was surrounded by extremely tall buildings of his society, but the fireflies, peacocks and birds' cute sounds made the park attractive, along with the bushy trees and long rows of flower bushes. The yellow lights brought more charm and peace to the park. Alex loved walking here. But something was odd. He couldn't find a person apart from him walking in the whole park. He didn't notice that until it was 6:15 and 20 minutes had passed of Alex's presence in the park. Nevertheless, he started to check the notifications on his phone, and the most astonishing part was, that his school didn't send a time table schedule for today, and also the school metro app didn't send the schedule of any metro to school today. He wondered what was wrong this early morning. He didn't have an answer. Because both his school and school metro apps never failed to send a notification, but they did fail today.

The sun started to rise up. Still, Alex couldn't find a person. Thinking that no one had the good lifestyle to show up for walking or jogging every day, he simply returned to his building, and then his apartment. He was dissatisfied with today's walk. Hearing not a person's voice made him feel weird. And not just weird, he was confused, and scared, of whatever was happening to him since this morning. He came to the conclusion that today, he'll go to school late, and will take the taxi to reach his school and not the school metro because he really wanted to share this all with his parents. The unusual incidents and everything. So it would pretty much take time.

"Uh. Elevis, are you there?" Alex entered the elevator and asked. "For you sir, of course! Anytime!" Elevis voice replied. "How many people have travelled with this elevator since 4AM today?" Alex asked this question with curiosity. "So yes! It's a fact, that for now, since 4AM today, this elevator has been used only once." replied Elevis. Alex was speechless. He was the only person to travel in the elevator the whole early morning, while on the other early mornings of other days, usually more than 100 people travel in it by this time. Now he was really scared. His goosebumps had risen. He simply commanded the elevator to take him to his floor, and he entered his apartment to find his family.

"Mom! Dad! Where are you? Please open the door." Alex started banging on his parents' room door. Then he went to his sister's room door and started banging it and knocking really loudly. No response from either of the rooms. Both of the doors were locked. Alex started to sweat a lot now. He was nervous and so scared now. He felt some unknown loneliness. He took out the emergency axe, and without even thinking for a moment that it could cost his parents' money to fix the damages, he broke his parents' room door with the axe. To his horrified surprise, his parents were not even in the room, and then he broke his sister's door and went inside. Again, her sister was missing too.

For a moment, Alex got the worst thought he could ever get. He went to all the other apartments on his 71st floor and tried to break the thick wooden main doors of all the other apartments, with the help of an axe which was placed for fire safety. After 10-15 minutes of continuous hard work, finally he was able to break one apartment's main door, but the security alarms started to beep on the whole floor. He didn't care, he went inside, and saw that his neighbours were also missing.

Minutes and even hours passed. It was 9 in the morning, and finally, he was able to break all the main doors of his floor in the building. But, didn't find a person. Tears started to fall from his eyes. He went to the ground floor of his building, got outside, and again, didn't see a person. "Hello!? Is anybody there?!" He cried. He ran to each building to find any person but didn't find anyone. He then ran to the apartment complex's main gate, to ask the society personnel why was everyone missing. To his another surprise, not one security personnel was there, but all their tools like registers, sticks, guns and everything were lying on the ground. Then he saw, that the route of the drone expressway in the sky, through which all the drones travelled from one place to another, was devoid of any drones. No drone was travelling through it.

He exited his society and kept running in the streets, roads and then the main roads of the city. Cars were there on the road, but they were not on. They were stopped, and so many cars simply stood in silence, with the lights and engines switched off, and there was no person in any of the cars. Alex kept running on the main expressway too, where there are over 10,000 people travelling through it every hour, but again unexpectedly, he couldn't find anyone. The drone traffic was zero. No one was travelling through any of the vehicles. No aeroplanes, no helicopters, no helicars (flying cars), or no drones were there. Not even the school metro was operational. Alex ran to the India Gate, where finally the National Park came, in front of the India Gate. Even one of the most populated areas of Capitrolis was empty today. He continued running, and eventually entered a mall named The New Capitrolis Mall. As Alex knew, even in the earliest morning hours and last night hours, there are hundreds of people in the mall, but still, he didn't find a soul, nor a person.

He came out of the mall, sobbing, and crying, and tears were falling out of his eyes. After all, he was just a 12-year-old child. "What is happening?! Where the heck is everyone?! Am I the last person here?! **Am I the last ME?!**" Alex cried and fainted with shock.

FIVE

WHERE IS EVERYONE?

For the next 2-3 hours, he remained unconscious and fainted outside The New Capitrolis Mall. Then he woke up, and it was 3 in the afternoon, with cloudy weather. He was still with tears in his eyes. "How the heck is it possible?! Everyone just disappeared. Were all of them kidnapped or something? Then what about me?! Plus no one can kidnap the people of the whole city! Wait a minute. Just the whole city? No, no, no! Don't tell me!" Exclaimed and cried, Alex. He went to the mall again, went to the top floor that had a terrace, and stepped out of the elevator. He saw a helicar's helipad, with a helicar parked on it. He went to the helicar pad, and as soon as he stepped on the helipad of the helicar, the helicar began to turn on, and the engines started to work, the red lights started to blink on the helipad, and he opened the helicar's door, and sat inside it, on one of the six seats in it. "Destination please." the automated voice of the helicar spoke. "Uh-um. Evergreen County, South Capitrolis." Alex replied while wiping the tears from his cheeks. The helicar's air conditioner started, and it started to fly. Alex quickly wore his seatbelt and closed the door. The helicar in not more than 5 minutes, landed on the helicar's helipad of his society, on the top of a building's terrace.

Alex quickly went to his building, and his apartment, and it was 4 in the afternoon. He immediately went to his parents' bedroom. Same as before, his parents were gone. So was Sierra, his sister, and so was everyone. They had disappeared into thin air. Alex realised this after he opened his SateRadar gift, and switched it on, and saw only one red dot, representing only one person on the whole planet earth, and that red dot was where Alex was, in Capitrolis, in his society, in his building, in his apartment. That is, the red dot was no one but Alex. Rest, every human had vanished from the face of the world. No dead bodies, no traces, no clues, nothing. They just disappeared. Alex didn't see the face of a person today. He forgot about his school, his meeting with Jessica, his birthday, his football match in the evening, his Educity examination preparation, everything, for everyone was gone, who was left on the planet besides him?

Now, Alex, cried a lot. He screamed, cried while shouting, and wailed for hours. He couldn't just express his pain. He was so shocked. He wished whatever he saw today was just a nightmare or a dream at night, while it wasn't. He went to his room, and started to hit his hand again and again on the hard concrete wall, so hard, wishing that this is just a nightmare and he wakes up in real life. But while it pained on his hand, he realised, that this is reality. In his real life, everyone is gone, disappeared, and where? He doesn't know. He doesn't know if they're alive or dead. If they even existed before or those were just illusions, or they existed before, and whatever he is seeing write now is an illusion. He was so so overwhelmed, that he simply went to his balcony, and fell on his knees, only experiencing his pain and depression.

"What the heck? Where did everyone go?" exclaimed Peter, after listening to William's story with so much interest. "Yeah! What happened to everyone?" asked Garima. "That's a really creepy story, William." said Sandeep. "And is that the end of your dream you saw?" asked Rhea. "Guys just stop. Let him tell his story–" exclaimed Aryan. "Well, the thing is, half an hour has already passed, and it would become dark and would be evening time, till the time I finish this. Still, you would like to continue listening?" asked William. "Yeah. We really are interested in it. We don't mind even if you keep narrating it till night time." replied Aryan. "Oh great. So, this is what happened:

Alex cried the whole evening, and when it was almost 8, only the power supply was working in Capitrolis. Except for Alex's society, most buildings' lights were switched off, because no one was there, who needed light or power. Alex was broken from the inside. This was the worse that could ever happen to him. He didn't know what was next, what he had to do, how will he find anyone, or thought that he simply entered into some creepy parallel universe. But his conscience kept telling him, that something big is behind all this, and he had to survive among all this.

"There's no one I can talk to. There's no one I can see or hear. There's no one I can say hello or goodbye to. There's no one I can sit with, play with or meet with. How am I supposed to live in this freaking world like this?!" cried Alex. He was now frustrated and depressed. But he believed his conscience, which said that he was hungry, and didn't eat anything from last night, almost 20 hours. He went to his refrigerator, only to find that a few cheese rolls were remaining. He simply microwaved the cheese rolls and ate them, however, the tears were still coming out of his eyes. To distract himself from this empty world, he switched on his Airtop. He switched on his favourite web series, but it couldn't interest him. He had his dinner, but the only thing he could simply ponder and think was- Where is Everyone?

The night passed, and depressed Alex slept while watching his series. In the morning at 7:00 AM, he woke up. With a sad face, he was simply overwhelmed and burdened, with the question, where is everyone? He again called, "Mom! Dad! Sierra!" just with the hope that they will come to him or answer back, but it was a pin drop silence. Not even the noise of traffic in the city which kept the city alive was heard. He didn't understand a single thing which was happening with him. He stood up from his bed and went to his balcony to see the city of Capitrolis. The beautiful city was shimmering with shiny skyscrapers, with the morning sun's light rays falling on the windows was seen, but no traffic, no drones, no moving cars, and no person. He went back inside, and again checked the SateRadar, but the same result was shown. No humans.

For a while, Alex literally started to feel that he should kill himself. But deep down in his heart, something else was telling him to keep going. So he removed that thought and feeling from his mind. He went to the living room and saw a cake box which he probably forgot to notice the previous day, on his birthday. On it, an electronic cake cover was kept, made of strong plastic with a blue light slowly glowing. He removed the cover and saw a beautiful cake in it. "Mom and Dad must've got it for me." he sniffled and tried to control his tears. Gently, with care, he lifted the cake's plate with the cake on it and put it in his refrigerator.

SIX

ALEX BLOWS UP A BUILDING

He then took his phone, got out of his apartment, to see and then recall that he had broken all the doors of all the apartments on his floor. He got into the elevator, went to the parking basement, and got to his parent's car, a white NeutronX Model Y45, a luxury and fast hovering car. He got into it, sat and commanded the self-driving car to head to the Capitrolis Library. Now, why was he going to the library? Well, Capitrolis Library was not just a typical library. It has holo-books, which are made from holographic books and typical books as well, and has the access to all the public and private information of major companies, corporations, industries and even the government. Alex wanted to access the Security cameras of Capitrolis to see what happened to all the people which were in the security department of the library, and gather information on why there are no drones, and most facilities are switched off, except water and some electricity supply. For he studied in history that it was the old period of time when facilities failed to be provided, but 2162 was a year of extremely developed cities, where such things were extremely rare.

Even in the car, he was sobbing quietly. On the way to the Capitrolis Library, he talked to himself. "I mean, why the heck? And if everyone is missing, why not me? And really, where is everyone." but on the other hand he also said to himself, "Alex, just calm down. You already spent one day just crying about it. It's a big deal for sure, thus it must have a big cause." Now this was his conscience talking to him. For he knew that it can't be true that all of a sudden everyone dies or becomes extinct.

His car reached the Capitrolis Library. He stepped out of his car, and looked at the large building with ancient Indian architecture. "The Capitrolis Library - Established in 2087." He read the title. He was surprised by the title of the building as the library was too old. But it was the most reputed library in Capitrolis. He had no time to think how the library was. He ran to the library entrance using the staircase, entered the building. He went to the library map first. He observed the map, and saw where was the Security and Inspection department of the library. He clicked a picture of the map from his phone and followed it to reach the Security department hall of the library. "Security and Inspection Personnels Entrance only." The LED display over the hall gates showed. Alex didn't care, he simply entered the hall, to see so many computer screens and monitors with live security cameras streaming. He went to the main screens and monitors and entered the date and time of his birthday, the time of 3:00 AM, before people disappeared. And he played the CCTV Cameras' recording of that night. The cameras were so high quality, that he could see the slight hovering cars travelling at night, and even people in some buildings and skyscrapers. These cameras were installed on drones which keep on flying 24/7, operated with wireless charging. These drones were facing the city's major viewpoints. So Alex sat down on the chair, with the hope of finding or understanding the disappearance of the people of Capitrolis and the whole world.

Minutes went by, and everything was normal in the cameras. Except it was seeming like the earth was slightly shaking and there were slight tremors. Alex suddenly remembered something. "The tremor in the night!" Alex went to the computer screen to check this thing out closely. The land was actually seeming to shake very slightly, but not enough to cause even a major tremor. Like it seemed that the land was tilting and shaking slowly, but no one was disturbed because this was very very slow. In cameras, it was noticed as the recording was in fast motion. Alex then noticed something weirder. There were a few maroonish glows above the clouds in the sky. And not just any glows. There were patterns. So many maroonish glowing lights were rotating above the sky. It was like some drone show was occurring above the clouds, drones glowing with maroon colour, but not visible clearly as they appeared to be behind or above the clouds.

Alex just got frustrated. After some minutes, at nearly 4:13 AM, the land was still moving slightly, and the maroon patterns were still occurring. But then suddenly, a super white and bright flash came on all the screens which were showing the recordings. Alex couldn't look at the screens. It was too bright to even open his eyes, even though the flash was a part of the recording itself. And this flash stayed for 10 seconds, and then something unimaginable happened. Whatever cars and vehicles which were seen travelling, came to a stop, and all the people which were somewhat visible in buildings disappeared. Alex was confused. He repeated the recording, and lowered the brightness. He saw the flash occurring, still it was bright, but now the brightness level was low in the computer display. Alex saw that nothing was visible in this flash, but just then the flash ended, but everyone disappeared.

Alex came out of the hall, understanding that the people's disappearance is somewhat related to this flash. But then he suddenly had an emotional breakdown. He started crying loudly. And then he screamed in frustration. His voice was echoing in the large building of the library. Alex cried a lot, and just lay down on the floor, crying. He just stood up again, just took the security hall's recording in a transfer drive, and took the drive with him. It was like a Pen drive. He went to his car, unlocked it, and ordered his Car AI to head home. The hovering car started its journey. Alex just wanted to solve whatever major glitch this was. He wanted to find the root of this problem. He wanted his old life back. He wanted people to be back. He wanted his parents, his friends, his crush Jessica. Alex just made himself clear that he has to stop cribbing and crying about what happened, because that is really not going to solve anything. On the way, he saw the building of the Parliament of India. He immediately commanded the AI to stop, take a U turn and head to the Parliament of India. "Are you sure? Your new destination might be restricted to only some people." the Car AI said. "Just go to the Parliament of India!" shouted Alex to the AI. "Okay sir." the AI responded.

The hovering car took a U turn and entered the parliament of India. There was actually restricted entry. But no humans was equal to no security of the parliament. His car continued driving and stopped at the entry of the parliament building. Alex knew, that Parliament of India has access to the unthinkable resources. India being the top country in the whole world, must have something related to what happened. Maybe some major kidnap, war or something. But war, "it can't be", he thought. After all, there are deaths in war, and he couldn't even find one body. He entered the parliament building. There he saw a big hall, with different pathways leading to other halls. He went to the pathway mentioned "For Highly-Positioned Officials only".

He walked through the pathway and was astonished to see the parliament being so large in size, and its interior being so royal. It was literally made of marble and limestone. He again, didn't have time to focus on these things. He ran to the hall, and was amazed to enter a dark hall with blue windows, neon lights glowing on the ceiling. "This hall is really some high technology stuff." Alex murmured.

He observed the hall more, it had all major details of the secret information of the government, and all the information of the government, and all the status of the city, and the country as well. However Alex was most interested on a large screen which showed a picture of the IndWatch Satellite. The satellite of India, orbiting the Earth, which recorded a lot of videos and photos of earth, having more than a billion photos and videos. It was just launched a few years back. "If I could get access to what happened, then it would be super. The satellite might help me in understanding what happened. It's camera's video recordings of the Earth and space would just be perfect." Alex said to himself. He was a genius. And he knew that to solve this problem, he first needs to understand what is the actual cause and problem, and really what the heck happened.

Alex takes all details of the satellite from the parliament with him to his house. Blueprints, launch details, mission status, and literally everything. In the evening, he starts his research after reaching back home. He removes all studying material from his soft board and starts to pin all these blueprints and papers and switches on his Airtop to access the transfer drive. However Alex, while removing everything from the soft board, becomes emotional at two things- his picture with his parents and Sierra, and the number of Jessica written by her on a paper slip. He lets these two things still be pinned up. He switched his Airtop on, and first read whatever he could find about the IndWatch Satellite. "IndWatch satellite is the largest satellite India has ever built in history. It was launched for private operations for the government like security in terms of national security as well as the geographical observations, and climatic observations. IndWatch has high resolution cameras which can even show what is written on a paper in someone's hand, even though IndWatch orbits in space, around the earth. It also records videos always while orbiting the earth, and has a large memory as well." He found this information on the Internet.

However, he failed to understand how can someone access the IndWatch Satellite's data. He then recalled that he could access IndWatch Satellite's all details from one place entirely anyway- the parliament. He observed that today itself. He decided to fly to the Parliament. Fly? Yes, he decided to go the parliament via Helicar. It was 9:24 PM. He didn't want to sleep. He wanted to find the problem, and the people. He didn't care about his sleep. Alex took his phone, Airtop, and PC's screenshots in a printed form with him, and reached the helipad where the Helicar had landed before. He entered the Helicar and told the AI the destination, "Parliament of India Helipad." The Helicar took off. He could see the whole Capitrolis City being so dark. He wondered if he could make himself feel better by lighting up the whole city with lights entirely and completely, that is, switching on all electricity power supply switches from the Capitrolis Power Supply Headquarters. But first he wanted to access the IndWatch recordings, and he was stuck to this determination.

The Helicar landed on the Parliament's helipad. The parliament's power was on. Alex ran to the same hall, the technology and security control hall of the parliament. He entered the hall, switched on the main computer. It had access to so much information and direct chats to the leaders of different countries. On the Messages icon, there was even a message from the president of the United States. But Alex cared for himself more than for the message. He opened the IndWatch icon, and a login panel opened up. Now he was stuck. "What the-! How could I possibly know the password or username?" He clicked on the 'Forgot details' option. Another window opened up stating that he must go to Cheniaros city Government Security Office to find the details of the login.

"Are you freaking kidding me?! Cheniaros city?! 2,000 kilometres away?!" Alex said in frustration. Cheniaros city was the new name of the city of Chennai. Alex screamed in frustration and pushed a red button by mistake in his frustration. "BOOOOM!" Just in front of the hall, from a window, he observed a large skyscraper exploding. The skyscraper fell down to the ground. It was a 112 floors skyscraper, perhaps an important building. "Now, have they put bombs in their own city?" Alex said in confusion. He now understood that the parliament he is standing in is just not some random parliament. It was a building which majorly in fact controlled India, and as India controlled most of the world, not politically but economically, the parliament he was standing in was a super dangerous and prominent building of India.

SEVEN

CYCLONE IN CHENIAROS!

"Now how am I going to Cheniaros? The helicar I have is really uncomfortable and I don't even trust it for flying so much." Alex murmured. Then he recalled another thing. He took all his stuff, and ran to the helipads zone. Just opposite of his helicar's helipad, there was a bigger helipad with a larger helicar, and with the label on it 'President and Prime Minister of India'. He understood who the helicar belonged to. The current yet missing president and prime minister. Who cares? Everyone was missing except Alex. He boarded the black helicar, checked the fuel, and first went to his home for bringing some food with him, and as well as the documents related to the satellite he is researching about. He took 10 chips packets, and came back to the black helicar, and then took off for Cheniaros!

"Whoa! Sounds too majestic!" exclaimed Peter. "Well, I don't understand. Why did Alex do all this so fast? If I had been in his place, I would've cried for years. On the other hand, he just started his research and stuff? How is he able to control his emotions?" asked Rhea. "Yeah! What makes him so different?" asked Garima. Aryan was embarrassed again that his team was interrupting William. William replied, "Well, I guess some questions do not have answers, as I have not written this story, I just know some parts of it. How can I possibly answer–" "You just go on with your story. Guys stop disturbing him!" said Aryan. William continued, "Yeah so...

Alex's journey to Cheniaros was hectic. He had never travelled outside Northern India, and was nervous, going to another city, all alone, knowing that no one is there too. He was tired as well. He slept while the helicar was flying and continuing its journey. The tremors, the maroonish glowing lights, and then the flash, he was seeing all that again in his sleep, like in his nightmare. And then he woke up with shock. Then he again started to have tears in his eyes, just thinking where is everyone. He was hungry as well. On the GPS he looked, that he had reached Madhnais State (Madhya Pradesh). There were still bunch of hours before he reaches Cheniaros.

He opens up his Airtop, and starts reading more articles regarding IndWatch Satellite. He finds many videos of various Vidubers, the people who created videos and posted them on a website named Viduoz, a famous video streaming app just like YouTube, of the year 2162. The Vidubers told about the government's new satellite of IndWatch and how it will help India to research information. They all mentioned the features of the satellite like scanning temperature, clicking pictures of the earth, researching and communication, but none of them mentioned the untold features like what Alex got to know at the Parliament, that the satellite can even spy on other countries, and is a satellite to have the clearest and most zoomed images of the earth.

Alex knew, that if he gets this information, he would get half of the information regarding everyone's disappearance, and at least would get an idea what to do next. He knew that without the help of this satellite, it would be close to impossible to even know what happened. Suddenly on the screen of the helicar, and on the class, a notification popped. Alex touched the notification by clicking on the screen, and it said: "Flood Alert in the following cities: Momuras (Mumbai), Soruta (Surat), Kelisorett (Kolkata) and Cheniaros." "Oh great! First everyone's disappearance, then THIS! I mean, wow!" Alex exclaimed in frustration. He still thought if he should stop his journey, as flood warning was shown for Cheniaros. But his doubt had no match for his dedication, which was extremely high.

After some time, he then again checked the GPS, and it showed only 1 hour left to reach the city. He then changed the destination to the exact building he had to go to in Cheniaros, the Government's Security Office Building. The time now immediately reduced to 47 minutes, as the building was in the outskirts and in the north of Cheniaros. "Well, that's great." said Alex to himself. However even while he was doing all this, finding the root of the problem, he was still missing his parents, and friends and Jessica. He was recalling all the memories he had with all of them earlier, and started to get tears in his eyes again. But he smiled at his fate sarcastically while having tears and closing his eyes, for he had a problem to deal with- "Where is Everyone?"

After some time, an AI Voice announced in the helicar- "We have reached your destination." Alex opened the doors of the helicars, pushed them above, took out his backpack and Airtop, and entered the Government's Security Office campus, and sees the whole campus with wide eyes. He doesn't believe that the campus was so large, probably as the size of four parliament buildings. "How could I possibly find the IndWatch Satellite's Password information here?" he murmured to himself, seeing the size of the building. The Cheniaros city's temperature was cold, Alex wondered why was so cold, even though it was the Summer season. He entered the reception hall, as expected, with no security, and noticed that there was no power in the building except a few emergency bulbs. He switched on his phone's torch and tries to look for the campus map.

He finally gets a torn campus map printed on paper, which was folded and crumpled. He looked for the IndWatch room. "Where is it? Ugh!" he exclaimed. He finally finds a floor of the building where there are Space Security Department of the building. He ran to the building where this floor was. Alex was tired now but didn't want to give up. He reached the floor through the elevator and now had to find the exact room.

"MissileOrbiter... NucleSpace... SafeIndia.... RISAT-3... IndWatch... IndWatch! " Alex found the exact satellite room. He became energetic, and immediately goes to the computer and switches it on. Opens up the same software, of IndWatch. He quickly browses the application and tries to find the information about the password to access the satellite. But then he screamed out of frustration! Why? Because of a message displayed on the screen of the computer- "Sorry, but the Password cannot be shared with anyone except the Parliament. However, to extract details from the satellite manually without password, lower the Satellite Orbit and with the help of Picker Rocketcraft (a hybrid of aircraft and rocket), bring the satellite safely back to the ISRO Launch Base." Now of course this whole operation of sending a Rocketcraft to the satellite and bringing it back to the surface of the earth was very overwhelming and complex for Alex, after all, he was simply a 13-year-old teenager. Also this Picker Rocketcraft was not a considerable option as it anyways required a large team of actual people including pilots, astronauts, engineers, scientists and mission controllers to launch, operate and use it. And in contrast, Alex was literally a one-man-army here.

Alex groaned. He sat on a chair sobbing. He had no idea what to do next. He couldn't get the password for the IndWatch satellite access, and now how can he use rocket science and bring the satellite to the Earth's surface. But he didn't give up. He knew that he was close to finding the problem. He took his backpack, and was just coming out of the cabin or room when suddenly, there were red lights blinking all over the campus.

At first Alex thought that he triggered some sort of alarming system by entering the room or something. But later he realized when he saw on his phone: "Cyclone and Flood Alert in Cheniaros. Evacuate the region or seek higher ground." Alex reacted, "Shit! I almost had forgotten it!" Alex ran to the Helicar he came through, and it was raining heavily. Far away he could see a cyclone coming towards the city of Cheniaros. He opened the Helicar door, climbed in it and ordered the AI system to start the Helicar. "Sorry, due to high winds and cyclone alert, the Helicar wouldn't operate." the automated voice responded. "What the hell?!" Alex exclaimed. He tried commanding the AI system repeatedly, but the Helicar won't just start. He then just took an emergency umbrella from the Helicar and took his belongings, and got out of the Helicar.

In frustration, he kicked the helicar, "What a waste vehicle!" and exclaimed. He then noticed that the flooding water had started to get collected in some places. He had no idea what to do now. He ran here and there and then ran on a hilly road, to seek higher ground. His phone had no network. He couldn't still see anyone, so no one could possibly help him. The road was very steep. Alex slipped 2-3 times but still got up and ran to seek higher ground. He suddenly heard a blasting sound and looked behind. He saw the black helicar of the Parliament he came in, breaking into pieces due to the high pressure of water and debris falling on the helicar.

The city of Cheniaros was turning into hell. Alex couldn't see the low-heightened buildings of the city, and the floods were so destructive. His only motive was to stay alive and not die. He kept running and then finally his fortune smiled on him... Alex found a Railway station, a perfect way to escape the city! Alex ran inside the railway station. It was a small local railway station but in a hilly area. Very few trains were at the railway station. Most of them were facing Cheniaros city, towards the floody city. Alex then finally found a small train engine, a sleek, modern, and hi-tech one though, as the year was 2162. This engine was facing the opposite side. Just to be on a safer side, Alex went inside its cockpit and checked its route. "Perfect! This is the train I want!" Alex exclaimed with relief. He switched on the train's start button. The train controls of that time were very simplified and easy. Thus Alex was good at controls as in his school many times there were workshops on operating such vehicles. And the rest complex controls of the train were controlled by the AI system. Literally, every vehicle had an AI system at that time!

The train started, Alex also pressed the Horn of the train as a result of being happy that he almost escaped Cheniaros. Then he changed the route of the train on its computer monitor screen, and changed it to Capitrolis Railway station. The train, slowly increasing its speed, started running and then finally got Alex out from Cheniaros.

He sat on the cockpit chair of the train engine, but was still worried about finding information about- "Where is everyone?" He tried to figure out some other way to know about what happened on the night when everyone disappeared. But the beautiful and scenic views kept him busy in seeing the beautiful views outside the train's window. He was delighted at least for the first time since everyone's disappearance. The train engine on its full speed, was heading towards the northern India. It was so fast that the 40 hours time which takes normal trains currently to travel from southern to northern India, now only took 6 hours! The train was smooth as well.

However, Alex failed in figuring out some other way to find the problem's cause. He was extremely curious. The sun had risen above the horizon now. It was the time of sunrise. Frustrated Alex, he said– "Ugh! Going to Cheniaros was a waste of time!" And he immediately throws his backpack in frustration, under his chair. Suddenly when the bag falls, something else comes out of the backpack. It was Jessica's Mepama, which she gave to Alex! Alex sees it, and holds it in his hands and becomes emotional. But then he realizes something. When he spent his first day with Jessica and both Alex and Jessica were talking about Mepama, he remembers something that Jessica told him. He tries recall more, and remembers the following conversation–

"So you are sure that this thing isn't dangerous in general?" Alex questioned. "Well, it might be if you use it for troubling people, but I have my own vision for this Mepama concept. I am developing more ideas about this Mepama, and I'd like it if this concept becomes a development for the world! I want this concept to do something great one day! That's why I won't call it dangerous, but powerful, because this little thing might have the capabilities to do something tough to do or do something which is needful!"

Alex's light bulb switched on! He quickly went to the train's monitor and changed the route to the town of ISRO Launch Base, not a city but a small developed town near the ISRO Launch Base, where the rockets and space missions are controlled and launched. He had a plan! A plan that probably would unfold the mystery of everyone's disappearance. The ETA (estimated time of arrival) was showing 45 minutes. Finally Alex took a nap.

EIGHT

A NON-HUMAN FRIEND?

When he woke up, the train was at a halt. He looked outside the window that he had arrived at the SpaceVillage town of India, the town near the ISRO Launch Base, and the train engine was at its railway station. Alex checked his phone and was surprised that it was 11 'o' clock! He had been sleeping for hours, even after the train had arrived at the SpaceVillage town. He wore his backpack and took the Mepama in his hand, and got out of the train engine cabin. As he came out of the train, he noticed that while Cheniaros has a massive cyclone and storm, SpaceVillage's weather was sunny and beautiful. There were green trees everywhere, and the flourishing nature, untouched by humans' hands. The hilly region was beautiful, and far away he could see various waterfalls falling from steep hills. And when he looked on the other side, he could see bungalow-like buildings which were short-heightened, and empty and silent.

He came out of the railway station and again, didn't find anyone in the town. He sighed, and walked on a road, where he looked for signs for the directions for the ISRO Launch Base. When many minutes passed and he couldn't find a way, he opened up the directions app on his phone. It showed that the ISRO Launch Base was still 11 kilometres away. Alex groaned again, but he knew that he had to go to the Launch Base. He tried to find a self-driving taxi, but as this was a town, either the taxis were manual or there were bicycles. He took a bicycle, and with the help of his phone's GPS and navigation, rode the bicycle towards the ISRO Launch Base, on a wide road. As it was a sunny day, Alex was sweating a lot. After just 4 kilometres, he decided to take a break. He parked the bicycle on the edge of the road, and sat on a large rock. Far away he could see the ocean with the seashores and the sea glimmering with the sunlight's reflection. But there was not a single house or building nearby where Alex was at that point of time. He played a song, one of his favourites from the MusiZ app on his phone, named- 'In the Middle of Nowhere', pretty much relating to his situation currently.

After 10 minutes of break, he again sat on his bicycle, and suddenly noticed something, that the bicycle had gears! That is, he could change the gear to the highest gear, and travel faster. He did so, he changed the gear to number 8, pedalled, and travelled faster as well. He was getting less tired now, yet travelling faster now. Finally, after 7 kilometres of consistent cycling, he reached the ISRO Launch Base.

However, as soon as he reached the ISRO Base, he saw a large entryway with its large gates closed. It was electronic and the whole base was surrounded by fences. "You gotta be kidding me-" murmured Alex. He had to get inside, in order to do whatever he had thought of. He tried to push the gates with his hands. Nothing happened. Turned out that the gates were made of thick and strong metal layers. He then knocked, loudly. Suddenly a tray popped out of the gates: "Requesting for a PIN." Alex obviously didn't know the code. So he tried to enter the gates through another way. He found a tree, a tall one. Its branches were going slightly on the other side of the wall of the gates. He couldn't climb the wall directly as there were sharp fences on top. So he thought of climbing the tree, climbing its branch leading to the other side of the wall, and jumping on the other side of the wall.

He somewhat tried tree climbing when he was younger, probably 2-3 years ago. So he had some confidence. He began climbing the tree. But slipped and fell on the ground as soon as he climbed half metre. He didn't give up. This time, he tried again, and successfully reached the top of the tree. Now it was super hot and sunny as it was 3 'o' clock in summers. Then he continued climbing the branch he was supposed to climb. Finally he reached the end of the branch and saw that the other side of the wall, had a few shrubs, and if he jumped on the ground, would get hurt. It was 5 metres high. So he was scared of jumping. But then he also saw a pond that was also just below the branch of the tree. Though it was also 5 metres down the branch, but it had water and Alex used his physics skills.

"If I fall on the ground, there's a hundred percent chance imma get hurt. But if I fall into the pond, there might be less chance of getting hurt." Alex thought to himself. He immediately jumped into the pond, splashing the water, and got fully wet. But he had a sort of achievement that he was now inside the ISRO Launch Base. From inside, he pulled the lever to open the gates and take the cycle inside, just in case.

Then he entered the building. It was a tall and wide building, with glass windows that looked huge. He went inside, and stepped into the main hall. There were framed pictures of ISRO missions in the main hall and beautiful furniture. Finally, he went to the reception table, where there was a map of the whole Launch Base. He searched for the IndWatch room.

"Where is it... Where's it... Where is it..." Alex mumbled to himself, finding the IndWatch room on the large map. He didn't find a specific room of IndWatch but found a large hall named 'Special Missions (Government-Based)'. Alex figured out that this might be the room he is trying to figure out. Eventually, he took the map and walked to the hall. He was having a hard time dodging through so many corridor walls and intersection barriers, but he was dedicated.

Eventually, he entered the hall, and it was majestic! Large Screens displaying slideshows of pictures of various satellites, and other large monitors displaying the stats of the satellites, like orbits, location, speed, etc. Alex was fascinated by all this. He had never ever seen such a majestic hall, in his entire life! He quickly went to one of the computers, opened the application menu, and selected the IndWatch satellite. On all the large monitors and screens, all the stats, orbit, location, height, speed were seen. He finally gained some hope for solving this mystery. He then selected one of the options, which was: "How to Lower the Satellite Orbit?" He read the complete instructions. To lower the IndWatch satellite's orbit, he had to first pull down a lever in the mission control centre, which was a large hall in the same base, but in another building of the premises.

Alex printed out the exact same instructions and then he started running for the Mission Control Centre. But then he suddenly stopped, as his smart wristwatch showed a notification labelled "Low Body Energy. Please Eat Something." So he simply went to the canteen of the premises first, and from the counter, he manually on a small touchscreen, selected a burger meal with fries. The tray of his order slid out of a vent-like space. Alex took the plastic plate and grabbed a chair to eat. While eating his lunch, he read out the instructions one more time, and then recalled his idea, to join both of them and put his idea into action.

He quickly finished his lunch and then went to the Mission Control Centre, in the other building, which he found out from the map. On his way, he suddenly heard someone speaking. He was stunned. "The heck? There's no one on this planet except me, but then who's talking?" he mumbled to himself. He tried to listen to the sound properly. "Hello? Anybody there? Help Me! I'm stuck!" He heard this sound. It was like some 7 or 8 year old saying something. Alex got diverted and went to the room from where this voice was coming. He opened the door, and saw that it was the storeroom. "Someone help! I'm stuck here!" the voice again said, in a high-pitched voice. It was coming from a closet in the storeroom. Alex was somewhat nervous, and was slowly leading towards the closet door, but nervously. He could not believe that there was someone else left apart from him! "Umm... Who's in there?" asked Alex to the voice. "Eee! You came! It's me! Gopiz!" the voice shouted excitedly. Alex took a second and then immediately opened the door to see who it was actually.

"Who are you?!" Alex shouted. "Aaaa what? Is it me? Yeah! It's me! Gopiz!" the voice replied. Gopiz was a tiny robot, with a large black screen, with two eyes and a small smile of cyan colour, appearing on the screen. He was a cute little robot, of less than a metre height. He had little hard plastic hands and legs. His head was actually a lot larger than his body. "Ugh!" Alex exclaimed, because he thought some 'human' was here, but it was actually Gopiz, this tiny little robot. "Who Gopiz?! Wait, not even who... What are you Gopiz?!" Alex yelled. "I'm Gopiz. I am a robot designed by the new-comers and students of the Technology & Engineers Committee of ISRO. In short, some cool, smart scientists made me." Gopiz replied with a cute smile. Alex had a frowned face, because his hope was again shattered.

"Whoever you are... Just go now, okay?" Alex told Gopiz. "No!" Gopiz said loudly. "I want to stay with you. Who are you?" Gopiz asked. Alex was stunned to see a robot requesting to stay with him. "I'm Alex-" "Okie-dokie! Mr Alex take me with you, I'll help in whatever work of yours!" Gopiz said and gave a cute smile again. "No. Whatever you are, I won't take you in anything so please stop talking to me or following me!" Alex yelled and stormed out of the storeroom. He took his map and instructions of the satellite, the printouts of them specifically, and continued his walk in the corridors, to the Mission Control Centre. He was feeling a bit weird and dull, but he was frustrated mostly. Walking in the corridors, suddenly Alex felt some pressure on his head, and within seconds it was Gopiz, who jumped from Alex's head, in front of him. Alex got scared for a second, and screamed to see someone immediately landing in front of him from the above. "Ta-da! Look, I'm here!" Gopiz gave an intriguing smile. Alex, after looking at him saying that in such a cute and funny voice, was about to laugh but his frustration took over that little happiness. "Are you mad? I told you not to follow me! I'm busy! I have work to do!" Alex yelled. "But I want to work with you–" Gopiz replied. "And where the hell did you jump from?!" Alex asked Gopiz boldly. "Your head. I was sitting on it the whole time you were walking and now, I've shown you a surprise!" Gopiz replied again in a funny and cute voice. He was naturally seeming too cute to ignore, too annoying to deal with, and too funny to not laugh at.

Alex just ignored Gopiz standing in front of him, and just walked past him. Gopiz became sad now, for Alex didn't need his help. But he knew that something was wrong because he too saw no other person apart from Alex. "I think I know what's wrong..." Gopiz said loudly when Alex walked just a few steps away from Gopiz, in the corridor. Alex stopped. He turned back and asked Gopiz, "What do you mean?" "Um. Um. People!" Gopiz replied. "What? What people?!" Alex asked frustratingly. "They disappeared right?" Gopiz said. Alex was shocked to see the tiny robot's awareness. He just took him out of the closet a few minutes ago, and Gopiz knew about everyone's disappearance.

After a few seconds, when Alex realized that Gopiz could be of some help too, Gopiz continued- "When 2-3 teenagers were locking me inside the closet, I don't know why, there was some slight earthquake occurring. And just when they closed the closet, there was this bright flash outside which I could see from the very small space below the closet door. And then suddenly the voices of those teenagers disappeared and the whole building fell silent." "So after that, you didn't hear anyone? Like no voice or anything?" Alex asked Gopiz. He replied- "Nope. Not a single sound or voice. I just met you after that, that is today. But please let me work with you. Pretty please?" and Gopiz made that cute face with pleading robotic eyes. "But how can you help me in my work? I am trying to do something so I can also know what happened to everyone." Alex replied. "Oh! I can help you in many ways. I know a lot of stuff, you see? I am an Ultra Artificial Intelligence Robot, and I can help you with directions, navigation, basic knowledge of places and all, and a lot of other stuff. PS, I can fly or hover too!" Gopiz replied excitedly. Alex sighed and then said- "Fine. Come join me." And Gopiz became extremely happy, and walked along with Alex, towards the Mission Control Centre.

After a while, they both reached the giant door of the Mission Control Centre. It was locked. Alex tried to push the giant doors but he failed. "Na-na-na! Don't strain yourself. Here, I got it." Gopiz said, and hovered higher a bit, and reached a fingerprint scanner beside the doors, and put his tiny hand on it. Within seconds, a unique fingerprint appeared on Gopiz's hand, and the doors unlocked. Alex was shocked. "What the heck was that?" Alex asked. "Oh, that? Well, I used to work with many scientists and administrative people, so I have the fingerprints of everyone I worked with. So pretty much, I can open any door in this campus with a fingerprint lock! So whenever I need to open a door with fingerprints, I just select the head administrative person's fingerprint, and my hand automatically constructs a fingerprint similar to the actual fingerprint of that person, on my hand! Then I scan and unlock it!" Gopiz explained.

Alex remained baffled and shocked. Gopiz was actually really useful. Then as soon as the Mission Control Centre doors opened, they both gasped. An extremely large hall, with very tall and giant windows, with a seaside view and a launch pad and a runway on the coast. The computers and large screens were displaying a lot of information about all missions. The orbits, altitudes, distances, speeds, and what not. There were all controls to all the missions in this hall too. Then there were so many tables and chairs, which were of course empty. Alex and Gopiz walked inside the hall, and then went to a table. There, Alex tried to explain his plan to Gopiz.

NINE
GOPIZ GOES INTO HIBERNATION

"Hmm... So you're saying that you want to get the IndWatch satellite's camera footage to observe carefully what has happened in the skies above the cities and land, right?" asked Gopiz. "Yep... And once we'll understand what was happening in the skies, we hopefully would try to figure out where everybody went, because as soon as that bright flash occurred, suddenly everyone disappeared. And I am one hundred percent convinced that everyone's disappearance is linked to this weird flash and patterns in the sky." Alex explained in detail. As soon as he finished speaking, he found Gopiz snoring. "Gopiz!" he shouted. "Aa! Yeah! What?" Gopiz woke up and replied. Alex stared at him and said, "Did you even listen to what I said?" "Uh... I listened till... Uh... The bright flash!" Gopiz replied. Alex placed his palm on his face.

"Why were you sleeping?! I didn't know robots sleep too!" Alex said loudly. "Well I have to take naps and sleep for a bit sometimes, as you see, to save my Battery for a while. My battery is 16%, so I am trying to save it." replied Gopiz, weakly. "Go charge yourself then." "Well, yeah I need to. Thanks Alex! Goodnight!" replied Gopiz. "It's still 7:00 PM." informed Alex. "Yeah I know, but I won't be able to say Goodnight to you later, it takes me 10 Hours to charge. So yeah!" "Well then... Goodnight." said Alex.

Gopiz went to his Charging Pod, started to charge himself, and shutted down. Alex continued to structure his plan in a better way. He had a big idea in his mind. He sat on a chair, pulled it towards a table, in the Mission Control Centre only. He switched on a Computer, and tried to gather more and more information. Alex continued his research on bringing down the

IndWatch satellite. He had in his mind on how exactly he can try to bring the satellite down. After a few hours, around 12:00 AM, Alex fell asleep, on the chair itself.

The next morning, Alex heard a lot of noise, as if a lot of furniture like chairs, desks and tables were moving. He opened his eyes only to find that Gopiz was moving all the furniture of the Mission Control Centre to one side, by pushing them all together. "What's all this?" Alex asked Gopiz, getting up from the chair, with still a sleepy face. "Oh! You're up? You slept late I guess." replied Gopiz. "Hmm... Yeah. I was structuring the plan more properly and generating better ideas, for the plan I told you about yesterday." replied Alex. "No problem. But hey, I saw that you slept on the chair itself. It is uncomfortable to sleep on it, so I am laying down some mattresses for you to sleep on from next time." said Gopiz. Alex was shocked to see Gopiz's observation and compassion for him. "So much care, for others, in a robot?" he thought to himself, still not believing the case.

"Hello! What happened?" asked Gopiz, waking up Alex from his deep thinking mode. "Yes! Uh. Thanks Gopiz. I really appreciate it." Alex thanked Gopiz, putting his hand forward to Gopiz, offering a handshake to him. Gopiz was smiling already, but he became happier to see that Alex liked something he did, and is friendlier to Gopiz.

Alex quickly helped Gopiz set up the mattresses and then both of them went to the canteen to get something for Breakfast. Of course, Gopiz didn't eat anything, and Alex just had a cold and dry burger. But both of them were discussing the final plan for the last time.

"Now look... After lowering the IndWatch Satellite's orbit from the Mission Control Centre, we're going to attract it to the ground using giant Mepamas, fixed on the wings and body of the Unmanned Aerial Vehicles or UAVs." Alex explained the final plan's summary to Gopiz. UAVs were basically remote controlled aeroplane-like vehicles, the only difference was that it was controlled from the ground remotely by a Human, and had no one inside it.

Alex's brilliant idea of using Jessica's invented Mepama with the UAVs was believable, and probably even practical. But for this required both Alex and Gopiz had to work really hard to manufacture Mepama on large scale, attach them on the UAVs and a lot of other work too.

"And we'll make the UAVs fly just below the IndWatch Satellite's location so it falls off from its orbit trajectory and starts falling to the surface, landing it in the Bay of Bengalia." continued Gopiz, to sum up the plan. "But is it safe to land in the ocean? What if it lands somewhere else like on land?" Alex inquired. "Ah! Don't worry about that. The satellite has an emergency parachute which we could activate when it starts falling from its orbit." Gopiz replied. They both agreed to this plan and started thinking how they will now execute this plan.

After Alex had his breakfast, he and Gopiz got out of the canteen, and started walking in the corridors. So where will we manufacture the giant Mepamas?" asked Alex. "Uhm... We can do it in the ISROEM centre, but it's a bit far away." replied Gopiz nervously. "How far? It'll take us 10 minutes... 15 minutes... 30 minutes max?" asked Alex. "1 day, 12 minutes." answered Gopiz. "The heck?! You gonna gotta be kidding me!" exclaimed Alex. "Nope. The estimated time is this if we travel by walking though." said Gopiz. "Bruh- Tell me how far is it by Helicar?" asked Alex, again. "Oh! Okay. By Helicar it will take us 20 minutes." "Now that's something believable." Alex commented. While conversing with each other, they reached the Mission Control Hall, once again. Soon they got ready, Alex changed his three days old clothes, and washed his face and took his backpack with him. After getting ready, they went to the helicar parking lot. Gopiz generated a fingerprint, pressed the fingerprint on the helicar lock sensor and the vehicle unlocked, and the doors opened.

It was a simpler helicar than the one Alex travelled in to Cheniaros. They both took their seats, and fastened their seatbelts. Gopiz entered the Location of ISROEM Centre, and after entering the details, he said: "So... Ready to go, Chief?" Alex sighed and replied, "Let's solve this mystery damn it!" and expressed the one and only purpose for what they both were working for. Gopiz pulled the lever and Alex clicked on the Start Journey button. The Helicar turned on, made some noise, rose up in the air, and flew away. Just a few minutes after their journey started, Alex asked, "ISRO, well I know, but what is ISROEM?" "Indian Space Research Organisation Equipment Manufacturing Centre." replied Gopiz. "Ah... I see. It's a pretty complicated short form." said Alex. "It is? Lol, I know millions of such short forms." told Gopiz. "Because you are a robot. A kind of computer." said Alex. Gopiz giggled in response.

They continued having a general conversation, while suddenly the Helicar monitor indicated- "You are about to reach your destination in 3 minutes." They both got ready to implement their plan. When they landed, Alex unfastened his seatbelt, and said, "Let's go bro. We've reached." But there was no response. "Gopiz?" he called and turned to Gopiz, only to see that Gopiz's digital eyes, mouth and face was replaced by a progress bar, and a Label saying- "Updating Artificial Intelligence System. Estimated Time of completion is 120 hours." Alex screamed in frustration and anger. He got out of the Helicar / slammed its door, closing it. Alex's face was full of disappointment and frustration. He looked at the ISROEM building complex, with a frowny face. Then he looked back at the stationary Helicar, Gopiz inside it, in deep sleep as if he's hibernating.

"What a useless robot!" Peter said, mockingly. "Peter, shut up!" Aryan shouted at him. "But yes, poor Alex. Finally he got someone to talk to, and now he's gone too."" said Garima "Not 'gone', actually, just hibernating." replied Rhea. "Guys it doesn't look nice if we keep interrupting the flow of narration of the story." said Aryan. "Oh okay. Please continue William." said Garima. "No, like it's actually great if we discuss and take breaks in between the narration. Like this shows how deeply you guys are lost in listening to the story. Seems nice!" said William and then he continued, "Anyways...

Alex was now in complete despair, for he knew that Gopiz's revival was impossible, not at least before 120 hours. "Dang it man! Why the heck did I even believe that I finally have a companion?" Alex shouted to himself. "After all, he is just a stupid AI robot!" he then exclaimed. He kept blaming himself because he trusted Gopiz that the latter could help him in his attempt to solve the mystery, and the cause of their disappearance. It was now that Alex experienced the actual loneliness, after his trust shattered into a million pieces. It was a frustrating feeling that he didn't experience before, not even after everyone just disappeared when he was in Capitrolis, but now, after his mind was surrounded by clouds of fear. The fear of lack of hope.

Alex knew that if he tried to cancel the update of Gopiz's software manually, it might revive him and wake him up again. But he did not want to take any risk because then the matter would not be just of a few days, but forever. Any error in interfering with Gopiz's hardware to stop the software update could lead to complete shutdown of Gopiz's systems, forever. Hence, again, Alex had no option but to move ahead alone, at least for those 5 days- 120 hours.

TEN

ALEX SURVEYS THE ISROEM CENTRE

It was afternoon now. Being summer, it was super hot. Alex was sweating a lot. So he finally accepted the situation and wore his backpack, and then started to walk towards the ISROEM centre complex. He tried to overcome the feeling of loneliness by pushing himself to do what was required. But even though Alex just spent one day with Gopiz, his absence halved the motivation to implement the plan. As soon as he reached the main gate, the large steel gates automatically opened.

Alex entered the complex, after once again turning back and looking at the distant parked Helicar. The complex was large, with modern and factory-like buildings and roads connecting different parts of the complex. Now Gopiz had the knowledge about the ISROEM centre. Alex, on the other hand, didn't even know a thing about it. So he himself had to first visit the reception and then find a way to the manufacturing department factory building. And so he did all this. After half an hour of studying the complex map, Alex had learned the entire map of the complex and now remembered everything on his fingertips. He got out of the main building which had the reception area, and then started walking towards the manufacturing factory building. It was a bit far, a kilometre away. He became thirsty and hungry now. Yet, he thought to himself, "My silly hunger is just gonna waste my time that I could use instead to implement my plan." In this way he tried to ignore his natural requirements.

After some twenty minutes of walking slowly, he reached the Manufacturing factory building. With a sigh of relief, he entered. All his tiredness was gone after he saw the interiors. Large aluminium alloy wings, carbon fiber parts, rocket engines, steel components lifted by cranes or hanging from the roof. It was a very spacious and large factory. Next-gen machinery Alex didn't even know about, were placed on large tables with messy stuff of iron, screws, tools, and blueprints of spacecrafts and rocket designs. Weird lookings machines rocket engines and spacecraft parts were lying here and there, on tables, chairs, stools, desks, and even on the floor. There was barely any space on the floor to even walk comfortably. Nevertheless, Alex walked towards the main, long and broad table. Immediately, he saw something familiar that made him feel astonished and excited- "Is this... Is this Genera 9Xi?" He saw a massive 3D-printing machine, a model that only two major space companies possessed- GoSpace, of Akstonea, and ISRO, of India. It was the most advanced 3D printer, in the entire world, of that time.

"I don't believe this. All this time, they had hidden it here?!" He exclaimed in excitement. Now he realized that by using this 3D-printer, how easy could the manufacturing of the giant Mepamas be. All those things that had to be done manually, like making each giant Mepama part individually, now could quickly be processed and made using this 3D-printer. The hope and confidence that he lost was now regained by him. He started to believe that he can himself make the giant Mepamas, attach them with the UAVs and bring IndWatch down. He became self confident at this point of time.

It was not that he forgot the absence of Gopiz, but that he could go solo now, because his trust for Gopiz was broken anyway. After all, he was just a machine or computer. Alex further began exploring the factory. The giant spacecraft parts hanging from the cranes, inside the factory, with extremely tall roof made of steel and concrete, were making Alex realize that he was in an extremely important place, especially for ISRO. Since childhood, he was a big fan of space exploratory missions, rockets and spacecrafts. But he never saw them in real life before. But now seeing them, and that too in their manufacturing and developmental stages took Alex back in time. He recalled how much he enjoyed watching space and sci-fi movies with his parents. Their memories made him severely emotional. He felt like crying out loud, but knew deep down that doing so would get him nowhere. It would just be a time wasting action. So with just one or two drops of tears flowing and then falling from his eyes, he wiped his eyes and focused on the present, again. "Stick to the goal, Alex." he mumbled a few times.

Right now, his only goal was to find out if there are the basic materials here, at the ISROEM centre, to make the giant Mepamas for the UAVs. He had taken screenclicks (the future name for screenshots), of whatever research he did about the materials of Mepama by clicking and searching its pictures online using image search engine, just like we have Google Lens. He took these screenclicks the last night when he did research about what the Mepama is actually made of, by clicking its picture and searching it up on the internet to identify its material composition. This research was important for him to understand how exactly Mepama was made and how can he make more. So he kept on exploring the factory. He saw so many different shelves, trays, and benches with a lots of industrial items in all of them. He surveyed the entire factory to ensure the presence of at least all the basic materials that he'll probably use to make the giant Mepamas.

He did this for quite a lot of time and spent almost two hours, just surveying. Finally, after checking out the entire factory building, he was really hungry now. He went to the vending machine, in a corner of the factory. Alex didn't know how to cook much, hence he always looked for fast food or processed food from superstores and shops, after everyone disappeared. However the vending machine items were not free; it demanded money. So Alex just opened his Digital Payments app and scanned the QR code of the vending machine. After the payment was done, he got a sandwich, a small cupcake as dessert and a bottle of drinking water. He then had his lunch.

After lunch, he looked at his wristwatch, only to notice that it was almost 3:00 PM. He wondered if he should get some more sandwiches and water bottles to take them with him back to the ISRO Launch Base, where he and Gopiz came from, so he could have those sandwiches there. And it seemed like a great idea because he was bored of the canteen food there and this sandwich was far better than the stale and cold food of the canteen of ISRO Launch Base. Eventually, he decided to go to the vending machine, and buy a few more sandwiches and water bottles. He did so, paid to the vending machine, got the items and packed them in his backpack. When it was almost 3:30 PM, he concluded that he'll manufacture the giant mepamas here only, in the ISROEM centre. And finally, he left the manufacturing factory building.

While walking back towards the main gate, which was again, a kilometre away, Alex thought and worked out with his brain- "Yeah sure, I have got the place to make the giant Mepamas. And, yes, I know the basic materials and stuff which I probably need to make them. The only problem now is that I don't have the exact structure and configuration of Mepama. And without that, I can't make the Mepamas because I wouldn't know how and what to join and prepare to make the Mepamas." He thought and thought and thought, and finally he got the idea to go to Jessica's house in Capitrolis, and get the Mepama configuration charts because he recalled another conversation from the past that Alex and Jessica had in the School Metro while going back to their metro stations from the School:-

"So this Mepama thing... How did you plan and manage the idea to make this?" Alex asked. "Well, I did a lot of research, studies and planned a lot. I made entire diagrams of the components, design and configuration of the Mepama's Structure on big charts and stuff." replied Jessica.

Hence, Alex decided. "I'll get those charts, perfect!" While thinking and planning all this, he reached the main gate. Soon, after exiting the complex he saw the Helicar, still parked. He got in, and saw Gopiz, still with a progress bar on his screen, still in deep sleep. Alex sighed, and closed his Helicar door. Unexpectedly, there was an alert that the Helicar needs electric recharging. Its battery was almost over, and the Helicar could only fly 10-15 kilometres more. Alex got more worried. Nevertheless, he searched for any nearby Helicar charging stations. He found one, which was just 3 kilometres away. He programmed the Helicar to land at that charging station, and started the journey. Once again, the Helicar took off and flew away, but this time, with Gopiz unconscious. Alex put his head on the headrest of the seat, relaxing after an exerting day.

He then looked at Gopiz, who was of course, still with the progress bar on his screen, which used to actually be his face. With the distance between ISROEM centre and the charging station being quite less, very quickly the Helicar landed on a cemented Helicar Pad. It landed in a Helicar parking lot, with several other Helicars parked on the adjacent Helicar pads, all parked in a row. Alex saw a charging machine, and he took the charging cable from its handle, opened Helicar's charging port, by first opening a hatch, and connected the charging cable to the charging port. Estimated full charge time was 25 minutes, which he saw on the Charging machine's screen.

While the Helicar was charging, Alex kept walking in the Helicar parking lot of the charging station, looking here and there, at the surroundings, seeing the small town and its quiet atmosphere without people around. Suddenly, he saw something horrifying. A shiver ran down his spine. He saw something he never expected. A large airplane crashed into a building, and was broken into two parts- the front and the back portions. The debris was lying all around. And this crash site wasn't much far from the Helicar

Charging Station. It was just a few hundred metres away.

Alex, out of curiousity, ran to the crash site. When he reached, he saw that most of the plane was already burnt due to the fuel blash. There was however a broken space in the fuselage of the plane, and he thought of going into the crashed plane from this small entrance. It felt scary at first, but Alex's curious nature most of the time suppresses his fears. He entered the burnt and crashed plane from the broken space, only to find more debris, broken stuff, and bags fallen. It seemed like the plane crashed into the building very horrifically. However there was not even a single dead body, not even one. So Alex soon got out of the crashed plane, and thought that everyone must've disappeared first, and then because no one was actually flying the plane anymore, it might would've crashed. He got out of the crashed plane and started walking back to the charging station, still not believing the massive destruction and the crash he just saw.

He thought, "What a person feels is not completely what they realize." He thought this with relevance to the context of what a person feels, or the emotions of a person are often generated only due to the circumstances right in front of them, and not due to the entire realization. In other words, the emotions are incomplete. When Alex understood that he's the last person remaining in the entire world, he felt the loss of what was in front of him, the lack of his family, parents, new crush- Jessica, and all the other people he knew. However, his feelings didn't include the emotions of what other things would've happened in the world and the other consequences and outcomes of this event of disappearance of everyone.

When he walked to and finally reached the charging station, he noticed that the Helicar was now fully recharged. He disconnected the charging cable, closed the charging port and the hatch, and restarted the Helicar. Gopiz was in his deep sleep, unconscious, as Alex expected him to be. It was now almost 5 in the evening. Hence, Alez decided to head back to the ISRO Launch Base. He quickly entered the destination and location on the driverless Helicar's computer monitor and flew away from the eerie atmosphere of the crash site of the plane he saw. While in the sky, flying and heading to the ISRO Launch Base, Alex wondered whether he should go back to Capitrolis tonight, to get the Mepama design and configuration charts from Jessica's house, or he should go tomorrow morning. He knew that Gopiz is hibernating, so he'll be on his own. The night travelling plan seemed scary and uncomfortable too, as he already encountered the unwelcoming and eerie situation just some time ago- the Plane Crash. So he was already anxious and hence thought to spend the night at the Launch Base only, and head to Capitrolis tomorrow. Another reason for taking this decision was that he was really tired after exploring the ISROEM factory, travelling and all of that. Plus going to Capitrolis tomorrow would give him tonight's time to relect further on his plans and ideas, and he could do more research.

Alex then gazed at hibernating Gopiz, with the progress bar being only filled with a small percentage. "Why Gopiz... Just why?! Why did you have to leave me on my own, that too now?" said Alex in a frustrated tone. He was saying so as if Gopiz was awake and could hear him. "But you know what? I don't care. You broke my trust? Fine. Now I am gonna show you that even a 13 year old boy could alone, do big things, like solving mysteries. Sure, I don't need you anymore!" exclaimed and shouted Alex. He was determined to boycott Gopiz and stop taking his help, even in future. He made a decision that he'll do everything from now on alone, and by himself.

They finally landed in the Helicar parking of the ISRO Launch Base, and Alex went to the Mission Control Centre room. Gopiz was still in deep sleep, hibernating. Meanwhile, Alex reached the Mission Control Centre doors but remained standing in front of the automatic doors, because it required a valid fingerprint, which only Gopiz could generate. "Wow! I literally forgot about this-" murmured Alex, sarcastically. Then he got an idea, which was a bit vandalistic. He went to the area outside of the Mission Control Centre room, which was basically a green garden with a few rocks. It was almost sunset now. Alex picked up a rock, and threw it powerfully towards the Mission Control Centre's large glass windows. It shattered the top portion of a glass window pane. He threw a few more rocks, until the entire glass window pane broke and shattered. Now there was an entrance to the Mission Control Centre room, made by shattering and breaking a whole glass window pane. Through this entrance, Alex could now go inside, simply by walking through the entrance. He felt an increase in his confidence as he accomplished something, without the assistance of Gopiz. He stepped over the shattered pieces of glass and entered the Control Centre room.

He then decided to open the automatic doors of this Control Centre room from inside and make them get stuck, by placing a small desk or table between them, so he does not have to use the broken glass window entrance again and again, and the automatic doors remain open. Hence, he dragged a small desk, opened the automatic main doors of the Mission Control Centre from inside, and placed the desk in between the doors. Now these doors were unable to close completely, and there was enough gap between the doors for Alex to climb onto the desk and walk through the doors. After it was 7 in the evening, the sun had set and it was night time. Alex opened and switched on his Airtop, and estimated the duration of the Helicar flight from where he was to his home back in Capitrolis. The GPS Navigation app indicated that the duration of the Helicar flight was 1 hour and 45 minutes. "Not bad." said Alex to himself, after looking at the duration of the flight.

Another thing that clicked in his mind was that he wanted to check out the UAVs he was going to use for his plan. They were parked in an aircraft hangar of the same place, that is, the ISRO Launch Base. "Well, so I guess I'll sleep early today and wake up at 4 AM, early in the morning tomorrow." He wanted to see the dimensions and size of the UAVs to see if they are large enough to get a lot of giant Mepamas fixed to them, so they could attract and pull down the Indwatch satellite effectively. So as planned, Alex got ready to sleep early. He quickly had his dinner meal, which were the sandwiches he got from the ISROEM centre vending machine. Then he had some water, attended nature's call and finally got ready to sleep. As he came back from the toilet, he noticed the mattress that Gopiz laid down for Alex to sleep on. He again started to miss Gopiz's presence. But no, he wanted to boycott him. So he tried to suppress this feeling. He took a pillow and a blanket from a storage cabinet; lied down on the mattress, and went to sleep after setting an alarm scheduled for 4 AM in the morning for the next day. Alex slept, and he knew that he was another step ahead towards the goal to find everyone.

ELEVEN
VISITING JESSICA'S HOUSE

At 4:00 AM, the awaited alarm rang on Alex's phone. He woke up, still feeling sleepy and drowsy. However, he pushed himself to get ready early, to first go and check out the UAVs, then to head back to Capitrolis. So he switched on the Mission Control Centre's lights, and the entire hall lit up. Then he went to the washroom and finally got ready. He took his phone, and walked to the UAVs parking hangar. He got out of the building and started walking on the proper cemented asphalt, where a lot of spacecrafts and space planes were parked. The Launch Base outdoors was almost like a large airport outdoors, with plane parking spaces, taxiways, runways and launchpads. Alex followed the map and after ten minutes, reached the UAVs hangar. He pushed a beeping blue button, to open the shutter gates of the UAVs hangar. The shutter gates went up, and it was all dark inside the hangar and nothing was visible due to night time. So he switched on his phone's torch for a better view.

He slowly walked inside the hangar, and pushed a little glowing switch to turn on the hangar lights. One, two, three, four... One by one each of the large lights switched on. Alex's eyes sparkled with surprise and awe. Ten to twelve Modern UAVs, with a redesigned look, perfect for Alex's plan, were parked in the large UAVs Hangar. Alex went further ahead to get a closer look. All the UAVs were painted snowy white, and a fantastic good-looking ISRO logo was printed on the body of each UAV. Each of the UAV had a large surface area and large wings, exactly what Alex hoped for. "What a blessing! These are perfect." he exclaimed after checking out the UAVs. He then went back to the gates of the hangar, and said to the UAVs- "I'll come back soon boys. Get ready for the action!" And then he closed down the shutter gates once again, using the same beeping button. Alex felt like although he was in a miserable situation, all the odds were in his favour. He got the exact place he was looking for- the ISROEM Centre, and now the perfect UAVs.

It was almost 5:00 AM in the morning when Alex was packing all his stuff in his backpack for his journey back to Capitrolis, so as to get the Mepama configuration charts from Jessica's house. He had his morning meal, the same sandwich, and had some juice by getting it from the Launch Base canteen. Finally, by 6 AM, he was ready to go. He was just wearing his socks and shoes when something clicked in his mind- "It might take me more than 3-4 days to come back here." he thought. "Then this stupid robot would wake up and look for me and think that I have gone missing." Despite wanting to boycott Gopiz, he thought this for him. So he wrote a short and rude letter for Gopiz, went to the helicar in which Gopiz was hibernating, in the helicar parking. He opened the Helicar, and placed the letter on Gopiz's left hand. He then got out, and realised- "Oh crap. Helicars require fingerprints." And the only helicar that was already unlocked was the one in which Gopiz was there, in deep sleep.

So Alex thought for a while. First he thought of taking Gopiz with him to Capitrolis. But because he was angry at Gopiz, he called off the idea. So he simply lifted Gopiz from the latter's seat, and got out of the Helicar once again. Surprisingly, Gopiz was quite light. "Prolly he's made out of Carbon Fiber." he mumbled as he held Gopiz in both of his arms. He finally put Gopiz down, on the floor of the building corridors. Then he sighed, and walked away to Helicar Parking. There he boarded the unlocked Helicar and started it. He entered his apartment society's helipad's location and started the Helicar by pulling the lever. It rose up in the air and started flying. "Battery? Check. Weather? Check. Software? Check!" He completed his general Helicar checklist as it started flying. And eventually, it reached high in the sky, almost soaring above the clouds, and the journey began.

Alex decided to rest for a while, so he took a little nap. When he woke up, there was still a lot of time was left- 1 hour and 18 minutes. So he switched on his phone, and reviewed his sequential plan that he typed in the notes app of his phone. He kept reading and scrolling, and added a few more bullet points in it. His plan was to first arrive at his home, have his breakfast, get a shower, then head to his school. There he would search Jessica's home address so he could finally go and reach there. He also wanted to visit the Library once again, but this time to get books related to manufacturing, aviation, and other books related to the concern. He had a lot to study, understand, and experiment before he could actually implement his plan to bring the IndWatch down.

Alex was still sad about Gopiz's temporary shutdown, but remained ignorant to the thought of using his help further later. He checked the time remaining once again to reach his home in Capitrolis. "55 minutes?! You've gotta be joking!" he murmured. So he decided to listen to some songs while travelling, on his MusiZ app. So he started listening to some motivational and energetic songs to boost his confidence and stay focused and determined for his mission- to bring the IndWatch down. He put his head back on the seat's headrest and closed his eyes to relax as well. "I don't know... What it takes to succeed... What it takes to believe... What it takes to be the real me... All I can do is, fight for it!" These were the lyrics of the kind of songs Alex was listening to. He spent quite a lot of time listening to music, and then got bored of it. So instead of playing another song, he played a podcast, just to hear actual other people's voices, in a world where everyone was just gone. It was an interesting motivational podcast, about the stories of a person who was being interviewed by another person, how he overcame his challenges, how he dealt with failures, and finally succeeded.

After listening to the podcast for a while too, he checked the time remaining to land. There were still 21 minutes left. Although the main capital city of Capitrolis was still far away, Alex saw the entire National Capital Region down there on the land surface. He could see the developed towns and urban areas. The NCR (National Capital Region) was as developed as Capitrolis- the centre of NCR, with modern buildings, city features and infrastructure. Alex was flying over the NCR at this moment of time. So he removed his headphones and looked out of the window to see the beautiful and glittering modern towns and small cities of the NCR. The view was enough to tell that he is about to reach Capitrolis, for it was just like the capital city looked like. Seeing the glittering skyscrapers, and the beauty of the infrastructure and city-like features of the NCR region even from the sky, from the Helicar made Alex feel optimistic. The NCR was welcoming him back home. He now had an urge to quickly and positively do what he's here for. So he was happy to come back to Capitrolis, despite not seeing any other person.

Finally, the helicar landed on the helipad of Alex's Residential Society. He immediately unfastened his seatbelt, wore his backpack and ran towards his building. "Hey Elevis! How have you been doing?" Alex asked his elevator's voice recognition AI, as he entered the elevator. "Hi Alex! I've been doing well. Let's head to your default floor- Floor 71st, shall we?" the voice AI replied. "Uh... Yeah. Thanks!" Alex confirmed the floor, and the elevator started moving up. He got excited to see his house once again after a bunch of days, although he also wished that his parents and sister would be at home, which was as expected, not possible.

The elevator dinged, and Alex went inside his apartment by simply pushing the main wooden door, as its lock was already broken by Alex in frustration when he was breaking other apartments' doors with the axe. His home made him feel comfortable as he entered and stood in the living room, but the loneliness of course, bothered him. However, he kept his feelings aside and went to his bedroom. He took out a trolley bag and stuffed a lot of his clothes in it, as he needed to go back to the ISRO Launch Base near SpaceVillage for a longer period of time now. He also took a few rough notebooks for calculations and rough work too. Suddenly, his eyes fell on a paper slip with Jessica's phone number on it, which she gave to Alex in the school metro while going back home. He became emotional, unpinned the paper slip from the softboard, and kept it safely in his wallet, as her memory. He also kept his Educity Level 1 Physics Workbooks, just in case, for practice. "All packing done, finally!" He then lied down on his bed, not only because he was tired of travelling and then packing everything in his trolley bag, but also because he had a long day ahead. That was because he first had to go to his school, and then to Jessica's house to get the Mepama diagrams, structure and configuration charts. He switched on his phone only to notice that it was 9:30 AM already. So ignoring his lethargy, he went to take a shower, for he hadn't taken one since a bunch of days.

He finally came out of the bathroom after taking a bath, and got all ready for the day ahead. His dedicated perspective knew that he must do whatever it takes to solve the mystery of everyone's disappearance. So he got his backpack ready once more, and finally got out of his apartment. "Alright Elevis, let's head to the Ground Floor." prompted Alex, to the Elevator's AI voice recognition. "Sure, Alex!" The automated digital voice replied, and the elevator started heading down. He stepped outside the elevator as soon as it reached the ground floor and the doors opened, and was walking out of his building, through the luxurious reception area of his building. It was very sunny outside, being the second-last month of summer. The heat was so much that Alex got tired even before starting to walk to the Helicar Pad building. "Gosh... The heat!" he thought to himself. He wished there would be some sort of faster way to reach there so he won't have to tolerate so much heat for much of the time.

But well, his wish came true! His eyes suddenly took notice of a small area, with 3 to 4 electric kick scooters parked in that small area, near the entrance of his building. Those kick scooters were actually used by his residential society's staff and maintenance people, back in the time when everyone was present. But well, now that Alex was alone, they were abandoned. However, Alex made up his mind to use a electric kick scooter to reach the Helicar Pad's building faster. He picked up one of those kick scooters, tightened his backpack straps so it doesn't fall off easily, switched on the electric kick scooter by pressing the power button, and pushed off the ground with his left leg, and started to move ahead. It was a rejuvenating and exciting experience. The wind was blowing calmly and peacefully against Alex, while he was riding the kick scooter. After just a 2 or 3 minutes journey, he reached the Helipad building's entrance. He switched off the electric kick scooter, and before he could leave it, he thought, "Why leave it over here only? This could be useful in travelling through large complexes." So instead of just leaving the kick scooter right there, he folded it, and carried it with him, inside the building. It was quite heavy, for it was a fast-speed electric kick scooter, but Alex managed to carry it with him till the building elevator, and went up to the building's terrace, where his Helicar was parked. The elevator's doors opened, and he walked up to the helipad; opened the door of the Helicar and had a seat after keeping the folded kick scooter on the seat beside him. "Alright, let's head to Yartrunas International School." he said to himself, while entering the location on the Helicar's computer screen after closing its door and switching it on. The Helicar rose up, and whooshed away from the helipad.

The helicar was peacefully cruising in the sky. However, something unexpected occurred. Massive dark clouds started to settle in, transforming the clear blue sky into a sky full of large and thick dark grey clouds. Alex unlocked his phone and checked the weather forecast, only to find that there's this massive thunderstorm coming to Capitrolis, although the forecast was updated by the automatic AI weather analyzer server. "How is this even possible? It was so sunny and hot just a few minutes ago." thought Alex. But he hoped to reach his school just before the thunderstorm rain showers began. But it was too late. The dark clouds had already rolled in, and just within a few seconds, intense winds and rain began. At first, it didn't affect the Helicar much. But then it began to indicate an alert on its screen- "Potential Risk of Severe Weather Conditions." Alex gave the Helicar computer a command to rise further up, above the clouds to avoid being affected by the thunderstorms. Hence, the helicar increased its altitude. But this decision had its own challenges. Due to an immediate change in the atmospheric conditions and altitude, the core systems of the Helicar were affected. This flashed more and more alerts repeatedly on the computer monitor screen. "Warning: System Stress Detected - Overload Imminent!" This made Alex panic, as there was a risk of crashing. Although he was above the clouds now, the core systems of Helicar started to malfunction. So the only decision he felt was worth taking was to land the Helicar wherever he was currently, as an emergency landing.

Hence, Alex commanded the Helicar to securely land in an open space, wherever it was currently located. So finally, the helicar descended, came below the clouds once again, and then finally near the land surface. The thunderstorm was stronger than before. Visibility was extremely less. But luckily due to the precise GPS and navigation technology of the self-flying helicar, it landed in an open park. The helicar automatically switched off as soon as it landed over the green grass of the open park. When Alex checked the location, he realised that he was only halfway to his school. "Darn it, man!" he shouted. "Why did it only have to happen today?!" He was totally frustrated. He tried to look outside the windows of the helicar, but all he could see was heavy rain showers, and only the grass that surrounded the place where the Helicar landed. Everything else was invisible due to the dark thunderstorm and heavy downpour. He checked the weather forecast one more time, to see what the predictions say about the duration of the storm, and got even more disappointed and annoyed to know that the storm would persist for 3 or even more hours, starting that particular moment.

His helicar being caught in a thunderstorm, all he could really do was-wait. So he reclined his seat and tried to take a nap. But well, the repeated and loud thunder noises kept him awake. So I really didn't have any other option besides using his phone. So he switched on his phone, and checked out some old videos on Viduoz, just because there was nothing to do. So he was just scrolling through those short-duration videos which were just like Instagram reels that we have today, but then suddenly he found a video of a race car. Watching that video, he felt something odd, and then he realised and exclaimed to himself- "Oh god. What a fool am I! This is a Heli-car, not a Helicopter! Why can't I just drive it till my school?" You know, just for clarity,

Alex was super intelligent, but sometimes became the exact opposite of that, that is- super stupid.

So with the intention of making the helicar drive itself on land and roads instead of making it fly through the skies, Alex enabled the Road Self-drive command and switched to Land-Travel mode. And as expected, it successfully worked. Despite the difficulty of the massive thunderstorm which quite felt like a cloudburst, Alex decided to continue his journey to his school, but this time, via land. The Helicar's wings and flying components contracted and retracted as they were no longer needed, and the wheels came out even more, to navigate the Helicar properly. Alex clicked the start button and the Helicar started moving smoothly, just like cars travel on land. The helicar took a few turns to navigate out of the green park where it had landed, and finally took a last turn, merging onto the main road. Alex just kept his seat reclined and closed his eyes and let out a sigh of relief, as the Helicar speeded up on the main road, continuing its journey to Alex's school. It was still raining heavily, and the Helicar was driving itself. Alex unknowingly was sound asleep, as if the act of following through brought him relief to peacefully sleep.

After Alex woke up, he noticed that there were only 5 minutes left for him to reach his school. So he got all ready, meanwhile the rain became less intense too. It seemed like the thunderstorm was retreating away. So Alex packed up his backpack, put his phone in his jeans pockets, and finally drank some water before becoming all set to get into his school campus.

As the Helicar reached the main gate of his school campus, the rain almost stopped. Still, the ground was as expected wet and all, and riding the kick scooter on such a surface of course didn't seem like a good idea. "Alright then... I'll just walk." Alex thought to himself, and sighed. So he opened the door and stepped out of the helicar, only to feel tiny droplets of rainwater still falling on his face from the sky, but in almost negligible amounts. He walked up to the gates and tried to open the large metal gates, but they seemed to be locked. This frustrated him more. "You've gotta be kidding me... YOU'VE GOTTA BE KIDDING! FIRST THE THUNDERSTORM, THEN THE HELICAR WARNINGS AND SHUT DOWN AND NOW THIS?!" Alex shouted angrily, lifted his leg off the ground, and kicked the main gates with a strong force. Frustrated Alex, then stood in front of the campus gates, feeling pity for himself. Unexpectedly, he heard an electrical crackling sound coming from the portion of the gates where he kicked his leg. He turned back to the gates, only to find some electrical sparks with a crackling sound. This sparking persisted for a few seconds until it suddenly led to the burning of the circuit in the digitally-powered main gates. This eventually unlocked the gates just after a few seconds. Alex was stunned; how did one kick on the main gates lead to the burning and breaking of the main gates digitally-powered lock? And now the gates automatically opened, as its digital-lock system became broken and defective.

Alex, anyways, did not waste time overthinking. He went inside his school campus, being welcomed by the cool and pleasant winds blowing against his face, flags of Yartrunas International School waving along with the Indian flag in the large garden of the school, and the large School campus awaiting Alex's presence. It was a large campus, which of course tired Alex as he was walking in it. The building he was first heading to was the main Reception and Management staff building, including the Principal's office. But he looked in all directions again and again, mumbling to himself- "I seriously never saw this large school campus so silent and empty." The fact that even his school which was quite large in terms of area was devoid of anyone but Alex made him feel weird and uncomfortable. But he regained his confidence when he suddenly recalled that he alone had been to major places like Cheniaros, ISRO Launch Base, and ISROEM Centre, already. So visiting his own school should be a piece of cake anyway.

As he walked and came closer and closer to the Reception building, the sky cleared and the black storm clouds retreated almost fully. He quickly recalled his plan of what he has to do in his School. His plan was simple. In a nutshell, he just had to go to the Reception and Management Staff building, and get Jessica's residential address from the database or records, wherever the school staff would have kept them. He just needed to figure out if these records were written on paper or he would need to access a computer to get those records or that information. In the case of a computer, he was just worried if the computer had a login password to access it. So he hoped for either a password-free computer, or the records and information available on papers.

He finally entered the reception and management staff building, after climbing a few stairs. The beautiful architecture of his school buildings always mesmerised him. And just when the stairs terminated, the automatic sliding glass doors opened, allowing Alex to enter. And he finally entered the main reception area of the school. It was an extremely huge hall with luxury and comfortable furniture, and a large Reception desk, of course, this time with no one present there. Alex quickly walked to the management staff room of the building, and entered the room. There were lots of files, folders, documents and papers all scattered in the room. There were a few Laptops and Computers as well. For a few seconds, he felt overwhelmed, not knowing where to start. "Come on Alex! We have to find the address. For humanity's sake!" But he of course didn't know which computer to use to access the database. So he just went to the conference table and switched on every single computer on it, there being six or seven of them. He did so because the database could be in any of them.

After turning on all of them, he individually checked every computer that didn't have a password for login, but found no database. "What the hell man! Why'd they only put the database in a computer that was protected by password?!" He shouted frustratingly. But then, Alex isn't just Alex like that. He's himself, for a reason. His unique and smart approach came in handy. "The CCTVs..." he mumbled to himself, almost as he spoke to himself in mind. He looked for any CCTV and security cameras attached on the roof or ceiling of the room, and fortunately, found a camera, facing all the Computers which had passwords, all the three of them situated on the same side of the table. Alex quickly rushed to the Security and CCTV room. It was in the same building, just a few more rooms away from where he currently was. The excitement and impatience in Alex made him run like he never did. Just in a matter of a few seconds, he reached and entered the CCTV Surveillance Room. He walked to the large CCTV Monitor, and sat down on the chair placed near its desk. This being beneficial for him, the CCTV Surveillance monitor didn't have a password to log in. So Alex just accessed it, and opened up the Surveillance recording tab of the management staff room, and set a date of two or three days before everyone disappeared, and when his school was full of students, teachers and staff. So he got the recordings and he began to carefully observe the things happening. For a few minutes, nothing happened. It was a very monotonous recording. So Alex decided to speed it up from Normal speed to 1.5x speed. As he did so, just after a few more minutes of watching, he saw the management staff people come and sit down on those previously empty chairs of the Management Staff Room's Password-protected computers, and switch on their computers. So Alex slowed down the recording that very moment, and reversed the recording a bit so he could observe more closely. His super logical and intelligent nature made him trace the password of all those three password-protected computers! He zoomed the recording to the fingers of the management staff, closely watching their fingers, to see what they actually type. The very clear and high resolution camera allowed him to see their finger movements with precision and accuracy. One by one, for all the three computers he saw and noted down the finger presses on the keyboard, and noted down the password for each. Finally, in the end, he got the passwords of the three password-protected computers- "Azjv7ed, Mb294bd, Ok826eh3i" "Yes! Thank god." Alex exclaimed with the feeling of achievement. But then he thought- "Why to waste my own time trying to figure out which computer has the database access? Lemme check that also through this surveillance recording too." So he continued to observe, trying to find out which of the three staff members was working on the database and records, so he could figure out which computer had its access. For a bunch of minutes, all the three of them were working on other tabs and applications. Then finally one of them opened up a database. It was the computer that was in the middle of one computer each, on its either side.

Alex switched off the Surveillance Monitor and Computer and ran back to the Management Staff Room, this time, more restlessly eager and impatient. As soon as he entered, he rushed to the computer which had the database, and switched it on. "Come on... This has to work! Come on..." he kept mumbling, as he typed and started the Computer. He entered the password he noted for that computer. "Welcome!" The screen displayed. Alex managed to access the password-protected computer! He quickly tried to find the database file of the students, in the File Manager. Finally, after 2 or 3 minutes, he found a file named "New Students - Session 2162-63". He double clicked the file to open it, because of course, Jessica was a new student in his school. The file window popped up.

After scrolling a lot of students' names of different classes, he reached the section of his own class. And there, he found- "Jessica Smith, Residential Address- 703, Tower A, Marbella Towers, Capitrolis" After so much struggle, in the storm, the helicar, the management staff room and even in the Surveillance room, Alex got Jessica's home's address!" And with a deep sigh of relief, he clicked the photograph of the address and saved it in his phone. The stress and anxiety he had been bearing since a long time, about the uncertainty of getting Jessica's residential address, was finally gone now. He wore his backpack, once again, and walked down the stairs, coming out of the reception and administrative building.

"Finally!" Alex exclaimed with joy, "Let's go get those Mepama Charts." Being excited, he ran while heading towards the main gate of his school. After a minute of fast sprinting, he reached the main gates, but then suddenly stopped, as he noticed and recalled the unusual breaking of the electronic lock of the main gates, which broke just because Alex kicked it, that too just once. He thought to himself– "Neither I ever went to martial arts classes, nor I ever exercised or practised so much that my kicks became so powerful. Then how in the world could this electronic lock just- break?" He was lost in this thought, still perplexed. But just after a minute of deep thinking, he realised that his second part of today's plan was still remaining- To get the Mepama Charts from Jessica's house. By this time the sky cleared so much and the weather became so sunny, that it felt as if it had never rained since days! "I guess now the Helicar would be able to fly." said Alex. He was a bit nervous to actually 'fly', because of his experience that he had earlier today- the turbulence in the thunderstorm, the warning alerts of flight systems and the malfunctioning of core systems. But well, he felt confident enough because of his partial success in finding Jessica's address, and also because the weather, once again, was sunny and clear. So he decided to fly to Jessica's house, despite the bad experiences he had the same day. He entered the Helicar, slammed the doors which came downwards and closed, and entered Jessica's residential society address. He tried to find a helicar pad near her house, and found one just adjacent to her society. He chose that helicar pad as the destination, drank some water before taking off, and started his journey, in the pursuit of completing the second half of today's plan.

The Helicar was in the air, soaring through the sky when Alex felt hungry. And it was then that he realised that it was afternoon time, that's why he felt hungry, for he had his last meal more than 6 hours ago, that too at ISRO Launch Base. So being quite hungry, he searched up some superstores nearby to get some ready-to-eat food items or something. There being many of such shops and stores nearby, Alex clicked on the option of Slowing down the Helicar, on its computer screen. And within seconds, the Helicar reduced its speed. In his quick search of an open space or Helipad to land on, Alex could only find another Helicar Charging Station near the superstores he found on the Maps and GPS app. So he added a stop on Helicar's computer screen, and entered the stop's location as the location of the Helicar Charging Station he found. Subsequently, the Helicar landed on the surface of one of the Helipads of the Charging Station. He quickly got out of the Helicar and opened up directions for the nearest superstore, on his phone. He knew that he couldn't afford to lose much of the time, for he has to get to Jessica's house real quick, as it'll take much of the time there too. Plus, he has to go back to his house before sunset, because the large but lonely city seems uncomfortable to travel in, especially at night. He took out the electric Kick scooter he had with him, and unfolded it. It was safe to ride it as most surfaces became dry now because of the instant sunny weather after the severe thunderstorm. So Alex used his kick scooter to quickly reach the superstore he was going to, and once he reached there, he parked the kick scooter on its tiny stand, stepped inside the superstore as the automatic glass slide-doors opened, and started finding any ready-to-eat food items. At first, all he could see was some rotten fruits and vegetables and products. So he decided to check refrigerators for any fresh food items. Eventually, he only found microwavable garlic breadsticks and a microwavable tiny pizza. Upon searching more, he found a chocolate-flavoured milkshake and an energy bar. He put all these food items in his backpack and crossed the billing counter, without paying. After all, who the heck would pay for something, knowing that no one is there to use or collect that money. Funnily, everything available everywhere, at this point of time, was absolutely free of cost for Alex. But it wasn't funny for him. It was an insignificant thing for Alex, for he did not overthink about things that were irrelevant from his ultimate goal– To find everyone. Alex finally exited the super store, and started riding the kick scooter back to where he landed the Helicar. Just as he reached the Helicar charging station back, he folded his electric kick scooter, placed it inside the Helicar, and took off once again, this time to reach Jessica's residential society directly without any more stops in between.

It was only 6 more minutes to Jessica's house after he took off from the charging station. After all, the Helicar was flying, so it took lesser time to reach places than it would if he would've travelled by road. The Helicar started its descent as it was about to reach its destination. Meanwhile, he quickly ate the energy bar and drank the chocolate milkshake with it, to delay his hunger for some more time. "Alright Alex, one last thing to do for today!" He mumbled to himself after the Helicar landed, to generate more enthusiasm and willingness to find the Mepama Charts. He knew, the more he would search, the more and better charts and more detailed information he would get. The results he would get from his search at Jessica's house were directly proportional to his efforts. He had to search every possible corner, for of course, he himself doesn't know when Jessica exactly kept her Mepama Charts and other details and specifications.

He stepped out of his vehicle, took out and unfolded his kick scooter, and looked around to find a way to enter Jessica's residential society - the Marbella Towers. While looking here and there, he switched on his electronic kick scooter to stay ready to ride it and enter Jessica's society. Finally his eyes fell on an alley with an open gate, leading to the Marbella Towers society. Alex turned the scooter in that direction and rode it through the alley. The alley had beautiful lanterns and flower pots on both the sides, as if it was decorated for a function. "This probably is the secondary or back entrance of the society." Alex thought to himself, while riding the kick scooter through the narrow yet beautiful passageway. Finally, where the alley ended, was a large fountain with colourful flower bushes and trees surrounding it. Jessica's society was quite beautiful, even better than Alex, and he admitted the same. Behind the large water fountain there were only three yet tall high rising apartment towers. Alex looked at their labels and headed towards Tower A, in which Jessica's apartment was.

As soon as he reached the entrance of Tower A, he parked the kick scooter on its stand and walked inside the building. He was welcomed by a luxurious reception desk, facing towards a seating area with premium quality sofas and furniture, just like Alex's residential building. He saw two lifts in the lobby of the ground floor and pressed the button to call one of them. As the elevator reached the ground floor and its doors opened, he entered the elevator, which also had the Elevis system. "Take me to the 7th floor." Alex commanded the Elevis Voice recognition system, knowing that Jessica's house's Flat Number 703 would obviously be on the 7th floor. The elevator started to go upwards, and Alex was now full of energy and determination to get all the information, charts and diagrams related to the Mepamas from Jessica's house. While in the elevator which was going up, he was wondering where Jessica might would've stored those charts and information papers, and suddenly, the elevator dinged and Elevis announced- "Here is the 7th Floor." "Come on... Last task of the day!" he mumbled, and walked out of the elevator. But well, as he approached the Main door of Jessica's flat, he realised that he would have to break the door in order to open it. But well, he already experienced a closed door before. He took out the emergency axe from the Fire Emergency Glass Cabinet in the 7th floor's corridor, gripped the axe properly, and with a sheer impact, broke a major part of the teak wooden main door of Jessica's apartment. He felt sorry, for he was intentionally destroying his crush's house's part, but it was required. After hitting three to four times more, Alex managed to open the door lock from the inside by putting his hand through the broken door. And voila! He finally entered Jessica's house.

For him, it was a weird feeling, of intruding someone else's house, especially someone who probably would have trusted him. But after all, it was a necessity, and he knew it. Without the Mepama Charts, diagrams, specifications and information there was almost no way he could make the duplicate giant Mepamas. He went further through the entrance lobby, which led into the luxurious and large living room. Alex's own house was quite techy. It was full of automatically-operated things, like Curtains, automatic drying, ironing and folding of clothes, automatic sorting of dishes, utensils and plates, and whatnot. In contrast, Jessica's house didn't have these kinds of machines and things, but it was in its own way, beautiful, luxurious and large. There were antiques, a statue of Gautam Buddha and other sculptures, amazing paintings and beautiful textures on the wall. Alex took quite an interest in the appearance of her house. But then, he came back on his track, his mission. He walked up to the lobby that led into the bedrooms, and tried to identify which one of them was Jessica's. He entered a bedroom, which had a table with finance and investing books kept on it, magazines, etc. Of course, this wouldn't be Jessica's room. So he went to another one, but that was less of a bedroom but more of a study and store room, with huge cardboard boxes and a lot of packed things, with labels on them. "Probably Jessica and her family shifted to Capitrolis recently, so they didn't open all the things and boxes that they shifted from their old house." Alex thought, after looking at the boxes and labelled and packed stuff.

He got out of that room as well, and went to the last bedroom that was left to check out. And yep, that was Jessica's. How'd he know? Huge whiteboard with physics formulas, equations, and numericals written on it. He also saw very organised features like everything neat and clean, placed in their right places, and lastly, saw a photo frame with Jessica and her family's picture in it. He became quite emotional after seeing the picture, but well, he couldn't waste much of his time, so he proceeded with his search. He also looked at Jessica's study table, which had neatly organised and stacked books, and everything else placed tidily on it. He opened the drawer, in the hope of finding anything like Mepama Charts or information. But well, the drawer only had a tray with iron pieces, magnets, screws and wires. He then found a cabinet near the study table, which had a lot of files and folders in it. He took out each file and folder to check if any of them was related to Mepamas. He found Jessica's school documents, certificates, and different other papers that were of no use to him. He turned towards the bed's side table now, and there too, there was nothing useful. But well, Alex noticed something else, kept on the side table. Some weird, pyramid-shaped, small techy decoration item like thing. It was glowing purple and white, again and again. He lifted it from the side table, and took it in his hand, observing it closely. He looked for any buttons or switches on this techy decoration item, which seemed more like an AI device or speaker to him, because his room's AI speaker glowed in a similar manner. But then he noticed something- the lights that were glowing on that thing's surface, which were purple and white, faded and changed into red and black, as soon as he took the item in his hand. He was frustrated, and perplexed, trying to understand what this piece of techy item is. But realizing that he's just wasting his important time and distracting himself from his main target or goal for today, he kept that glowing decorative pyramid back on the side table, just commenting- "What a weird and dumb thing!"

Quite tired and frustrated after 15-20 minutes of searching for Mepama Charts and information papers, he started to make the room messy. Instead of putting back the things he took out, he just kept them at random places- on the floor, on the bed and the tables. He finally opened the closet of Jessica's Room, looking for literally anything related to Mepamas. And finally, after some more searching deep inside the closet, in its lowest shelf, he found a shoebox, but with the label "Mepama and Stuff". To his surprise, everything- from Mepama diagrams, blueprints, configuration charts to all the information and specification papers, was kept inside that shoebox. She had collected all the papers and charts related to her Mepama Invention and stored them in this shoebox. "Thanks to Jessica's organising skills and nature!" Alex said to himself, with a sigh of relief. It was around 5:15 PM now, less than an hour left until sunset.

Alex first took a look at all those charts and papers related to Mepama, and he appreciated them seeing that everything was written properly and in detail. He then packed all those charts and papers back into the shoebox, satisfied with their quality. The feeling of accomplishment and success of acquiring the Charts and information he needed, made him feel proud of himself. He smiled, as he left Jessica's apartment, not only because he completed a significant task he alloted to himself, but also because he fulfilled the main purpose of coming to Capitrolis. He wanted those charts and information, and hence travelled a thousand kilometres back, from SpaceVillage. And he got what he was looking for, even before he could actually believe so. With a sense of pride and increased confidence, Alex went down the elevator and finally came out of Jessica's residential building, wearing his backpack, and holding the shoebox with the Mepama charts and information he needed.

The confidence he acquired now was so much, that he decided to abandon the electric kick scooter right there, in Jessica's Society! "It's a great idea to reduce the dependencies, especially in such a situation." he thought to himself, still smiling because of his achievement. He decided to walk through the alley he came from, and walk till he reaches his Helicar. Now of course, leaving the kick scooter just there wasn't a big deal. And what he called a 'dependency' was nothing but an 'efficiency', that he ditched. In my opinion, it was an insignificant, yet dumb decision." And William took a pause, after sharing so much of the story to the NDJJC members.

After the members noticed that he took a pause, Rhea, being compassionate, said, "William, would you like to have some water? You have been speaking for almost an hour now!" William replied, "Oh, yes please! I was actually gonna ask for it. Thanks!" "It's nothing, come on!" Rhea smiled and said, while pouring some water from a jug in a glass, and then she gave it to him. "Thanks again!" William thanked Rhea, and drank some water from the glass. "Oh look, guys! I had ordered some starters from Zomato. It's almost here!" Sandeep told everybody. "You–! You used NDJJC's savings once again for ordering food?!" Garima shouted at Sandeep after being irritated of his doings. "Uh yes? Come on, it's a great occasion." Sandeep replied to Garima. "Absolutely! I hope you have ordered Paneer Tikka and Spring rolls as well." Aryan added to the conversation. "Ugh! You boys..." Garima exclaimed. "Well, it wouldn't hurt to, you know, eat a little." William said. And Garima became embarassed of her previous comments. Nervously, she giggled and said- "Lol. Yes, I guess... Nevermind." And everyone was looking at each other's faces. And suddenly they all bursted into a loud laughter of the awkward scenario they created. And meanwhile, someone knocked at their cabin's door. "Oh, its here!" Sandeep exclaimed excitedly, for he was a foodie. He went to the door, opened it, and took his food order. He even gave a tip to the delivery man, and the latter smiled, thanked and left. Closing the door, Sandeep came back and noticed that it was another time, that Garima was staring at him, this time being more irritated because of him. "Oh, so now NDJJC is so wealthy that we give tips even for paid orders!" Garima said sarcastically, indirectly commenting on Sandeep's action. "Come on darling, stop being so stingy. Chill a little!" Rhea jokingly said to Garima.

"Yaar, I am not being stingy. I am just trying to save NDJJC's money for our future endeavours. How will we be able to–" Garima said incompletely as William interrupted her and said- "Please don't mind but let's forget about all this and continue with the story." "Pfft! Savage reply! Destroyed in seconds! Dude, give me a high five." Peter giggled and laughed at William's statement, and gave him a high five, mocking and teasing Garima. Aryan was also laughing but silently. After a few seconds, he cleared his throat and said- "Alright William... Please go on." And William continued-

"Right, so now that Alex successfully achieved his goal, his confidence increased dramatically. He walked through the alley, ditching the kick scooter, reached the Helicar and simply sat in it, and got ready to go home. He still had one confusing thought, about that glowing pyramid. "Neither it had any charging port or battery slot to recharge it, nor any buttons or switches. But it had glowing lights. What the heck was it actually?" But the thought of actually starting the Helicar and getting back home, made him forget the confusion and start his journey. Thus, after the great accomplishment of getting the Mepama charts, Alex flew back home, to his own residential society.

The sun was setting on the horizon now, and Alex could view the sunset from his Helicar while it was cruising in the sky. The city lights suddenly automatically turned on, as there were automatic systems involving sensors and stuff, for turning on and off the city lights, during nights and days, respectively. Capitrolis looked more beautiful at night from the sky, and Alex appreciated his beautiful city. "What a view! I bet this view would have been even better if everyone was still here." He said, missing everyone's presence. It was 11 more minutes to his society helipad. He had the frozen garlic breadsticks and pizza with him, which he planned to eat as dinner for today, after microwaving them at home. Soon, as the Helicar started descending from its cruising altitude, the sun had set completely and Alex could see the beautiful twilight in the sky. Just when 5 more minutes were left to land, Alex thought to celebrate his small yet significant achievement. "What can I do? Hmmm..." he mumbled and thought. He wanted to low-key celebrate, although himself, but because he wanted to pat himself on his back for the great job he had done today, despite difficulties like the thunderstorm, getting to his school, finding Jessica's address there, and cracking the password. "You know what I can do is, play some party music and songs in my Room on my AlexRoom AI Speaker, microwave and eat these garlic breadsticks and mini pizza, and have some of my birthday cake, which is many days old now, though kept in the refrigerator." He made the plan for his low-key celebration, and meanwhile the Helicar landed, gently touching the surface of the helipad, and turning off its engines and motors. Alex switched off the Helicar, came out of it, wore his backpack and finally entered the elevator of the building and went down from the terrace, where his Helicar landed. The Elevator dinged, and he came out of the building on which his Helicar landed.

Walking towards his building, he enjoyed the calm wind blowing against his face and hair. The yellow street lights of his society were looking beautiful. The sky was quite dark now, as it was night time, and the silence made the atmosphere more uncomfortable. But the street lights and other beautiful and bright lights of his residential society provided Alex some consolation. After walking till he reached his building, he turned and entered his building's reception area, walked to the lobby, and went to his apartment via the elevator. He entered his home, and blocked the main door of his apartment by pushing a chair against it, as the lock of the door was already broken but he wanted to 'feel' safe.

After blocking the main door, he entered, and quickly went to the kitchen. He switched on the Microwave, which could talk, being futuristic. After being switched on, the Microwave taunted Alex- "Hmmm... So this time it's King Alex who's here to do something using the microwave. Finally this person stepped inside the kitchen, wow!" "Can you please shut the frick up? Here, microwave these two boxes, one of frozen garlic breadsticks and the other one of a frozen mini pizza." Alex replied. "Sure thing, bud! Microwaving as per frozen food requirements. By the way, consider eating something healthy too, dum-dum!" Microwave said, mocking Alex once again. "Ugh! This talking shit!" Alex murmured. After his food was microwaved, Alex switched off the microwave, not wanting to hear more from it. He then went to his room, and said, "Hey AlexRoom! I'm back. Please play some party songs." The AI system switched on the room and ceiling lights, giving Alex's room a colourful and party-style appearance. And then it played some party and upbeat songs, as Alex wanted it to. Alex had his dinner and enjoyed his solo party and tried to generate more positive vibes in the wider negative situation he was in. It was a silent night outside, but inside Alex's apartment, there was an energetic and optimistic atmosphere, with party songs, Alex vibing to those songs, having his dinner, and later eating some of his birthday cake as a dessert.

Alex felt slightly rejuvenated after his minor celebration. The confidence and hopes he had before almost doubled, and he felt that he was another step closer towards solving this mystery. After he finished with his dessert, he was tired of the loud and party music and wanted to make a peaceful atmosphere now. "AlexRoom, play some meditation and peaceful music." he commanded. "Sure. Here's some meditation and peaceful background music you might like!" the AlexRoom AI Speaker replied, and played a soothing and peaceful meditation music. It was around 9.30 PM now. Alex switched on his Airtop, sat down on his bed, placed a cushion behind his back for support, and got ready to do further research. He wanted to know what study materials, topics and books shall he read to be able to understand, make and manufacture the giant Mepamas.

So he typed and typed and entered the description of his purpose and plan to the Text-based AI Model he was using, and it gave out the results. There were many core subjects he needed to study and research about like Advanced Physics, Electrical Engineering, Mechanical Engineering, Control Systems, Electromagnetism, Physics of Magnetic Materials, 3D Printing and Additive Manufacturing and Materials Science. Plus there were 2 to 3 books that the AI Model recommended for each of the subjects. Alex took the screenclicks of the list of subjects, topics and books he needed to study and research on, and tried to understand more. He understood the fact that he must have a strong command on at least the fundamental topics in all these fields and subjects, then only he would be able to manufacture the Mepamas successfully.

After taking the screenclicks and noting down what all he needed to study, Alex wanted to see if he could get these books from the Capitrolis Library. So he went to its website on his Airtop, and searched up every book's name to check book availability for all the books he required. In total, there were five books that were not available at the Capitrolis Library, for those books were actually quite rare, and were found at only limited places. "Nevermind, I'll get the rest of the books which are available from the library tomorrow," he thought. And finally, Alex felt sleepy. He stopped the music on his AI Speaker, switched off his room lights, took a blanket, and slept peacefully, after achieving his main target for today."

TWELVE
STUDY TIME?

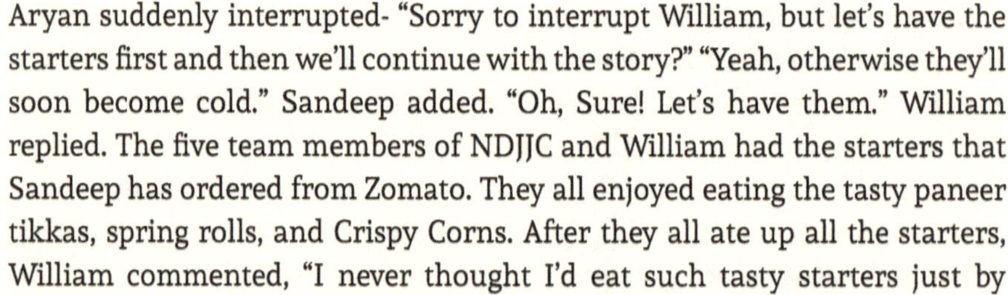

Aryan suddenly interrupted- "Sorry to interrupt William, but let's have the starters first and then we'll continue with the story?" "Yeah, otherwise they'll soon become cold." Sandeep added. "Oh, Sure! Let's have them." William replied. The five team members of NDJJC and William had the starters that Sandeep has ordered from Zomato. They all enjoyed eating the tasty paneer tikkas, spring rolls, and Crispy Corns. After they all ate up all the starters, William commented, "I never thought I'd eat such tasty starters just by telling a story, lol!" "Well William, it's not just a story, you know! It sounds like a complex situation, and something not fictional. And just like we have history for past events, this seems something like- Futurstory!" Rhea said. "Well, I don't think it's real or non-fiction, but certainly it's an amazing and engaging story!" Aryan replied. "Well, yes! It's a complex and amazing story. I can't wait more to tell you guys the rest of it! So let me continue.

It was the next morning now. A new morning, a new day, with the new goal- To get the study materials and books from the Capitrolis Library and start studying. Alex woke up, and went to his balcony, to see the morning view of the city. Although there was no sound of any human, as expected, there were so many birds chirping and flying, as if the stoppage of human activities gave way to nature to flourish again! He then went back inside his room and started packing his backpack. He also knew that he'd require a large luggage bag too for bringing those 15-20 books from the Library he was going to this morning. So he went to his parents' room, opened the closet, and brought a large black colour luggage bag to his room. It was empty, and he wanted it to be so. This was so that later he could bring home and carry those many books from the Library easily. Finally, he went to the Kitchen and opened the refrigerator only to find some Cucumber and Onion Salad remaining in a large bowl. He didn't like it that much, but considering that he has been eating too much junk, frozen and processed food, he decided to eat the leftover salad. Plus he had a more emotional thought regarding the salad- "It's the last thing that Mom prepared with her own hands!" So though he didn't like the salad, he took it out and ate it with joy because it was made by his Mom, just before everyone disappeared. He became quite emotional while eating the salad as breakfast, but then he wiped his tears. He knew that he couldn't let his emotions come between him and his goals to delay his actions. After 5 minutes of eating the salad as if he loved it a lot, for it was actually made by his mother before she was gone, just like everyone else, he was finished with his breakfast. He was ready to go now. He wore his backpack, took the empty luggage bag with him, and headed out.

"Alright Elevis, let's go to the Ground Floor." he commanded the Elevator's Voice Recognition AI. "Sure! Heading to the Ground Floor." Elevis responded. The elevator doors opened as it reached the Ground Floor, and Alex got out with his phone in his hand, walked out of his building, and headed to the Helipad building of his society. While he was walking to that building, he entered the location of the Capitrolis Library in the Navigation and Maps App and checked how much time it was taking to reach there via Helicar. "What?! 5 minutes?! Wow!" he exclaimed, seeing the duration of the journey which was so less. He had his phone in one hand and from the other hand, he pulled his luggage bag which had wheels attached to it. After walking a distance, he reached the Helipad building. He quickly went to the terrace of the building, went to the Helicar which was parked on the Helipad, kept his empty luggage bag inside the Helicar, and finally sat inside it himself. He slammed the door, started the Helicar, and flew away.

"If it's just 5 minutes away, I'll be back home quickly. And that'll give me more time to go through all those books, and see if they're relevant and useful, or not." Alex reflected. He was super damn serious about learning all the advanced engineering, physics and what not, despite being quite young for all those topics and subjects. He knew that he didn't have any other option besides this, for building the giant Mepamas and using them to bring the IndWatch Satellite down to the ground was the only way he could uncover the mystery of everyone's disappearance, by closely observing the IndWatch Satellite's Camera Footage that was facing the earth. He was thinking all this while the Helicar descended from the sky, intending to land at the place where Alex specified, which was the broad main road in front of the Capitrolis Library. And finally, the helicar touched the ground and landed successfully.

Alex got out of the helicar, slammed the door, and took the empty luggage bag with him. He walked up the stairs of the large Library building, and eventually entered the building. As he came there before as well, he knew the way to many of the different shelves and cabinets. So because he had an idea about where such Physics, Engineering and Scientific books were kept, he quickly navigated through the different bookshelves and books sections, eventually reaching a books section of subjects and categories like Science, Engineering and Physics. After he reached the place with books of such types, he unlocked his phone and read the list of books given by the AI Model, through the screenclicks he took yesternight. Then, he one by one tried finding the books he needed, by searching on each of the shelves. As he kept finding the books that were mentioned in the list, he kept packing them in the empty black luggage bag that he brought with himself. With time, he kept collecting the required books, and once he was done, he went to the reception desk of the library, switched on its computer and searched for any holo-books available of the similar topics he had to study, in its database. It only responded that there were only 3 holo-books for 2 of the topics. Holo-books were hologram-style 3D and techy ways of reading books, by actually visualising 3D objects and reading text at the same time. There being only 3 holo-books, Alex got demotivated, because the time that took for reading a holo-book was a lot lesser than the time that took for reading a regular book. But well, he didn't give up. He went to another desk nearby to collect those holo-books that were relevant to the subjects he was about to study. He knew that no matter how monotonous, frustrating, boring or difficult the process of studying all these topics of these subjects will be, he has no other option, but to learn, understand, and apply this knowledge that he's gonna receive. Making the giant Mepamas pragmatically was not even an easy task for a team of expert engineers, yet Alex believed that he himself alone could succeed in building them, and using them with the UAVs to attract the IndWatch Satellite towards the ground, and eventually bring it down as well. It was not overconfidence, but the fact that this was his last hope for finding out where did everyone else go, compelled him to set such a goal, that was extremely difficult to achieve.

So, after Alex packed all the books and holo-books in his luggage bag, he was ready to head out. He came back to the reception area of the library, but then he thought- "It's just 1 PM in the afternoon, and I've already completed today's task, so why not go through and study these books and holo-books here only for a while? The Library offers a good and motivational environment too!" Agreeing with the thought, he unpacked all his materials like his Airtop, Airtop Charger, Notebooks and Blank papers for rough work and calculations. He sat on a comfortable chair in the reading area of the library, set up his study materials and Airtop, and opened the first book- 'Introduction to Electrical Engineering'. He expected it to be written in a difficult to understand language, using complicated and advanced vocabulary and words. And well, he wasn't wrong. But he was able to understand the texts and paragraphs of the book partially, if not fully. Wherever he had a doubt or lack of clarity, he would stop reading there, use his Airtop AI Model, search the meaning of the sentence or word he didn't understand, read the response in a simpler language, and finally understand and continue reading. At first this cycle and process seemed monotonous and different from how Alex learned stuff till date, for the content was too technical and scientific for Alex and his age. But as Alex kept understanding the book and started making progress, he got the hang of learning, studying and understanding content from these kinds of books.

After an hour reading the first book, he closed it and took a break. He went to the Library Cafe, and grabbed a ready-to-drink cold coffee from its refrigerator. He sipped the cold coffee for a while, and after 10 minutes, he began reading another book, to diversify his learning of different topics. He spent 3-4 hours studying in total, and when it was around half past 5, he decided to pack all his things like his Airtop, study materials, and books that he has been studying till now. He decided to study further till late at night tonight.

Alex didn't expect that the topics he would need to study, learn and understand to make the Mepamas, would actually be so interesting. At first what he thought was boring and complicated, turned out to be surprisingly engrossing as he studied and understood more and more. Now that he was heading back home after studying for 3 to 4 hours straight, he wanted to quickly reach back home, have his dinner for tonight, and then continue studying. The fact that he had to stop studying for now as he had to return home, made him more restless and curious to know and understand more about the content given in the different books he studied from. So finally, he came out of the Library Building, stepping down the large and long building stairs, with his worn backpack and black luggage bag with books and holo-books held in one of his hands. He reached the Helicar, lifted and put the now slightly heavy luggage bag inside the Helicar, stepped inside it himself and closed the door. It was almost sunset now, and the sky turned orange, pink and purple. Meanwhile, Alex entered his society's location, and the Helicar began its brief journey. It rose up in the sky, and headed towards Alex's society.

He reclined his seat a little bit to relax, as he was tired of continuously sitting on a single chair while he was studying in the library. As it didn't take long to reach back home, Alex decided not to take a nap as he could take it when he reached home. However it was evening time already, so there was no point in taking a nap, because just after a few hours he would sleep anyway. While Alex was thinking all this, the helicar landed on his society's helipad.

He got out of the vehicle, lifted the heavy luggage bag from the seat, took it out and kept it on the ground. Slamming the Helicar Door, he wondered what he would have for dinner tonight. Although it was almost 6PM now, he didn't plan anything fresh for tonight's dinner. Nevertheless, he walked up to the elevator lobby, went down via the elevator, and walked out of the building, at least to first reach home and then decide what to eat. Now that he was on his way, he was pondering about his choices. "Well, after all, till when will I keep finding my food like a scavenger everyday? And that too frozen and unhealthy foods like pizza, sandwiches, garlic breads, and what not. For tonight, I guess I can settle just for corn flakes or something, but for everyday meals, I must have a healthy and consistent solution for my food and snack requirements." he thought deeply. And because he was so lost in thinking all this, he didn't realise that he walked even further from his building, walking past it and missing it. As soon as he realised, he ran back to his building with the wheeled-luggage bag and his backpack. He went to the lobby, pressed the elevator button, and went up to his apartment, finally reaching back home.

As he entered his apartment through his unlocked main door, he just kept the luggage bag near his dining table, and just lay down on his long sofa, after being tired. He still tried to figure out a solution for getting food everyday. But for now, that was secondary, and a much more important thing was to study, till late at night. Alex wanted to quickly finish understanding and learning everything that he had to learn. He wanted to implement his Mepama-UAVs plan as early as possible. He knew that learning such complex and difficult subjects would take some time, probably a few days, weeks or probably even a month. But he himself wanted to finish learning all of these topics and subjects as soon as possible.

So without wasting much time, after resting for enough time on the sofa, he went to the kitchen to make his dinner hastily. He entered the kitchen, opened up a cabinet where generally food items were stored, and took out a box containing corn flakes. He went to the kitchen slab, took a plastic bowl, added some milk with sugar in it, and switched on the microwave. "Wuiiii! Finally Alex bro is having something somewhat healthier. Hehehege..." The microwave started talking as soon as Alex switched it on and opened it to heat his bowl of Milk. After heating his bowl of milk, he took it out and added corn flakes to it. "Noooo! Bro what?! Corn flakes? That's not at all healthy!" Microwave exclaimed, just a second before Alex switched it off again. He stirred the bowl, took a spoon, went to the dining table, took out a chair and started eating his dinner. He unlocked his phone with his retina-scan lock, and searched a few things related to what he was studying. While having his dinner only, decided that he would anyway study late till night, so before he would start studying, he could consult with his text-based AI Model to ask for solutions for getting food everyday without cooking. Within 5 minutes, he finished with his dinner. He kept the empty bowl in the kitchen's sink, and went to his bedroom. After switching on the lights, he took out his Airtop, and opened his AI Model on it. He typed- "I am alone in this entire world, even though it might sound unbelievable. I have to find food everyday for all my meals and food requirements like a scavenger. I am located in Capitrolis, India, and wish to find a solution for myself, to start getting cooked food everyday, for all my meals without cooking myself. List out any solutions for this or similar purposes."

When Alex sent this prompt to the AI Model on his Airtop, the only solution that it provided was- ChefMate. "Oh yeah! Why didn't I think of this before?!" Alex exclaimed after suddenly himself recalling a good solution for his needs. ChefMate was a large machine, as tall as a refrigerator, and as broad as half of Alex's bedroom. It automated the cooking of hundreds of food items, from a variety of multi cuisine dishes. In other words, Alex could use it to automatically cook food, and get ready-made healthy and tasty meals. All he would need to do is refill the machine storage with the ingredients like wheat, grains, pulses, maida, and vegetables, and that was something only done once or twice a week. Alex understood that ChefMate was the perfect solution for his everyday food and meal requirements. He searched more about it on his search engine website, and understood more about how to actually use it and operate it. "This is Perfect!" he thought. But now, the real challenge was to find a ChefMate. The machine was rare, as it wasn't widely used due to its extremely high cost of buying. But now its price doesn't matter, for Alex has to pay no one. Alex searched for availability of ChefMate Machine in the entire city of Capitrolis. As the machines were rare, the results had only 2 stores that were selling it. Alex took a screenclick of the names of the two stores, and decided that his mission for tomorrow will be to get a ChefMate machine, from either of the stores.

But then, transportation was an issue here. After all, Alex couldn't simply 'get' Chefmate all by himself. It was a very heavy and large machine. Plus, in 1-2 days he anyway has to go back to SpaceVillage, so it wasn't a good idea to first bring such a bulky appliance to his own society, and then somehow ship it to SpaceVillage. And how exactly would he ship it to the SpaceVillage? He can't take it with him in the Helicar, as it does not have sufficient space to store Chefmate.

This was another challenge for Alex. ChefMate was really bulky and huge. "Via train?" he thought, but then immediately discarded the thought as he realised that the same purpose would be solved by a truck. Obviously, trucks of that time also became driverless and self-driving. So now, thinking about trucks, Alex searched a Truck Depot nearby. When he got the results, he took the screenclick of the list. He sent all the screenclicks he took till now to his phone, and then finally decided his final goal for tomorrow. He'd first go and get a ChefMate appliance from one of the stores where it was available, then he'd call a 'BulkShift Mover', a robotic machine that lifts, keeps and moves heavy stuff. It was more like a mini truck, with an extended robotic arm with its own wheels, that could detach from the main BulkShift Mover, go to the material to be moved, lift or hold it, and bring it to the main Mover truck. BulkShift Mover was somewhat a great way to move heavy and large things, including machines. So Alex decided to use this BulkShift Mover to shift a ChefMate appliance to the Truck Depot, and then allow the machine, as well as the BulkShift Mover inside the trailer of the truck.

It was a long process, consisting of three stages. But Alex's determined attitude didn't make it seem difficult. He once again reviewed the plan and then closed all the current tabs, except the AI Model one, and decided to start studying now. He rose from his bed he was sitting on, and went to his study table with his Airtop held in his hands. He kept the Airtop on the study table, and then went to the living room to unpack the luggage bag which had the books that he brought today from the Capitrolis Library. He brought the books he was reading today, to continue reading them. Dedicatedly, he focused on reading, understanding and learning. And from 7:30 PM till 12 AM at night, he continuously studied, that too, with interest. He finished half of the first book he began reading today, which was 'Introduction to Electrical Engineering', and read 3 chapters of the other book, related to Electromagnetism. When it was past 12 AM, Alex was done studying and he wanted to use the toilet before sleeping. He had another mission to accomplish tomorrow. The last one, before heading back to the ISRO Launch Base, near SpaceVillage. So he went to the washroom, and screamed unexpectedly, because of a lizard. The lizard fear was still common, even in 2162. He ran out of the washroom, slamming the door hard and closing it from outside. "What the f–?!" He almost swore. So he ditched his own washroom, and went to his parents'. Fortunately there was no lizard there. So he did his business, came back, drank some water before going to bed, and finally slept. His mind at night was calm and satisfied, as he felt that he was progressing in his 'Mepama Studies' and all those subjects he was learning. So he slept peacefully, in his air-conditioned bedroom.

THIRTEEN

FIRST AUTOMATED MEAL

Another morning, another day, another mission. But this one was tough, mentally for Alex and physically for machines and BulkShift Mover. Alex woke up as his alarm rang at 8:30. Today he woke up a bit late, probably because he slept late at night. Dismissing the alarm that rang on his phone, he readily went to his washroom to quickly get ready for his last big day in Capitrolis. Finally, as per Alex's desire, the washroom was devoid of any lizard. So he peacefully attended nature's call, took a shower, and brushed his teeth. Just in 20 minutes, he was all ready and set to go. He decided to skip his breakfast and directly eat something a few hours later as brunch. He took his phone and backpack, and rushed out of his apartment. He went down his elevator, and as his purpose was to save time because today he had decided to come back before 3 PM maximum so he could study too, he was in a hurry. Hence, he decided to use another electric kick scooter that was available in the kick scooter parking lot. So he switched on one of the kick scooters, turned it, and rushed to the Helipad building. While he was about to reach the building, he saw black clouds advancing in the sky. "Rain?! Again? Ugh…" he exclaimed. This led to another stress in his mind, that the rain or storm might hinder him from his today's objective. He still retained his willpower, and continued heading to the helipad to take off with the Helicar. He finally reached the helipad building's bottom, where he parked the kick scooter, entered the lobby, and went to the terrace. Finally he reached the helicar helipad, got into it, and despite the clear sky turning into a stormy one, Alex took off with the Helicar. He was confused, because the monsoon season was quite far from the present days these storms were happening in Capitrolis. It was still the mid-Summer season, yet there was such intense and heavy rainfall in the region. He noticed that the time left to reach his destination, which was the ChefMate store, was 12 minutes. Meanwhile he also searched on the weather forecast app about when the thunderstorm would begin, and it was saying 20 minutes later. "Well, at least I would reach the store before the storm would begin. That's a plus point." Alex thought to himself. After checking the weather, he browsed the old news stories that popped on his mobile feed, which he never saw before. But what an unusual thing, you do things that you didn't before, sometime or other. Alex wanted to avoid the feeling of extreme loneliness and fear of being alone, so he tried to fill up his mind with at least the memories of people, which though disappeared now, by looking at the news stories. "World's new fastest Helicar launched by Anderneas Pandey- CEO of Werghia Aviation International", "Yartrunas River levels to decrease due to heavy water usage in the Capitrolis NCR." "New President of India Madhu Devi to give speech at Old Red Fort" were some of the old news stories he saw and read.

Finally, when only 5 minutes were left to reach, Alex opened the BulkShift Mover app to keep the shifting process handy and ready to execute, to call it as soon as he reached the Store and found ChefMate. The sky was becoming darker and darker as the clouds covered up the bright sun, hiding the beautiful and clear blue sky behind those greyish shades of colour. This worried Alex, but what worried him more was the thought of being unable to complete today's important task. It was not just about food or survival. It was about efficiency and saving time. So he was all geared up to start the process of finding and shifting the ChefMate appliance.

The helicar landed at a Helicar Charging Station near the ChefMate store. Alex quickly got out of the vehicle and rushed to the store, to reach there before it started raining. As he approached the store's glass doors, the raindrops started falling on the ground, and the raindrop spots started appearing on the dry pavement surface. He was briskly walking ahead. Alex finally entered the furniture and appliances store, and walked through the beautifully decorated hall of the store. There was modern and luxurious furniture, home decor items, and general-purpose home appliances, all placed in a very organised manner, in rows. Alex walked to the home appliances section of the store, intending to find ChefMate. As the place was unfamiliar to him, it took him a while, but eventually, he made it to the Chefmate. As he approached the magnificent machine, he noticed something- a large rear portion of the ChefMate appliance was dismantled, with screws and many wires and a circuit board fallen on the floor. "Now what's with this dismantled Chefmate?!" Alex expressed his frustration, after noticing another problem on his way. He understood, as it was pretty obvious, that a partially dismantled ChefMate would be of no use to him. He had a closer look, but it didn't make it any better. He observed that not only it was partially dismantled, but some wires inside the ChefMate were cut as well which he could see through the partially opened space in the rear of the appliance. "I probably can reassemble this ChefMate, but it'll waste much more of my time." Alex thought to himself. It was raining heavily now, due to the unexpected thunderstorm occurring in Capitrolis and nearby regions. He thought once again, but then made his decision now- he'll be going to the other store where ChefMate was available. Now because it was raining, he decided not to fly, but to go there via road. He picked up his backpack and walked out of the store, frustrated but hopeful about the second one.

Outside, the rain was very intense. As he got out, he ran to his Helicar, to avoid getting too wet. In this hurried run, his leg slipped off the wet and slippery pavement and he fell on his chin. The rough concrete surface of the pavement scraped Alex's chin's skin causing a minor injury. But the fall was much more painful. He groaned for a second and then got up, and got off the slippery pavement and decided to walk on the road, for it had much more friction and a lesser slipping chance. He hastily reached the Helicar charging station, ending up all wet, with his clothes and hair dripping the rainwater. He got into the helicar, switched to 'Drive Mode' from Flight mode and entered the location of the other store he had to go to. The helicar's electric motors turned on, and the vehicle started the ride. Alex searched for a medical First-aid kit in the helicar's storage compartment, and fortunately he found a small pouch of the same. His chin was hurting, as the skin was scraped and there was slight and slow bleeding as well. Alex opened the First-aid kit pouch and took out a cotton roll, plucked a piece , added some antiseptic on it and put the cotton piece on his injured chin. It burned a little but it was necessary, as he remembered the first-aid procedures he learnt back in his school workshops. He ended providing himself first-aid by putting a band-aid on his chin. After he was done, he looked at the ETA. "21 minutes?! Even with no traffic? Ugh!" he said, after noticing the ETA from the helicar computer screen. So he just put on his headphones, connected them to his phone and played some calming songs and music, while leaning his head back on the headrest of his seat. He listened to a playlist with mixed types of songs, romantic, rap, EDM, and even phonk. But as he was listening to songs, he unknowingly drifted into sleep, just like he always does.

When he woke up, he noticed that he had already reached his destination minutes ago, and that the thunderstorm was gone, except that a few remaining dark clouds were retreating. He took his backpack and phone and opened the helicar door, came outside and closed the door. He was shocked. Why? To see the extremely luxurious and large electronics and appliances store he had come to. He approached the main glass sliding doors, which opened automatically as he entered the store. Unlike the previous store, this store had premium-styled interiors with beautiful and smooth carpet flooring, polished wooden desks and display racks, and vintage luxurious lamps placed in the corners. Alex was mesmerised by the beautifully maintained and decorated store, that too just for electronics and appliances. However as he recalled his goal, he proceeded and went to the home appliances section. He saw washing machines, Auto-Laundry systems, Refrigerators, many talking microwaves- whose cacophony was very irritating to him. Finally, he approached a display of 2-3 ChefMates. Fortunately, this store had multiple ChefMates, unlike the previous store which only housed one. This provision relieved Alex as he knew that if one ChefMate was dismantled or not in working condition, there was another he could take away.

Alex went to one of the ChefMates, the first one he walked to, and noticed that it was looking normal from outside, that is, it was not dismantled or anything. Finally, he pressed the power button of the ChefMate, hoping for it to switch on and start as he expected it to. And with a startup music tone, the appliance turned on! "Thank my lovely god! Finally!" Alex cheered up and felt blessed to finally have a working ChefMate. The final test he had to conduct was to find out whether this ChefMate could actually cook something. He opened the Ingredients Storage Compartment, from which the ChefMate took the ingredients and made delicious meals, as Alex knew. He saw that the Ingredients Compartment was already loaded with food ingredients for its first use. All the main ingredients like wheat flour, pulses, milk products, salt, sugar were present in their respective compartments. So he closed the compartment's drawer and locked it. He decided to test it by commanding it to make a healthy meal, a kind of meal that he never had since everyone disappeared. "Alright ChefMate, let's see what you've got." he mumbled. He kept on swiping on the ChefMate monitor screen, finding a meal to select and command it to make. He saw an option which had an icon of a divided meal plate, and the title of 'Customise your Meal'. He clicked the option, and got three lists to select his main course curry or pulses, vegetables and flatbreads- which we call Rotis for now. He selected specific options in all the three lists, adding Arhar Dal, Jeera Aloo and Butter Flatbread to his meal. Finally, he clicked on the 'Make it' button. The monitor displayed a countdown of 10 minutes, and a bunch of whirring sounds started coming from the ChefMate. Knowing that it'll take 10 minutes for him to try his first ChefMate meal, Alex went to a nearby armchair and sat on it. He unlocked his phone and browsed his Mesocia feed. Mesocia was the social media app of that time. He was scrolling through 'Strings'- short clips just like we have reels on Instagram currently. Passing his time by watching motivational clips and short videos, he spent the next 6-8 minutes doing the same. When only 2-3 minutes were left. He locked his phone, got up and went to the ChefMate once again.

After waiting for those few more seconds, Alex witnessed the output of the ChefMate. The monitor displayed a 'Food Ready' message, and suddenly, a large drawer akin to a tray automatically came out slowly, and Alex saw a professionally packed, divided meal plate made of plastic, also covered with plastic sheet. His food was packed properly and neatly in the meal plate, and after the drawer came out fully, the monitor displayed the message- 'Please collect your Order. Enjoy your meal!' Alex picked up the meal plate, and as he did so, the drawer went back in. He came back to the armchair, peeled off the plastic cover of the plate, and broke a piece of his flatbread, dipped it in his dal, and tried the first bite of the ChefMate food. He couldn't believe the taste- it was exactly the same as the food he used to eat at home which his mother cooked. He was very delighted and satisfied with the quality and taste of the food the ChefMate cooked, and he concluded that it's perfect for the purpose he desired to use it for.

Alex finished his meal, kept the finished meal plate on the floor, and after some minutes, he switched the ChefMate off, and opened the BulkShift Mover App, to call a Mover to shift and take the ChefMate to the main Capitrolis truck depot. The app opened, and prompted Alex to enter the location, and so he did. He found in the app that the nearest BulkShift Mover was 5 minutes away, and to call it, he clicked on the 'Confirm your Shifting' button in the app. His Mover was confirmed and the app displayed the message- 'Please wait for 5 minutes, till your BulkShift Mover arrives at your location!' Alex closed the app, and once again, went and sat on the armchair, waiting for the Mover to come.

Five minutes later, Alex's phone got a notification from the BulkShift Mover app, indicating that the Mover had arrived. Alex walked out of the store, only to find that there was a yellow and blue colour minitruck-like vehicle, with many robotic arms and parts that lift, carry and load the things in that minitruck. The computer monitor screen was beeping, prompting him to scan the QR code displayed from the app, to confirm the shifting process. Alex opened the app and quickly scanned the QR code which was given on the Minitruck's computer monitor screen. The user was verified and a tick mark was displayed, and suddenly, a mini wheeled-robot came out of the Minitruck and greeted Alex- "Hello! I am following you. Please show me the things to be carried and shifted." Alex guided the mini robot and led him inside the store, and eventually to the ChefMate. "This is the appliance to be shifted." Alex told the mini robot, pointing towards the ChefMate. The mini robot analysed the Chefmate and the space and dimension of the path that led to the ChefMate inside the store, to determine which size of the robotic arm wheeled-machine would be compatible to go inside the store, reach the ChefMate, lift and bring it outside to the minitruck. Alex noted this entire process with surprise, not knowing that this process was that complicated and detailed.

After the mini robot scanned the path inside the store that led to the ChefMate, and noted down the dimensions, it came back to Alex, and said- "I have analysed the dimensions and space of the path. I am now calling a compatible robotic arm machine to come, lift and load the ChefMate into the BulkShift Mover. Shall I Proceed?" "Yes. Proceed immediately." Alex commanded. Within seconds, a robotic wheeled-machine came to the same place where the mini robot and Alex were standing. The robotic machine had many parts, holders and a robotic arm. Just when Alex started observing the Robotic arm machine, it drove itself to the ChefMate, extended each of its holders to more than a metre, lifted the ChefMate with its strategically working robotic arm, and added temporary wheels to the appliance, attaching these temporary wheels below the ChefMate. The robotic machine then with the same robotic arm, and its holders, held the ChefMate Appliance properly, and pushed the ChefMate and started moving and taking it, heading outside the store. The robotic arm machine was taking ChefMate with it as if the appliance was a trolley or something, just because additional wheels were attached to it below. Alex and the mini robot walked behind the forward-moving robotic machine that held the ChefMate. "I hope no damage will be done in the transit. Will you take care of this?" Alex asked the mini robot. "Absolutely sir, we'll take very good care of it. Don't you worry!" the BulkShift Mover's mini robot replied. The mini robot was some sort of supervisor and manager of the entire process, handling and managing different robots and machines together. Finally, Alex, the mini robot, and the robotic arm machine came out of the store, with the ChefMate of course. The mini robot commanded the machine with the ChefMate to go back to the main BulkShift Mover mini truck, and then made the crane load the appliance in the Mini truck. After this happened, the mini robot asked Alex- "Are you going to receive the shipment at the destination or someone else?" "Yes, I will be receiving this shipment at the destination- the Truck depot." replied Alex. "Got it, I'll be boarding my mini truck back now, see you there!" the mini robot said, went back to the mini truck, and got attached to its body. And finally, the mini truck departed, heading to the truck depot.

Alex saw in the app that it was taking the BulkShift Mover 25 minutes to reach the Truck depot. It was now 11:45 AM. Surprisingly, much of the process was completed early. "Lemme reach the depot early so I can quickly find a truck for transporting the ChefMate to the ISRO Launch Base." he thought. So Alex went to his Helicar, and switched to Flight Mode, and entered the location of the truck depot. The helicar drove itself ahead, to a much more open space before flying, because it couldn't take off immediately, for the place where it was parked while Alex went inside the store, was surrounded by tall buildings and the road was also not very wide. After it reached a place with shorter buildings around and open sky above, the helicar increased its speed and took off. On checking, Alex saw that it was taking only 9 minutes to reach the truck depot via the helicar. This meant that Alex was reaching the destination, that was- the truck depot, way before the BulkShift Mover was reaching. So he would have plenty of time to search and choose a truck to load the ChefMate in. So while he was on the way, he opened some screenclicks in his phone's gallery and started revising a few topics and concepts that he had studied yesternight, for his Mepama Studies. Minutes passed by, and the helicar's computer beeped, notifying Alex that the helicar is about to land near the destination. So he once again got ready to land, locked his phone, and packed whatever he took out from his backpack during the flight back into the bag. And subsequently, the helicar landed on a helipad on top of a building, near the truck depot. Alex got out of the helicar with his backpack, realizing that he was standing on top of a 6-8 floors building. He looked for an elevator on this terrace, only to find that there was only a staircase going to the floors below. He stepped down the staircase, reaching one floor below the terrace. There, in the main corridor, he saw two elevators from which only one was operational. He called that operational elevator by pressing the button, and waited for it to come. As the elevator doors opened, he went inside and went down to the Ground floor of the building.

He came out of the elevator and walked out of the building he was inside. He briskly walked to the main truck depot area, and saw hundreds of trucks parked in a systematic manner. Each truck had a unique number, written on its doors. Alex wanted to find just one out of these hundreds of trucks whose door was unlocked, so he could go in, set up the truck's navigation system to go to ISRO Launch Base, and send it away with the ChefMate. So he went to each truck one-by-one, pushed the door handle (now the door handles were pushed instead of pulled), but the doors remained locked. He checked more than 20 trucks like this, and when none of them opened, he got frustrated. But just like yin yang's message of there's darkness in light, but also light in darkness, the situation also had some light for Alex. He was standing in the truck depot parking, but as he turned behind, he saw a small office, which was a single-floor building. "The office is probably for depot management and stuff." Alex murmured to himself. But what attracted him towards the office was not exactly the office, but a fire axe stored inside the office building, which he could see from where he was standing because the lights inside the office were on. He got a violent idea, and thought twice if he should do so. But the circumstances eventually made him go inside the office building, step up the stairs, get the fire axe, and finally come back to the truck depot parking. Now, his aim changed from finding an unlocked truck to finding a reliable and good truck. And there were many options available that qualified in this criteria. So finally, he chose a truck numbered- '1445', held the axe properly and hit the truck's door for the first time. The loud alarm of the truck started making noise, but- who cared? Alex kept striking the truck door's boundary until it finally broke off and fell on the ground. Just as the door broke apart and fell, the BulkShift Mover arrived at the same place, near Alex's truck. "What a timing." he thought. Alex climbed into the truck and sat on the main front seat. Now he turned on the truck by pressing the power button, and entered the location and details of ISRO Launch Base on the computer touch screen monitor of the truck. After entering the inputs of all the details, he reviewed the duration of the journey, which was- 1 day 2 hours, which was fine by him. He selected the options of- Auto Recharge at EV Stations whenever required, Non-stop Journey, and Follow Fastest Route available. Finally, after setting up the navigation system of the truck, he climbed down the truck, and went to the BulkShift Mover mini truck that had arrived already. As Alex approached the BulkShift Mover, the mini robot detached and jumped off the mini truck, and came to Alex. "So, where to shift this appliance, Sir?" the mini robot asked. "Uh. Inside this truck." Alex replied, pointing to the truck he had chosen and made ready to go. The mini robot quickly commanded a robotic arm machine once again, this time to unload the ChefMate from the BulkShift Mover mini truck, and load it inside the truck. The robotic arm machine unloaded the ChefMate from the Mover, took it to the main truck and loaded it by lifting the ChefMate and pushing it into the truck's trailer. However, even after it kept the ChefMate inside the trailer, and detached the temporary wheels from it, its holders did not stop holding the ChefMate. Alex was confused to see this, for he thought that the machine was malfunctioning. "Why isn't the robotic machine leaving the ChefMate? Its holders are continuing to hold it." Alex asked the mini robot, in confusion. "Our terms of use state that before payment, we do not leave the shifting material. So, your total is 2,500 rupees." the mini robot replied. "Huh. Weird terms." Alex replied, as he unlocked his phone and checked his payment app. He had insufficient balance, of just 924 rupees. He got worried, but at the same time, irritated by money-mindedness even in a world where there is a bigger problem to solve- to find where everyone is. Alex looked at the ground on his right side, and he saw the fire axe he used to break the truck door. And well, what he did now, is obvious. The mini-robot broke into two pieces and hence powered off, and as it was the main coordinator and the brain of the entire BulkShift Mover system, everything else of the BulkShift Mover, including the mini-truck, and the robotic arm machine, turned off as well. The holders of the robotic arm machine also released the ChefMate as a result of turning off. So Alex simply went inside the truck once again, opened its computer screen, clicked the button of 'Close Trailer Door' and then wrote a command- 'Wait 15 seconds and then start the journey.' And just as he submitted the command, he came out of the truck, and waited for it to depart. The truck's trailer's door got closed automatically, and just after 15 seconds, the truck started moving, slowly speeding up, took a turn and finally departed from the truck depot. Alex loudly sighed, in relief of course, that finally his last task in Capitrolis was completed. He could now begin the real mission- of building Mepamas, after going back to SpaceVillage. He advanced back to the building on which his helicar landed, and realising that it's just 12:30 PM right now, he thought he could utilize much of his time today doing his Mepama studies. "Wait a minute. There are still 2 more days remaining for Gopiz's software update to complete?" he realised. "That means, going back to ISRO Launch Base just tonight or even tomorrow, is of no use. I guess then I'll just go back the day after tomorrow." he decided, postponing his journey back to SpaceVillage, and deciding to spend some more time in his home city- Capitrolis. As all this was going on in his mind, he reached the building on top of which his helicar landed. He went inside it, went to the elevator, and went straight up to the highest floor of the building. Finally, he came out of the elevator and took the staircase to reach the terrace of the building, where his helicar was parked. He opened the helicar door, sat on its seat, entered his society's helipad location, and started his journey. As the helicar lifted in the air and started flying, he reclined his seat, and took some rest after completing the final task. No, this time he wasn't sleeping, but he just closed his eyes, giving his body and mind some rest. While his eyes were closed, he tried to visualize what he had already achieved in his journey to bring the IndWatch satellite down. He reflected deeply on the milestones he reached and crossed, and appreciated himself, though non verbally.

After he gave his body enough rest, he opened his eyes to check time remaining to reach, and still 13 minutes were left. "I already had my brunch, but let me also get something for today's evening snack and dinner." He changed the destination to a nearby superstore, and the helicar automatically selected the nearest helipad to the superstore. It now displayed that only 4 minutes were left to reach the new destination- the nearest SuperStore. Alex watched the city, buildings, parks, and skyscrapers pass by beneath him as the helicar sped through the air. Below he saw the India Gate, the National Park, and the New Capitrolis Mall, eventually getting left behind while the helicar propelled itself forward. Finally, the 4 minutes passed somehow, and the vehicle landed on a helipad in the Charging Station. Alex got out of the helicar, and went to the superstore adjacent to the Helicar Charging Station. He went inside, and grabbed some frozen snack packets of Fries, Fritters, Potato Wedges and Cheese nuggets that can be air-fried and cooked easily. He put these packets in his backpack and rushed back to the Helicar. He decided that he'll just have fries and cheese nuggets for an evening snack and rest everything for dinner. He also wanted to reach home by 1, so as to start studying early and make use of the time that he had got. He reached the helicar, sat inside it, closed the door and finally took off for his society. It was 12:50 now, and exactly 6 more minutes were left for the helicar to reach Alex's society. During that time, Alex came up with a timetable for the rest of the day, for studying and research, of Mepamas and concepts he needs to understand in order to make the giant ones. He decided that from 1:30 PM, till 4:00 PM he'll study continuously. Then from 7:00 PM till 10:00 PM will be his Study plus research time. After planning today's schedule, he unlocked his phone, and suddenly, a notification popped up- a photo memory. He clicked on the notification, and got emotional by seeing a family picture of his parents, his sister and himself, with a title- 'Your memory, an Year ago from today.' It was the regular gallery app, which stores pictures. It just did what it sometimes did, showed him old memories or pictures of the past. But this time, it brought tears of sadness in his eyes, because of his grief and longing to meet his family again. His mind flashed so many memories that he made with his parents and sister, like the trip to Dehra City (formerly known as Dehradun), where among the mountains and hills he and his family stayed in a beautiful resort near a river, the times he and his family dined out and had pizza parties, and what not. But he tried to calm himself down, for now it wasn't the time to weaken his heart, but to strengthen it and be determined to make the giant Mepamas, and finally bring the IndWatch down. Just when Alex finally became normal and tears stopped falling from his eyes, the helicar landed on his society's helipad. "Finally reached!" he said, with a sigh. He opened the helicar door, took his backpack and phone, stepped out and slammed the door. He went to the elevator, pressed the button, entered the lift, and went down to the ground floor. He saw the electric kick scooter he had parked at the bottom of the building, and so he got on the kick scooter, switched it on, and started off to his tower building. He could feel the air rushing against him as he sped up the kick scooter.

Finally, he reached the kick scooter parking at the bottom of his building. So he parked, turned off and got off the scooter. And via his elevator, he went to his floor, and finally entered his house- his apartment. He was tired of today's exertion, but also wanted to study as much as he can today. "Oh, yeah! Why don't I make that?" he exclaimed, just as he recalled something. He recalled that he can make coffee for himself, so he could wave off fatigue and get the energy to study for hours straight. He sat on the sofa for 2-3 more minutes, and then went into the kitchen to make a mug of coffee for himself. It was 1:15 PM now, and while the milk was being boiled on the induction cooktop, Alex went to his bedroom and got his books and study material ready for his studying session. Just as the induction cooktop beeped and announced: "The milk has boiled, turning off the induction," Alex came back to the kitchen, added milk to the coffee and sugar, and finally finished making his coffee. He poured it from the vessel into his mug. And when it was 1:25 PM, he was all set, just like his coffee. He put his phone on 'Do Not Disturb' mode so that the notifications won't disturb him, switched on his Airtop and opened his AI Model's Chat page, so he could ask him doubts whenever he felt stuck or confused. At 1:30 sharp, he opened the Electrical Engineering book and started studying. Minutes passed by, and those minutes soon turned into hours. Now hours passed by, and the study session extended beyond the time Alex had planned. Instead of just ending at 4 PM, it was now 5:15 PM, and Alex was still reading the chapter of 'Microcontrollers'. He was so well immersed in studying that he didn't even realize that so much time had already passed by. Finally, when the chapter was finished, Alex decided to take a break, thinking that it's almost 4 PM. To his own surprise, it was 5:57 PM then! "What the heck? I had been studying more than I had planned? Wow-" he exclaimed, and was shocked, but also proud of his capability to be so interested in things that he wishes to pursue.

Seeing that the sun had started to go down, he thought, why not go to the terrace and experience the remaining beauty of the city, at least? This way, at least I'd see a beautiful sunset, though alone. So he grabbed his phone, sipped some water before leaving, sprayed some perfume for a nice and beautiful feel and sunset experience. And finally, he left his apartment and went to the Terrace using the elevator. The elevator dinged, and the doors opened. Alex came out, and witnessed the large, beautiful and serene green terrace garden, with real grass growing in real soil. There were flowing water fountains made of polished stone, even fruit trees growing, and beautiful yellow lamps, and lights hanging from these trees. And finally, the glass railing of the boundary of the terrace allowed him to see the entire cityscape of Capitrolis. Alex went to one of the benches, and had a seat. Some light background music was also being played. "What a strange thing. Not strange in fact, but a great thing, that I live in the year 2162. Almost everything works automatically! From music to lights, from elevators to vehicles." Alex said, and reflected. "Our history book said that in the previous century and as well as in the first few years of this century, even these things had to be switched on and off and controlled manually. I wonder how much more difficult my situation would have been if I existed in those times, facing these circumstances."

He kept looking at the sun that was sinking below the horizon. He took a few deep breaths, to relax and calm his mind. But then, he saw something unexpected. As he looked closely at the glass railing of the terrace, he saw that the same triangular or pyramid-shaped techy glowing item that he saw at Jessica's house, was kept on the railing. The pyramid thing was glowing purple and white. He suddenly stood up from the bench and went towards it. "What the-" he murmured. But he remembered that if he touched it, the colors would change to red and black. So he had a plan. He removed his Jacket and held it in one hand, and took one of the elongated pebbles lying in the terrace garden and held this pebble stone in the other hand. He brought the jacket near that glowing pyramid thing, pushed and moved it slightly and made it fall on the jacket that he kept in his one hand using the pebble. The color did not change, as it was not directly in contact with his body or skin. "Huh, it changes its colour only with a human's direct touch? What the heck is this?" Alex said, as he was perplexed. He also felt a bit suspicious. So he just carefully wrapped the pyramid thing with his jacket, took his phone, and went back down to his house.

When he entered his apartment, it was 6:24 PM. But well, he was curious about figuring out what this pyramid-shaped glowing thing was. He went to his dining table and kept the pyramid, wrapped with his jacket, on the table. He finally went to his kitchen and turned on the advanced air fryer to heat it up, so he could cook the frozen stuff he brought from the superstore. As the air fryer started to warm up, Alex went to his Airtop, opened the AI Model chat page, and texted the AI about the pyramid-like thing he saw twice, and this time even got. He mentioned that it glowed purple and white lights but turns into red and black once it gets a human touch. However, the only reply of the AI Model was- 'The pyramid-shaped item you are referring to might be a special lamp with sensors that could identify human touch distinctly from other things' touches and then respectively change its colours. It might be available in some local places as kids' toys or lamps.'

"Kids' lamps? Seriously? Then why did I never see them before?" Alex questioned, while being dissatisfied with the AI's answer. He tried searching the same pyramid-shaped lamp with many keywords on various search engines too, but there weren't any great or relevant searches. He also went back to the dining table, and carefully removed the corners of his jacket to uncover the pyramid once again, only to see that the pyramid lamp was still glowing just purple and white- its normal colours. He then clicked a bunch of pictures of it and even searched these pictures on the image search engine for similar and relevant results. But again, there were no great results. He was frustrated, and he felt quite strange too. Nevertheless, he thought to ignore this pyramid thing for now, and focus on having a delicious dinner instead. So he went to the kitchen, opened the packets of fries, fritters and cheese nuggets, and emptied the packets into the air fryer. He decided to have the potato wedges later, probably tomorrow for breakfast. He set the air fryer timer for a few minutes, and went to his living room's recliner sofa and sat down on it. He unlocked his phone and once again started watching some Strings on Mesocia. He passed those few minutes doing the same thing, and finally when the Air Fryer dinged, he went to the kitchen, took out the fries, fritters and nuggets out in a plate, added some tomato sauce and mayonnaise to the plate, and finally sat down on the dining table to eat.

He enjoyed his tasty evening snack which was also his dinner, and finally finished his meal, around 7:15 PM. "I should go back to studying now, but this time, doing some research alongside as well." he thought. He wanted to now use the AI Model and internet to see where he can apply the knowledge he gained by studying these books' few chapters, in making the giant Mepamas. So his Study Plus Research session started, after he finished with his meal. He read and learned more, and then tried to give prompts to the AI Model via chat and got responses, gradually understanding what he'll do in making the Mepamas, and applying the knowledge he gained by studying these books. He also opened and watched the holobooks that he brought from the Capitrolis Library as well. He once again spent hours doing the studying and research simultaneously. Around 8:30, he went to the kitchen and made another mug of coffee, came back to study, and continued his study and research. Alex had this trait, that he often becomes worried or anxious. But when it was time for action, he was the best action hero- that is, he did what he had to properly.

After a few more hours of study and research, it was almost 11 'o' clock, and as the 23-Sleep Rule said that for energy and electricity conservation, the power supplied will be limited, Alex decided to finish today's studying and research session, and go to bed. He closed the holo-books, and regular books, shutted down his Airtop, and switched off most of the lights of his house, went to bed and drifted into sleep. The final significant and necessary task he had to finish was completed today, and he was all set to go back to ISRO Launch Base, although the day after tomorrow. But the relaxed and calm feeling of having the ChefMate shipped to SpaceVillage and getting the other two tasks done- Mepama charts and getting books to study, made Alex's tonight's sleep more peaceful. So he slept, around 11:10 PM, and the silent world's atmosphere did not feel so silent after Alex's positive thoughts of progressing in his journey chirped in his mind.

FOURTEEN
LAST DAY AT HOME

The sun rose up, just like every new day. Around 7:30 AM, Alex woke up and got out of bed. "The last 24 hours remaining for staying in Capitrolis!" he said to himself, while entering his balcony, admiring the cityscape and view. He didn't want to leave his homeplace, but his desire to find and get back all the people was stronger than his obsession with his city. He continued to admire the view, but at the back of his mind he also remembered that today was an extra day that he got in his journey of making the Mepamas and the IndWatch Mission, and hence, he should utilize it to the fullest. He had his plans all ready to study the entire day and make the most of this additional day, before heading back to ISRO Launch Base the next day's morning. So he went back inside his bedroom and the sliding balcony door automatically closed. He went to the washroom, took a quick shower after attending nature's calls and got ready by 8. He came out of the washroom, and hurriedly made his breakfast- coffee and toasted bread and butter. He added a bit of oregano seasoning on the bread butter to enhance the flavour, and finally sat down to have his breakfast. "A simple, tasty and quick breakfast option- bread and butter!" he said to himself, as he took the first bite. Within just minutes, he finished the breakfast and the coffee as well, and began studying once again. But this time, a question kept on popping up in his mind- "Will the attractive force of giant Mepamas on the UAVs be enough to pull the IndWatch down to the surface of the Earth from its orbit?" He tried answering it himself, but was unable to get a clear and proper answer. During his entire study session, till 11:00 AM, he was confused and worried about the same question. He made a plan, but it was rough. Not fully including all scientific considerations, forces and laws. Yes, he was intelligent, but he was underconfident that he might have ignored other aspects of the process of attracting the satellite towards the earth's surface. However, his will-power told him to keep going, and have faith in his plan and idea. He continued his study plus research session, noting down and understanding where he could apply the concepts he learnt and was learning during the study session.

"Hmmm... This means that the Mepamas' force of attraction must be strong enough to knock down the IndWatch from its orbit, slowing down its velocity or speed, decreasing its altitude, and pull it towards the surface of the earth." he thought to himself, understanding and making the conclusion in his study and research session. He tried to understand the concepts more clearly, reading topics like Electromagnetic Induction, Magnetic Attraction and Electromagnetism. Finally, around 12:30 PM, he finished his first Study Session of the day. And he felt like it was worth it, because he learnt and understood a lot of important things in this one. After the study session, he started to feel more knowledgeable, and now he was able to connect various scientific concepts and aspects together with each other. Anyways, after hours of studying and research, he unlocked his phone for the first time today. For the sake of a break, he opened the Mesocia app, and started watching some Strings- the short clips and videos, for entertainment. But much of his feed was filled with scientific explanations and videos instead, just as one would have expected. He spent a few minutes scrolling those short videos, for it was one of his developed habits, good or bad, he didn't know. After 15 minutes of scrolling strings, he kept down his phone, and walked up to the living room. He believed in the quote- 'All work and no play creates a mind too tired to create.' So he thought- "Of course I never did study this much, ever. Not even in my exams. Fine, this is an important mystery I have to solve, but I can't make myself go insane by studying for the whole day without any entertainment or relaxation." And finally, a good idea popped up in his mind as he just sat down on his living room sofa. "Let's watch a movie. Let's enjoy this last day in Capitrolis too!" he murmured. He commanded the TV with his voice- "Alright Televo, play 'Kuchh Palle Na Pade' movie." And the movie played the movie from the very beginning. 'Kuchh Palle Na Pade' was a comedy movie about a few college friends, who have different personalities but have the same struggle, that they can't study easily. It was similar to the movie we had in the present time- "3 Idiots." Alex had seen the movie, but 2-3 years ago, so he thought to see it once more because it was a nice and humorous movie.

He watched the movie till its interval, and then switched it off by voice-commanding the TV once more. He was enjoying it, but he had an unsatisfactory feeling that made him want to go back to studying. It was maybe because the value and benefits he was getting from his Mepama Studies was more than the value of amusement he got by watching the movie. He couldn't believe the situation, but it was the first time ever that even though he studied for hours, he wanted to study more. It was, anyway, a positive thing for him. Where he had thought that he would need to motivate himself or push himself to study these thick and complex books, there was this unexpected and naturally occurring boost of motivation. So it was in fact good for him. And predictably, he went back to study, and started his second study session.

Once again, hours passed, and now it was 5:40 PM. Alex got up from his study table's chair, and stretched his arms. He finished off his second study session. "Wait a minute. I didn't have lunch today! Wow." he realized, and laughed at himself as he forgot such a basic thing. He went to the kitchen, and took out the potato wedges packet from the refrigerator's freezer, turned on the air fryer and made the potato wedges as his evening snack. He thought about making coffee, but for a change, decided to make tomato soup, of course using the instant-soup powder. When both the things were made and ready, he took out the wedges in a plate and the soup in a mug, and took both of them to his balcony. As the sun was setting, he sat on the chair in his balcony and had his evening meal, seeing the silent but illuminated city as the sky started to become darker and darker, and the city's bright lights switched on one after another. It was a view that he used to love in the past, because now it turned into a glimpse of the crisis- the crisis and catastrophe of everyone just... disappearing. Finally as he finished his meal, he went back inside, kept his plates in the kitchen sink, and came back to his bedroom's study table, and started his third study session.

It was not just his own perseverance that pushed him positively to study, but something else as well. He felt a feeling inside him that automatically made him want to continue his Mepama Studies, without much break. Finally it was night time, around 10:15 PM. Alex thought to simply end the study session right then, and go and prepare a light dinner for himself. "I guess just some corn flakes and milk would be enough for my appetite." he said to himself, and went to the kitchen to make the same. He warmed the milk with sugar in the talking microwave who still talked nonsense like usual, commenting on Alex's choice for dinner. After warming the milk, he switched off the microwave, added corn flakes to it, and started having his light and simple dinner. Knowing it was his last night in Capitrolis and he had to go back to SpaceVillage tomorrow morning, he thought to sleep early tonight. But the studying sessions he completed today made him feel more enlightened, knowledgeable and proud of himself. After finishing his light dinner, he turned off almost all the lights of the house, went to his bed and slept, however, with the aim of waking up early tomorrow so he could do the packing and finally depart from Capitrolis."

FIFTEEN

BACK TO SPACEVILLAGE

"Wow. I mean. Just one word I'd wanna say again and again- Wow!" said Sandeep. "Seriously! Just look at Aryan, he can't even study for 10 minutes continuously, without checking his phone." Peter commented, after which Aryan gave him a death stare. "Probably he keeps waiting for his crush's reply." Rhea added and bantered. "Come on, Rhea! You too?!" Aryan replied. "Guys come on, we can't be disturbing the flow of the story like this. We already have exceeded half of the time we had in this interview. Let him complete his story first." Garima said, being annoyed by the distractive comments. "It's okay, Garima. A little fun is needed between such long stories. But yeah, let's continue-

The morning of Alex's departure began, and the sun rose up indicating the new day. The sunlight's rays entered Alex's room and touched his hand while he was asleep, as if they were bidding him farewell from his home-city. The birds started chirping, and it literally felt like the beautiful morning was calling Alex to wake up and get ready for his journey, but he remained asleep. Soon, his phone's alarm rang, but surprisingly, he didn't even wake up when the alarm rang, and continued sleeping. When finally he opened his eyes and touched his feet to the floor for the first time this morning, waking up from his sleep, he looked at the clock and shouted- "Holy fish! It's 9:45 AM? I am so late!" He immediately got up, went to the washroom, attended nature's call quickly, and came out to just change his clothes and get ready for his departure. Taking a shower and a proper bath seemed pretty frivolous to him right now. He hurriedly started packing his bags- the trolley bag with his clothes and essential items, the luggage bag with the Mepama Studies books, and his own backpack that he took everywhere. He also packed the most important thing, the thing he came to Capitrolis for- the shoebox containing Mepama Configuration charts and specification documents, which he got from Jessica's house. Finally, after some minutes he was done with the packing, and all ready to go. "Oops! Almost forgot." he said to himself, after noticing that he forgot to keep his Airtop and wallet in his backpack, and subsequently did so. It was almost 11 now, and he was all set to go. He decided to skip breakfast and directly have brunch at the ISRO Launch Base. Taking a last deep breath inside his house, he loudly sighed. "I'll miss you, my sweet home. But I'll be back. Not tomorrow, not after a week, maybe not even after a month. But when I will, I'll be with Mom, Dad, Sierra and all those billions of people who disappeared." he made a bold statement, before heading out of his home. Wiping a tear as he was leaving his home for a long time, he walked out of the main door, went inside the elevator, reached the ground floor and left his building.

He took a kick scooter, and headed to the helipad building. "Oh yeah, the Helicar needs a recharge as well. I saw the indication the last time I travelled in it. How did I forget?" he thought to himself, recalling that he saw the notification of 'Low Battery' in his Helicar the day before yesterday while coming back from the Truck Depot. He reached the bottom of the helipad building, stopped the kick scooter and entered the building. He went up, to the terrace floor, walked to his Helicar and sat inside it after loading all of his baggage inside it. "I hope it at least has enough battery to fly to the nearest charging station." the thought appeared in his mind. Fortunately, as he powered on the Helicar, it showed that it could fly for 5 more kilometres, while the nearest Helicar Charging Station was just 2 kilometres away. "Thank goodness." he sighed in relief and clicked the button to take off and start the journey to the station. In less than a minute, the helicar reached the charging station, and landed on one of the helipads. As it turned off, Alex got outside, and went to the charging machine, grabbed the charging cable, opened Helicar's hatch and the charging port, and inserted the cable's plug. It showed that the full charging would take at least half an hour. Now Alex was frustrated, because he was already late. But well, he couldn't blame something else, for he himself was responsible for forgetting that the Helicar needed a recharge.

While the Helicar was charging, he wanted to do something and not just stand idly. He looked around, and saw a small cafe just across the main road. "I didn't have my breakfast this morning, so let me get something from there." he thought. He walked to the cafe, crossed the road and entered it. The smell of coffee itself made him feel hungry. He further walked to the main counter, realizing that it was actually an automatic cafe. During these days, there were generally two types of restaurants and cafes- the manual ones, where humans prepared and made food, and the automatic ones, where machines made the food and beverages using appliances like ChefMate. He went to the kiosk monitor, added a vanilla croissant, a veg club sandwich, and finally a Latte to his order. Once he proceeded to the payment page, he realized he had no money in his digital wallet. But voila! He found a wallet kept with a house key card on one of the cafe tables, probably of someone who disappeared now, but was earlier sitting on the same cafe table. Now this wasn't really stealing, because of course, it was his helplessness or necessity, but Alex picked up the wallet, took out two-three notes, total being just a bit more than his order's actual bill, and inserted it in the kiosk. The kiosk, just like an ATM, gave back the remaining change of the money that Alex gave, and he, in turn, kept that change of money in that same wallet.

He waited patiently and explored the beautiful interiors of the cafe. Finally when his order was ready, he took it from the Collecting Counter, where his meal's tray with everything he ordered was kept on the counter by a humanoid robot. He sipped the Latte and had the croissant, followed by the club sandwich. When he was completely finished with his breakfast, he noticed that the 30 minutes had now passed, and assumed that the charging was completed. He got out of the cafe, crossed the road once again, reached his helicar and noticed the green light blinking near the Helicar's charging port, indicating that it was fully charged. He disconnected the cable, closed the port and the hatch, sat inside the helicar once again, and this time, started his long journey to ISRO Launch Base, near SpaceVillage. This time, the helicar rose to a higher altitude, in fact above the clouds, as it had to cruise for a longer period of time. Alex switched on and put on his headphones to listen to some music, to pass time. He listened to many songs, of different kinds and moods, for several minutes, closing his eyes and resting. While the calmness and restfulness engrossed Alex's mind almost completely, suddenly, Alex got jumpscared by an irritating and loud ringtone that was played as his phone rang. "What the hell?! An incoming call?!" Alex exclaimed, confused and not believing the situation he was facing. He thought that probably someone was still left, just like him, and was giving him a call. He quickly accepted the call and said- "Hello? Alex here. Who are you?" "Bro! Where are you?! Why did you leave me alone?" And the sudden feeling that almost turned into happiness eventually turned into annoyance. It was Gopiz, who had called him, after waking up from his 120 hours software update. "Gopiz, you just keep your mouth shut! Do you have any idea of how much I went through, all alone? You gave me a hope of a companion, although non-human, but at least someone. And then you yourself switched off?! Just don't talk to me now." replied Alex. "No... No... No! Alex brother, you got me wrong. My software update was not in my hands, at least not back at that time. The storage devices used in me have a periodic cycle of updating me, and they keep downloading new features in me with time. I did not have any control on my software updates then, but now, the new updates have given me autonomy and freedom, including the freedom to choose when I go through software updates and when I don't. I am so sorry that you had to stay and go through stuff without me. But I promise it won't happen again. Please forgive me." Gopiz apologised to Alex. "Well... If you are sure that it won't happen again, then it's okay. I was in Capitrolis to get some important stuff. I'll tell you everything in detail after I reach back to the Launch Base. And yes, I'm on my way." Alex replied. "Thank you for forgiving me! Now, let's uncover this mystery together!" "Haha. Yes, we will uncover it successfully! By the way, how did you get my calling number?" "Why? Do you underestimate this tiny robot? Hehehe. I might be small and irritating, but I have advanced technologies to track down computer devices' details, information, and what not!" "Wow. Didn't expect that. Anyways, here your voice is anyway not that clear. Talk to you after reaching there. Bye!" Alex said. "Bye Alex bro! See you soon!" Gopiz replied. And Alex hung up the phone.

Despite his frustration and anger due to Gopiz's shutting down, he thought to let it go because Gopiz is a robot anyway, and as he said, it was not under his control to stop the update from occurring. So, it's not his fault completely, in fact, it was just the fault of the situation back then, and no one else's. Anyways, the helicar continued to fly through its course, and its computer screen indicated to Alex that it'll take 50 more minutes. "In the meantime, I can read a Mepama Studies book." he thought. So he turned and leaned towards the backseat of the helicar, where all his baggage was kept, managed to open the luggage bag of the Mepama Studies books, and finally took out a thick book that he had already half-finished. He began reading the book to pass his time further. Whenever he was confused about the meaning of a word, definition or even a sentence, he would ask his

AI Model through chat. This way, he was understanding every single thing correctly and with clarity. He knew he'd need to continue his robust study routine consistently to finally be able to acquire all the knowledge to build the giant Mepamas and its systems. After some time, the helicar finally began its descent, propelling below the clouds and lowering its altitude. Alex looked at the time left on the computer screen of the helicar, and it showed 17 more minutes. After reading and studying for a while, Alex felt bored. He knew that he could not let his boredom overcome his studying, but it seemed logical to do so because he would have to stop studying after some minutes anyway, as the helicar will land at the Launch Base. So he closed the book and kept it back in the luggage bag. When 6 minutes were left to reach, Alex started seeing the small town of SpaceVillage below, from his Helicar window. The small railway station, winding streets, and the road to the ISRO Launch Base passing below, coinciding the Helicar's path. He also saw the glittering sea, just a few kilometres away from the same road. The helicar proceeded towards the Launch Base, just flying directly above the road to the same.

Finally, the helicar landed on one of the helipads in the ISRO Launch Base helicar parking lot, ending the long journey of almost two hours. As Alex opened the door and stepped out, he heard- "Finally my friend is here! Aaaaa!" Gopiz came hovering to Alex, after coming out from a door of the Launch Base Complex building. He suddenly reached Alex and hugged him tightly, as if he met his best friend after a long time, though the situation was somewhat actually the same. "You came back!" Gopiz said excitedly. "Uh... Chill bro. I was away for just four or five days." Alex replied. "Uh can you leave me now? I have to unload my baggage." He gestured Gopiz to stop hugging him. "Oh, right! I forgot, hehehe." Gopiz answered back, and ceased to hug him further. "I thought you got some new updates in there, but look at you, still forgetting!" Alex said and teased Gopiz, funnily, and laughed. He then opened the back door of the helicar, and took out all his bags and luggage. "So why did you go to Capitrolis?" Gopiz asked. "First let's go inside? It's quite hot and sunny." Alex replied. "Oh yeah! Okay. Let's go." Gopiz said, and started walking with Alex towards the door of the building, where Gopiz initially came from. Just after entering the building and the corridor at the same time, as Gopiz was super curious, Alex explained everything that happened after Gopiz's hibernation began. He also told him what he did in Capitrolis and why he went there. As they reached the hall in which they mostly used to be in- the Mission Control Centre room, Gopiz said-

"And yeah, I noticed how you made these automatic doors get stuck by putting this desk in between. So I understand how much difficulty you went through when I was in my Software Update mode. Again, so sorry about that." "Bro, now stop apologizing again and again. And tell me another thing- Has the ChefMate I just told you about arrived here? At the Launch Base?" Alex inquired. "Well, I am not sure about that. That truck you told to come here, can at maximum reach the main gate of the ISRO Launch Base, because as you know, the main gates are closed." Gopiz said. "Oh, right. So let's go check it now? Then we'll rest." Alex said, and Gopiz agreed. They both hurried to the main gate, and pulled down its lever to automatically open the large metal sliding gates. And as the gates opened, they both looked and then danced and shouted with joy. "Yay! It is here, it is here..." they both said and danced together. "I think you should give another command to the truck to come inside the ISRO Launch Base. This will make it easier for us to unload the ChefMate, I guess." Gopiz suggested. "Hmm yeah. Lemme do it." Alex replied, and went to the truck, climbed into it, and gave the command- 'Wait 15 seconds and then enter the ISRO Launch Base-' and he stopped typing further. He took his head out of the broken door's space of the truck, and shouted and asked Gopiz- "What destination shall I enter? Till where should it go so that it becomes easy for us to unload the thing?" "Ummm... Tell it to go till the Warehouse. There we have forklifts. We'll unload it there." Gopiz replied loudly. Alex entered the command completely, told the truck to wait for those 15 seconds, giving himself time to get off the truck, came out and went back to Gopiz. The truck started moving forward, entered the gates, took a slight turn, and drove itself to the warehouse. Alex and Gopiz hurried to the same.

Reaching the large and spacious warehouse, the truck stopped. As Alex and Gopiz reached there, Gopiz said- "You wait here. I'll get a forklift." Forklift was a lifting and moving machine used for industrial purposes, and it was useful for unloading stuff. Just within a minute, Gopiz was back driving a navy blue forklift and told Alex to sit beside him to just spectate, observe, and ensure if the unloading occurred without any issue. Alex followed Gopiz's instructions, and then Gopiz drove the forklift to the truck's trailer, whose door was opened after Alex pressed a button on the trailer before getting on the forklift. They both saw the brand-new chefmate inside the trailer, but the darkness inside the trailer made it less visible in sunlight. Anyways, Gopiz started moving the forklift's hands/forks, extended them to go under the ChefMate, and when they were fully under the ChefMate, he said to Alex- "Press that red button, please." As Alex did the same, the ChefMate magically lifted, and both of them watched it with amazement. Gopiz drove the Forklift back, bringing out the ChefMate from the trailer, as it remained lifted with the industrial vehicle's hands or forks. "Now can we take it at least to the nearest place to our Mission Control Centre where we generally stay?" Alex asked Gopiz. "Hmmm… There is a parking space outside the same building as the Mission Control Room, just outside the corridor. Let's place it there. Alright?" Gopiz asked for approval. "Sounds great! Let's go." They both travelled with the lifted ChefMate using the forklift, to that parking space. When they reached, Gopiz slowly pulled down the lever of the forks control, lowering the ChefMate with the vehicle's forks/hands. And finally, the ChefMate was established, where it was supposed to.

It was almost 2:30 PM now. "Thanks for the help Gopiz!" Alex thanked Gopiz for his efforts, from suggesting to driving the forklift. Alex was hungry now, and hence, he turned on the ChefMate, which successfully switched on with a beautiful intro music. Alex this time, added Shahi Paneer and Butter Flatbread to his meal. The ChefMate started making Alex's meal and displayed the countdown. While it was preparing his food, they both went back inside the building, into the corridors. They were busy diverting their minds from technical stuff to some time-pass topics. Just for fun, Gopiz asked Alex- "Did you have a girlfriend or crush?" This changed Alex's face from a laughing and smiling one to a serious and sad face. "Oh, was that something I shouldn't have asked?" Gopiz asked this another question. "No. It's nothing like that. It's just that, this same adversity made her disappear too. Jessica. Apart from my parents and sister, I miss her the most." replied Alex, emotionally. "Stay strong my brother. We'll unveil the truth of all of this. Don't you worry. You've already gotten this far!" Gopiz said and tried to motivate Alex. "Yes bud. We will!" Alex replied, gaining a slight smile. "Oh, I think that ChefMate's countdown must have been over now. Let's go get your meal." Gopiz changed the topic. Alex understood, but he was hungry too. So both of them went to the corridor door leading to the parking outside the building, opened it, and went to the ChefMate. Alex collected his plate from the machine, turned it off, and finally headed back to their default room- the Mission Control Centre. Alex and Gopiz both sat on the chairs in front of each other, and talked as Alex ate. After he was finished with his lunch, Gopiz asked- "So, shall we start the Giant Mepama-making process from tomorrow?" "Not tomorrow. Today. Although we don't have the materials here right now, we must start examining and understanding the Mepama Blueprints, configurations and specifications, and then plan a similar structure of the giant Mepama we're making, deriving almost everything except the size from the blueprints." Alex replied and continued- "What I've studied till now is enough to get started with understanding how the Mepama will work, but I need to study at least some important parts of the remaining books to understand everything and apply the knowledge properly." "Right. So what you can do is that you start studying those important topics, while the books you aren't reading, you give them to me, so I can scan them and store its contents in my memory, so I could assist you with all the knowledge and stuff while we actually make the Mepamas." Gopiz suggested. "Really? You can do that? Scan and store all the info? Wow, that'll be helpful. So, now I'll just try finishing up the important topics myself, and then let's work together to understand all the blueprints and info of the Mepama, so we can start making them ASAP." Alex replied. Agreeing to the plan, Gopiz was handed the books Alex wasn't reading at the moment, and Alex started reading and studying one of the books. He also used the AI Model for getting quick answers to his confusion or questions, meanwhile Gopiz was busy scanning the books' pages, storing all the information written.

This went on for hours, and by 7 or 8 PM, Alex was completely done with studying the important chapters of three books, while Gopiz was done with scanning all the remaining books. "So. All done for today?" Gopiz asked. "Of course not bro, I need to continue studying the remaining books." Alex answered. "But this way you'll mess up your brain. You can't just keep forcing knowledge continuously. You need a break. Plus, you don't need to know everything, because I've stored everything in my data memory, so I know all the things from all the books I scanned. I'll now just scan the books you finished reading too." Gopiz said. Alex understood that Gopiz's statement has a point. Why should he study every single thing, from one to all, when Gopiz already has gotten all the knowledge himself, and as an advanced AI robot, he can help Alex out in almost everything. "You're right. I should not study every single thing. In fact, this will waste more of our time. Let's have a Requirement-Return approach, in which only if required, I'll return to study the specific topic or concept I need to know." Alex said. "Yup. Now can you pass those three books you just finished reading?" Gopiz requested Alex, and so he passed and handed over those books to Gopiz so that he could scan those books as well.

After the scanning was completed of all the pages of those three books as well, with each book not taking more than 10 minutes due to Gopiz's super fast scanning speed, both of them took a sigh, and Alex literally lay down over the mattress, tired of all the work in late afternoon and evening. "Should we start studying the Blueprints and specifications from tomorrow?" Gopiz asked. "No. Not tomorrow. From tonight itself." Alex replied, extremely determined to immerse into the process of making the giant Mepamas as soon as possible. After replying this, Alex rested for almost half an hour, and then finally got up and noticed that Gopiz slept too. He went to Gopiz and shaked his robotic body, which made him wake up again. "Yeah! Sorry. My battery is low again. It's usually very long-lasting but maybe due to that 120 hours software update it's that low." Gopiz justified himself. "Go charge yourself then. Will meet you tomorrow." Alex said to Gopiz. "But what about studying the Mepama blueprints and charts?" Gopiz asked. "Don't worry. I'll manage on my own. I've been doing it for days. You go charge yourself for the big day tomorrow. From tomorrow onwards, we'll begin planning the exact manufacturing process of the giant Mepamas, answering the question how we'll do it. From the day after tomorrow, we'll start 3-D Printing of the basic parts, and so on." Alex replied. Gopiz thanked Alex for understanding his discharged situation, went to his charging pod and began his charging. Meanwhile, Alex went to one of the long tables of the same large hall-sized room, i.e. the Mission Control Centre room, pulled out a chair and had a seat. He turned on his Airtop, and brought the shoe box containing Mepama blueprints and charts. With the knowledge he acquired in these days when he studied a lot, he tried to understand the text, the diagrams and the information that Jessica wrote on the charts. He could pretty much understand everything. The structure of Mepama was not as complex as what Alex had expected. It contained a hard-plastic outer casing, an electromagnet- which is the heart of the Mepama, the rechargeable battery, a circuit board with a microcontroller, a signal receiver, the targeting system including many smaller parts, the magnetic base and finally the LED lights. "Okay, I think now I completely understand how it works. But then the real challenge here is making this structure of Mepama on a larger scale, and ensuring that it is compatible with the UAVs and attaches to them properly." Alex thought, while observing and studying the Mepama charts. He spent 45 minutes more just understanding and interpreting those charts. He also consulted the AI Model through chat on laptop, asking questions about how he could make the same Mepama of a larger size, and got detailed responses and solutions on the basis of the giant mepamas' usage in bringing down the IndWatch. Finally, when it was around 10 PM at night, Alex decided to sleep, so he could start his mepamas' manufacturing process with a fresh mind tomorrow onwards. He switched off his Airtop, kept back the Mepama charts in the shoe box, switched off the main lights of the hall-sized room, and went to his mattress to sleep. He got into the blanket, closed his eyes, and slept in the new place, peacefully.

SIXTEEN

DAY ONE AT ISROEM

A new morning, but with the old mission, emerged. Gopiz got turned on after he was fully charged, and he stepped out of his pod. He looked around, but couldn't see Alex. Then his eyes fell on the green garden outside the large glass windows of the room. Alex was drinking something in a mug, sitting on the grass of that garden, watching the morning sky with beautiful clouds. Gopiz went outside to the garden through the space of the broken window pane, hovered to Alex and asked- "Wow, you woke up early?" "Beautiful sky, isn't it?" Alex replied. "Hmmm... I guess so. Perfect for motivating us to get our mission started." Gopiz said. "So you ready? Let's leave for the ISROEM Centre." "And what about your breakfast? Would you eat it here or there–" "I already had it, Gopiz. I ate a cheese sandwich made by ChefMate. I'm already ready from my side." Alex replied. "Well, then let's go. It'll be great if we start early as it's just 7:15." Gopiz said. They both headed to the helicar parking, got into the helicar, and took off for the ISROEM Centre. While the helicar cruised, Alex told everything he studied about the Mepama charts to Gopiz. Both of them wanted to finalize the processes and schedule for manufacturing the Mepamas in the ISROEM Centre today, that is, decide what they will do, when, and how. Soon, the helicar landed on the helipad near the ISROEM Centre. Alex and Gopiz got out of the helicar, and went towards the complex. "So first, just for confirmation I need to go to the reception area to recall where the main manufacturing factory building is–" Gopiz was saying and suddenly Alex interrupted him- "Gopiz, Gopiz. I studied the complex map. I know where the factory building is. I explored and learned all about it during your hibernation, update or whatever." "Oh yeah. Well that's great!" Gopiz replied. They finally entered the complex through its automatic sliding gates that opened as they approached it. After getting inside, Alex and Gopiz directly went to the manufacturing factory building, bypassing the main reception building. As they finally reached and entered the factory building, Gopiz asked- "So what do we do now? If you've already surveyed the factory, what will we do today?" "It's simple. We'll decide the exact steps and processes, division of labour, and specific areas within the area for different purposes." Alex replied. They both went to a long table inside the factory, grabbed their chairs and sat. "So, from my analysis, this factory has 9 main areas from which 3 are specifically for assembling parts and making finished products. The remaining 6 of them can be used for other stuff, like making circuits, connecting wires, attaching smaller parts with each other, and even 3-D printing." Alex informed Gopiz. They spent much time further discussing how they can organise the manufacturing processes. Finally, Gopiz revised the process- "So let me just confirm the final process of making the giant Mepamas. First, we'll 3D-print the main components, then we'll assemble them, then we'll install the control circuits and connect them to other components, then we'll set up the power and remote control systems, and finally add the mounting brackets to the Mepama to make it attachable to the UAVs. This is the final process, right?" "Absolutely. It's the finalized process or plan." Alex replied.

They both quickly went to different areas of the large factory, and pasted large paper labels of the process specified, to each of the areas. They did this so that they could remember which area is for what exact process in the entire manufacturing process. When they were done, they went to the 3-D printing area, which was a smaller area relatively, with the large Genera 9Xi 3-D printer placed on a large table. Just as they took their seats on two small chairs, Alex informed- "Now we must start with the 3-D modelling of the individual parts." "Yeah, but won't it take long? It's almost noon already. If you start now, it'll take us hours to just design a single giant Mepama part." Gopiz replied. "Uh... Why do you think so? Bro, I know 3-D Modelling. I have been an expert at it for 3-4 years. Yeah, this might be a bit more complex, but I'll manage and finish it quickly." Alex replied, taking out his Airtop. After turning it on, he quickly browsed the internet and downloaded a 3-D Modelling software that was compatible with advanced 3D Printers like the Genera 9Xi. It took like 20-25 minutes to download, and while the downloading was in progress, Alex went to the same vending machine that he used before, and broke its display glass and took out some of the eatables for free, and had his lunch with a can of coffee. He did so because he had no money in his digital payments app. Gopiz was shocked to see Alex do this, but he didn't question him, because it was not a big deal. After the download was finished, Alex opened the software and began modelling one of the most crucial parts of the Mepama- the electromagnet- that attracts metal objects towards itself. His speed was remarkable, and Gopiz kept appreciating it repeatedly. He specified the materials that will be used for each part in the design. Alex used many tools to make his 3D model more detailed and effective. He designed the entire electromagnet by properly modelling the electromagnetic core, the coil around it, and created a well-developed model of the Mepama part. Finally, after spending like 40 minutes designing the digital version of the electromagnet, he was finished. "Let's print it?" he asked Gopiz. "Sure, I'll just turn on the 3-D printer." Gopiz replied, and went to the 3-D printer, and pressed its power button. An electrical whirring sound started to come out from the 3-D printer, as if they were the startup noises. "Uh, I think to pair it wirelessly with your Airtop, I should press this 'Pair' button. The LED light beside it is blinking. Should I press it?" Gopiz asked Alex. "Hmmm... Yeah, do it." Alex replied. Gopiz pressed the Pair button, and within seconds, Alex's Airtop received the Pairing request notification. He clicked on the 'Pair' option, and the Airtop was successfully paired with the 3-D Printer. "Perfect!" Alex exclaimed. "Uh, but one more question. Of what scale or size should the giant Mepama be? Because then according to that I'll print this electromagnet, right?" Alex asked. "I think the UAVs that we are going to mount these Mepamas on are 52 metres long, and 36 metres wide. So accordingly, if we want to mount some Mepamas on some portions of wings and the rest on the fuselage, then each Mepama should be around 25 square metres. That is, they can be square-shaped and should have all sides of 5 metres each." Gopiz calculated and responded. "Wow. Quick math!" Alex said. "And yes, accordingly giving space to other components of the Mepama as well, according to the blueprint and configuration you described, I'd suggest that the Electromagnet should be 4.6 metres long, and adjust the width according to the ratio." Gopiz told Alex the final size of the Electromagnet he would need to print. "Alright, so 4.6 metres it is." Alex said, typed and entered the Electromagnet size, and selected the option to adjust the width according to the ratio in the 3D Model itself. He finally clicked on the 'Print' button. Just as he did that, the 3D Printer started whirring more loudly, and displayed a countdown on its digital screen- of 32 minutes. "Also, the dimensions I told were just of the square-shaped Mepamas. If possible, to increase the overall magnetic strength of all the Mepamas together, according to UAVs' shapes, we can add extra Mepamas of varying sizes and shapes on them, to use maximum surface area of each UAV." Gopiz suggested. "That's a Brilliant idea, Gopiz! But I hope that doing so would not exceed the weight capacity of the UAVs." Alex replied. "Oh! Not at all. It's very unlikely that it'll exceed the weight limit or capacity of the UAVs. We can be chill about it." Gopiz informed. Anyways, Gopiz was busy observing the 3-D printer printing the first ever part of the Giant Mepama- the giant electromagnet, while Alex worked on another part of the Mepama, designing its 3D Model now. Finally, after some time, the 3D printing was completed, and Alex clicked the option to print another part of the Mepama which he was designing all this time. He tried to lift the newly made Electromagnet from the 3D Printer output tray, but it was too heavy and he failed. "Bro, you forgot that we're working in the ISROEM Centre. Every physical work can be automated here!" Gopiz told Alex, and pressed a button. Suddenly a big robotic hand came down from the ceiling of the factory, Gopiz gave the voice command to lift the Electromagnet and place it on a table next to the 3D printer's table. The robotic hand accepted the command, and did the same. "I had no idea that ISRO was so advanced. I mean, all the physical work is done by these machines?" Alex asked. "Of course. Why waste your energy at a place where robots and machines can help? That's the idea behind this automation." Gopiz replied. Alex and Gopiz carefully examined the large 3D-printed electromagnet which was now kept on a large table beside the 3D printer's table. "It's perfect! Much better than what I expected!" Gopiz said. "Umm.. Yeah that's great and all, but don't you think how difficult and time-taking it would be for us to print so many Mepama parts, join them together, integrate control circuits, systems and what not." Alex said, showing his concern. "Bro, I just said, we can automate stuff. Not everything, of course, but at least this 3D printing, assembling of parts, and fixing the wiring and circuits together. Our main work would be more of research and development. We would figure out how many Mepamas we would actually attach to each UAV, so as to get an accurate estimate of how many Mepamas we exactly need to make. So you know, we shouldn't work hard, but rather work smart." Gopiz replied. Alex understood that Gopiz made some sense. "Alright, so you know how to automate tasks and work in this factory? The physical work?" Alex asked Gopiz. "Yes, obviously!" Gopiz replied. "Perfect, so you'll help us make the possible processes automatic. Let's begin doing it." Alex said.

While the second Mepama part was being printed, they both went to each of the factory areas that they divided for specific processes, and commanded the robotic machines like robotic arms and AI-based machines to perform tasks based on conditions, procedures and explained to them what to do, how to perform, all by voice-commands. Finally, when they programmed all the machines and set them up for manufacturing the Mepamas in a synchronized manner, they were done with planning and getting the factory ready for making the Mepamas. Therefore, a major task for today was completed. After the second Mepama part was 3-D printed and the robotic hand kept it to the table beside the 3-D printer's, Alex packed up his stuff, including the Airtop, and together he and Gopiz headed back to the Helicar. It was almost 4 PM now. "You know another task for today is left." Alex said, while both of them were walking back towards the main gate of ISROEM centre. "What are you talking about?" Gopiz asked. "We need to count the total Mepamas we need to make, hence we would need to calculate how many Mepamas we actually would attach or mount on each UAV." Alex said. "Oh, that! Don't worry, it's an easy process. We'll just go to the UAVs Hangar, and I'll scan a UAV's surface area, and then with the help of my new updates, I'll calculate and let you know how many Mepamas we'd attach to each UAV." Gopiz replied. Alex sighed in relief, as if a major issue was sorted out. They both got out of the ISROEM Centre, through its automatic gates, and finally reached the Helicar. "Alright, Sire. Let's get in!" Gopiz exclaimed, opening the helicar door. They both got inside the helicar, turned it on, and took off back to the ISRO Launch Base.

20 minutes later, the helicar landed at one of the Helicar helipads in the parking lot of the Launch Base. "We've reached. Alex, wake up!" Gopiz said to Alex, trying to wake him up from his nap. Alex woke up and gave Gopiz a weary smile, both of them got out of the car, and went inside their building. Alex quickly drank some water, and then along with Gopiz, went to the UAVs hangar in the same ISRO complex. He remembered going there himself, and that too alone, a few days back. He saw those UAVs, but didn't observe them so closely so as to estimate the number of Mepamas that can be mounted on each one of them. When they both reached the hangar shutter gates, Alex pressed the blue beeping button that rolled up the shutter gates, they both got inside, and Gopiz pushed the glowing switch to turn on the lights of the hangar. All the big lights hanging from the ceiling of the hangar switched on one by one. "Well, here they are!" Gopiz said. "Don't waste time now. Go and start scanning or whatever you said to estimate the number of Mepamas on each UAV." Alex replied. "Ugh. Yes, bro. I am going." Gopiz said, started hovering and flew to the top of one of the UAV.

"Well, they're essentially the same model or variant of the UAVs, and don't even have a single difference, so one UAV's scanning would help us get the total number of giant Mepamas to be made. You know, the number of giant mepamas needed on one UAV multiplied by the number of UAVs." Gopiz said. "Bro, will you stop teaching me basic math? Just start your work!" Alex frustratingly shouted at Gopiz. "Chill bro. Am doing it. Duh!" Gopiz replied, and started scanning the UAV, from its front till its back, brom its top to bottom, calculating its exact width, length, height, and the estimated amount of Mepamas of the dimensions he told Alex of (5 metres per side). After spending some minutes doing the calculative scan, Gopiz completed his task and flew back down to Alex, landing in front of him. "19 Mepamas, including the square-shaped and irregular-shaped Mepamas, all mounted on a UAV. Hence, 19 Mepamas on each UAV. There are 11 working UAVs, so 209 Mepamas in total." Gopiz informed Alex. Alex sighed, and said- "That's a lot. Can it be reduced?" "Yeah, we can remove the extra irregular-shaped Mepamas, but reducing the number of them on each UAV means reducing the total effectiveness of all Magnetism combined." Gopiz replied. "Hmmm... You're right, we'll... We'll make all of them then." Alex said and concluded. They both finally also achieved the second objective for today, and returned to their Launch Base building, closing the UAVs hangar and departing from there. As they entered the Mission Control Centre Room, Alex literally fell and lay down onto his mattress, tired of all the work they both did today. "209 giant Mepamas. It's not easy." Alex murmured, although audibly. "It's super easy bro, automation is the key!" Alex sighed, and looked at his wristwatch which indicated- 5:52 PM. "I think you should eat something now. You kind of didn't have your lunch today, after all, I don't think a single sandwich and a can of coffee solves anything." Gopiz said to Alex. "Thanks Gopiz, but you don't need to take care of what I eat and when I eat. I can decide all that just by myself." Alex replied. Gopiz felt weird with Alex's answer, for it was somewhat a bit rude, but well, he did not take it too seriously.

An hour later, Alex told Gopiz to wait in the Control Room only, while he went and got his dinner meal from the ChefMate, kept just outside their building, a door in the corridor itself leading to its place. He turned off the ChefMate, and came back to the Control Room, where Gopiz waited for him. He peacefully had his dinner meal, and dumped the plastic meal plate in the dustbin after he was finished with it. "So... The manufacturing starts tomorrow. Ready for the big days?" Alex asked Gopiz. "Yeah, for sure!" Gopiz replied. "We've already set up all the automation today, just gotta start the entire manufacturing process tomorrow." Gopiz added to his reply. "Yep. Certainly! So tomorrow is a big day, shall we sleep early? You know it's just 8, but yeah!" Alex suggested, and by 'sleep' he meant 'charge' to Gopiz. "Good idea. Goodnight!" Gopiz greeted, and went back to his Charging pod. At the same time, Alex too turned off the lights, lay down on his mattress, got into his blanket and finally slept. And now, the most crucial part of the mission began!

SEVENTEEN

THE MANUFACTURING PROCESS

The new morning brought a sense of purpose into both- Alex and Gopiz. They woke up quite early, at 5:45 AM in the morning, maybe because they slept early last night. Alex got two meals from the ChefMate this morning, one for breakfast and one for lunch, both to eat at the ISROEM centre. By 6 PM, they took off for the ISROEM Centre. While in the air, they talked to each other. "I'm worried about this mission." Alex said to which Gopiz responded- "And I'm super excited for this mission." Both looked at each other, and then chuckled at the differences in each other's minds. "You know you're just a computer, that's why you are not emotionally linked to this mission, while I am. I am, because it's the only way that gives me hope to find everyone- my parents, friends, love, everyone." Alex said to Gopiz, after pausing and pondering for a minute. "I might not be emotionally linked, brother. But for me too, the success of this mission is as important as it is to you, because it will make you happy. It's my duty to help you out." Gopiz replied. Alex smiled at Gopiz's words, and both of them then looked at the rising sun, and its first rays filling the sky with some light. As the helicar touched down the helipad near the ISROEM facility, both of them got out and walked up to the complex. Entering the main gates, they both turned towards their left, and followed the road's curve, intending to reach their factory building. After they reached and entered their factory building, Alex pulled down two levers, turning all the lights of the factory on. "Ready Gopiz?" "More than ever!" They both exclaimed, and went into different directions. Alex went to the 3D Printer, turned it on and connected his Airtop to it, and with two designs of two parts of Mepama already digitally modelled, he put the 3D Printing of those two parts on loop, and gave the command to print 10 parts of each kind, among the two parts he designed on the software. 'Are you sure? This will take around 13 hours.' A message displayed on his Airtop. Alex clicked on the 'Proceed anyway' button, and started the automatic printing. "And it begins!" Alex excitedly said. While Alex did this all, Gopiz commanded the automated robotic machines once again, and told them what to do as the 3D-printed parts were printed, specifically first sort them according to their kind, and store them in an organized manner, and once all necessary parts were printed or available, assemble them together, making the inoperational yet basic giant Mepama, with its combined parts, although not having circuits or wiring for now. Then Gopiz headed to the designated area for Circuit Boards and their integration, designated by him and Alex only. He ordered the automatic robotic machines to start making the basic microcontrollers, Control Circuits and Circuit Boards, according to the requirements and specifications of the giant Mepama, that Alex approved yesterday itself. He gave them the order to make at least 50 such Circuit Boards today. After this, he finally went to the remote control and power systems area, commanding them to make Mepama parts of that kind. After both of them were done with the work they distributed among themselves, they met at the 3-D printing area, the main area where they sat. It was 7:30 AM now, and the manufacturing was automatically being carried out. Alex sipped the hot coffee that he brought from the ChefMate as well. "We made quite a bit of progress, didn't we?" Gopiz commented. "Truly! The automation idea was cool, but it's frustrating to see that 3-D printing is slow and only prints a single part in around 40 minutes. This slows down the entire manufacturing process." Alex replied. "Oh wow! I just got a great idea!" Gopiz exclaimed. For a minute, Alex's mind was blank, and Gopiz looked at him, as if he wanted Alex to guess his idea. "Ah! I got it." Alex exclaimed as he realized and then asked- "So let's do it?" "Absolutely!" Gopiz replied and then added- "Let's get you some more coffee from the reception area!" Alex facepalmed. "Bro, I thought you were talking about bringing all the 3-D printers from the entire complex to this building. And you're thinking about coffee?" Alex replied. "My bad, bro. But wait, if you're thinking like that, then why not use all the factory buildings for the manufacturing of giant Mepamas?" Gopiz said and suggested. "Bro the complex is so large. How will we be able to manage it? It literally takes 10 minutes to just reach the other side of the facility." Alex replied. "We have a super cool and fast transportation system here, you didn't notice?" Gopiz asked, getting up and going to a window of the factory building, and rolling up the roller blinds of it. Alex went to the window and gasped. His eyes fell on the large network of pipe-like structures, made of transparent material, at the centre of the circular-shaped ISROEM Centre complex. "What is this thing?" Alex asked curiously. "ISROEM Transpoloop, a network of ultraloop-based tunnel paths for short train-like vehicles called shuttles, made specifically to carry load and passengers to different places in the complex." Gopiz replied. Ultraloop was an extremely fast means of transportation, the successor of the hyperloop transport system, which is even currently under-development, in our real world. "That's incredible! Ultraloop is used very rarely in the entire world, and one of its networks is here? ISROEM is actually a super place!" Alex replied, still surprised. Alex agreed that they both can set up all the factory buildings throughout the complex for parallel manufacturing, speeding up the entire process. "Let me take you through this Transpoloop once, so you could get the experience, you know." Gopiz suggested to Alex. Once Alex agreed, they walked to one of the corners of their factory building and entered a small room, through a glass door. "Didn't notice this room before." Alex thought to himself. Alex was amazed after entering the small room, as it had the entrance to one of the tunnels of the Transpoloop, with a shuttle parked inside this tunnel entrance. "Come on, it's completely safe! Don't worry." Gopiz told Alex. Gopiz pushed a button beside the tunnel entrance, and the vehicle came outside the tunnel, entering the small room for boarding. "Get inside the shuttle." Gopiz said, and stepped inside, and had a seat. Alex did the same, and wore the seatbelt. "Dude don't worry about the seatbelts. They're just for formality- not a real necessity. Lol!" Gopiz said, for fun. Gopiz chose the destination- the building opposite to their own factory building- using the small computer screen inside the shuttle itself. And just as he finally pressed a small red button inside the shuttle, the shuttle's glass door closed, and it whooshed at an impossible speed. Within just 2-3 seconds, it stopped. Alex couldn't believe it. "Uh, what happened? It didn't work?" Alex asked Gopiz. "It did, and it has reached its destination already, the opposite building!" Gopiz said, proudly. "No way!" Alex exclaimed, so astonished at the superfast speed of the Transpoloop. "I love it!" he exclaimed further, stepping outside the shuttle, along with Gopiz. They both walked out of the small room of the building they reached now, and it was a factory building too. "This seems perfect! Even this factory building has a 3-D printer." Alex said as he noticed. Gopiz told him that every factory building possessed one. Impressed by this new possibility of using all factory buildings together to speed up the production, Alex asked the last question that popped in his mind, to Gopiz- "The 3D Models I made are only saved on my own Airtop, and it's currently paired with one 3D printer already. So, how will we share the 3D Models or designs to other 3D printers in different factory buildings?" "Ah... I see the problem. Don't worry. We have a centralised system for all the 3D Printers of the entire complex too. You can transfer the designs you made to the computers of the centralised system, and they can guide all the 3D printers to make those same designs. It's super simple and easy." Gopiz explained. Alex was now satisfied with everything that he got to know. He and Gopiz went to different factory buildings using the Transpoloop system, and guided and programmed the robotic machines to handle the manufacturing, just like they did in their first factory building. It took 4 hours, and finally, at noon, they came back to their original factory building. They were surprised to see that 4-5 giant Electromagnets were already printed and placed on another large table in an organized manner. "I'll bring my Airtop and then let's go to the Main Building." Alex said. Alex went to his Airtop, closed and picked it up and came back to Gopiz. The 3D Printing stopped. "Oh right! The 3D Printer is disconnected from my Airtop now. The 3D printing would stop now, wouldn't it?" Alex asked Gopiz. "Yeah, but not for long. I mean, we're gonna continue the 3D printing from the centralized system's computer, so just a 10 minute halt won't be a problem according to me." Gopiz replied. Alex agreed, and both he and Gopiz departed the factory building, and headed towards the main building which housed the centralized system's computers that connected all the 3D Printers and other components together. Once Gopiz guided Alex till the room where those computers were and they entered the room, Alex quickly turned on one of the computers alongside his Airtop. When he successfully paired the computer with his Airtop, he shared the 3D Models of the Mepama parts that he made to the computer. Once the computer received the files of those 3D Models, Gopiz took over the computer and went to the Centralized System software of the computer and commanded all the 3D Printers together to 3D-print the Electromagnets, i.e. the Mepama Part that Alex designed digitally. He mentioned the same quantity as before, hence instructing each 3D Printer to print 20 Electromagnets each. "Yo. It's done." Gopiz told Alex. Alex proudly smiled. "Alright, so we're all set for today's manufacturing, now we've done something on a large scale! Ten factory buildings printing and building like 20 Mepama parts each per day, that's like almost printing one specific part for all the 209 Mepamas, everyday! That's insane and amazing!" Alex exclaimed. "Indeed! It's almost like we can say that hey, on Day 1 we printed all 209 electromagnets, on Day 2 we printed all 209 Outer casings, and so on!" Gopiz replied. But the challenge was for such large scale 3-D printing to actually happen, i.e. to actually print around 210 electromagnets today, they had to stay in the ISROEM Centre till 8 or 9 PM tonight. But they didn't care about this, they were extremely joyful in easing the entire giant Mepamas Manufacturing. Finally, they returned to their original factory building, while all the factory buildings, including the one they were inside, continued with their 3D printing simultaneously, taking the first steps in manufacturing the Mepamas!

Hours passed by, and one by one, many Electromagnets with the coils and the cores started to get placed on tables, automatically after being 3D printed. It was now around 5:30 PM. "Bro, you didn't have your lunch today, even though you brought your Lunch meal from the ChefMate." Gopiz informed Alex. "I know Gopiz, and that's because I had my breakfast meal at 1 PM, so I am not that hungry, alright?" Alex replied, to which Gopiz nodded. When it was around 7:45 PM, Alex felt hungry. Now he opened his Lunch meal, went to the factory building's refreshments area, and heated his meal plate using a microwave oven. As he returned to the table where both of them were sitting, Gopiz calculated and told him- "Approximately, 192 giant Mepama electromagnets are 3D printed successfully. An hour more for all 210 to be printed." "I think it's time for you to go and see the computer in the Centralized System Control Room to check for any issues or problems." Alex said. "Me? Ugh! Fine!" Gopiz replied, frustratingly. "Bro why do you seem annoyed, tired or whatever? You're a robot. You can never be tired unless your battery is low." Alex sarcastically asked. Gopiz didn't reply, just left the factory building, and went to the main building to do what Alex suggested. While he went, Alex had his Lunch meal, which was Veg Biryani with some green sauce and tomato ketchup. Gopiz came back after a few minutes, and said- "No issues yet. 3D Printing will be finished in time as expected." "That's great then. After the 210 electromagnets are printed, we'll leave for the Launch Base." Alex replied. "Roger that." Gopiz replied. Finally, an hour elapsed, and Gopiz and Alex went to 2-3 other Factory Buildings too, through the Terminal Rooms (the small room with entrance to Transpoloop Tunnels via the Shuttles), to check and see the quality of Electromagnets that were made today. Alex saw the shiny iron electromagnets, arranged in rows, in a slanting and organised manner. "All 210 electromagnets successfully made!"

Alex said, excitedly. "Woohoo!" Gopiz exclaimed. They both shutted down all the machines and lights of every single factory and room they used. And after wrapping up everything, it was 9:15 PM. They headed back to their helicar and got out of the ISROEM Centre complex, exiting through the main gates. Reaching the helicar, Gopiz said- "My battery is low. Perhaps today was a long day!" "Oh bro, you should sleep or take a nap or do whatever you do when you need to save your battery. And yes, today was indeed a very long and tiring day. Goodnight." Alex replied. Alex entered the destination as the ISRO Launch Base, and started the journey. The helicar powered on, and took off. While the helicar was in air cruising, Alex noticed that Gopiz had slept, and an icon was blinking on his face which was also his screen. He tried to get a closer look, and perceived the icon as a Battery with a plus icon, probably indicating that Battery Saving Mode was on, and hence Gopiz was sleeping. Minutes later, the helicar landed in the helicar parking lot of the Launch Base. Alex shaked Gopiz's shoulder, trying to wake him up, but it seemed like his battery was completely drained out. So he lifted him with his hands, kept his phone in his pocket, closed the helicar door and walked into the Launch Base building, with Gopiz held in his hands. Once he reached the Mission Control Hall, he kept Gopiz on his Charging Pod, and turned on the pod to start charging Gopiz. Finally, he came back to his mattress, took out his Airtop, and lay down on the mattress as he was tired after a long day. Being 10:15 PM, he first considered sleeping to wake up early tomorrow. But then he recalled that he also needed to design the 3D Models of remaining Mepama parts on his Airtop. So he switched on his Airtop, took out the Mepama charts for guidance and worked for hours, designing the 3D Models of the other Mepama parts. When it was 2:25 AM, Alex was done making the 3D Models of all 3D-printable Mepama parts. However, realized that now that it was too late at night, he would get very little sleep tonight. Yet, he decided to sleep at least for a bunch of hours. So he turned off the 2 lights that he kept on when he was working, got into his blanket, and slept like a baby.

The next morning, it was Gopiz who woke Alex up. They were slightly late, because it was 6:30 AM already, while by this time they had already left for ISROEM Centre yesterday. Alex quickly freshened up and got ready, and by 7 AM, both of them took off for the ISROEM facility. They quickly reached, switched on the Centralized System's Computer in the main building, and gave it the command to 3D print the other kind of giant Mepama parts, using the 3D model that Alex made previously. "Make sure it prints 210 of these kind of parts." Alex told Gopiz when the latter was commanding the computer. The 3D printing began and Alex and Gopiz then went to each factory building using the Transpoloop system to ensure that the production was occurring smoothly and properly. By 11 AM, many more Mepama parts were already printed. "All these parts will only be assembled together once there are enough parts printed to make the basic Mepamas." Alex concluded. Hours elapsed, and the 3D printers were consistently making and printing the Mepama parts that Alex and Gopiz commanded to print. When it was 3:30 PM, Alex had his first meal for today, also made by ChefMate, this morning itself. Gopiz, till then, supervised all of the 3D printers by going into different factory buildings one by one. When it was evening time, or specifically 7:30 PM, Alex and Gopiz looked at all the newly printed Mepama parts, this time of a different kind and purpose. All the 210 parts were successfully printed, and hence today's quota was fulfilled as well. "Great job done, today as well!" Alex joyfully said, giving Gopiz a high-five. They then returned back to the Launch Base, and a somewhat similar routine was followed for days, printing different kinds of giant Mepama parts, though in bulk.

Days turned into weeks, and a great deal of production was already completed, and only assembling a few more parts together, and integrating the circuit boards and microcontrollers on the basic Mepama bodies were left. But they encountered a major problem- when they fully made one sample giant Mepama successfully with everything- control systems, signal systems, and even with all wiring and sensors, it wasn't working. This put Alex into a major distress, after they tested the sample giant Mepama, in the ISROEM Centre itself. "We'll figure it out, buddy! Don't lose hope." Gopiz kept telling him. "Man, we don't even know where the issue is actually!" Alex said, in a sorrowful voice. Gopiz went back to the sample Giant Mepama, which stood on a large table, turned it on once again, and tried once again to make it work, by pulling the steel utensil kept at a distance to it. The giant Mepama started whirring, but it didn't work, or specifically, it did not attract the steel utensil towards itself. And then the Mepama turned off by itself. "Alex-" "I had a feeling before as well. It won't work." Alex said in a broken voice. "Alex, listen-" "No Gopiz. You should've listened to me. Why did you keep reinforcing my hope for this mission, plan or whatever?" Alex said in a sorrowful and frustrated tone. "Will you please let me say?" Gopiz asked, boldy. "Whatever. You only speak now." Alex replied. "Yeah, so look. I think I understood where the problem might be. I mean I am not 100%

sure but–" "Well. You are never 100% sure about anything. As expected." Alex taunted. "Um, so please listen to me. The rechargeable batteries. They're possibly the problem." Gopiz said. "What do you mean? Now we'll replace the rechargeable batteries with what? Our heart? Lungs? Blood? Or your battery?" Alex said, venting out his frustration. "I kindly request you brother, please talk in a respectful manner." Gopiz replied. "Otherwise what? You'll hit me? Go ahead. Let's see what you've got." Alex boldly shouted. But this time, Gopiz didn't reply, just went to a chair some distance away and took a seat. Both of them didn't talk for like almost an hour. But later on, Alex felt sorry. He went to Gopiz and asked- "What about the rechargeable batteries? What's the problem?" "At least I expect an apology, first." Gopiz replied, not making eye contact with Alex. Alex, now that he finally calmed down, replied- "Sorry for my rude talking. It's just, I feel stuck. I don't understand what to do when you only have one way to accomplish something, and that way gets blocked too." "I told you already, we'll troubleshoot the problem. Why do you see this as the end?" Gopiz replied, and then continued- "So what I was saying was, that the rechargeable batteries are the problem. The tiny Mepama whose configuration charts we used to make these giant ones, uses rechargeable batteries. I don't know why, even though we both are geniuses, we both overlooked the fact that a bigger machine would need higher power output as well. In other words, the rechargeable batteries that we're using for the Giant Mepama, no matter even if they're fully charged, will be unable to supply enough electrical power to the electromagnets, hence creating an extremely weak magnetic field, making the Mepama ineffective."

"So you're saying that we can't use rechargeable batteries for powering the electromagnets?" Alex asked to confirm. "I mean this is likely to be the problem, because from my knowledge, it's almost impossible for rechargeable batteries to supply strong current to such big machinery." Gopiz replied. Alex realized that yes, Gopiz's logic is valid. "Yes, you're right. There's a high possibility that the problem lies with the rechargeable batteries. After all such large electromagnets obviously require higher electrical current." Alex said, reflecting deeply. Therefore, both of them started bringing different ideas to the table, thinking of what they can replace the rechargeable batteries with. After minutes of discussion with highly technical and scientific ideas, facts and stuff, Alex brought up another idea- "Ooh! And what about a generator?" Gopiz smiled, and then replied- "Now you're talking! Generators, especially those powered by powerful fuel, will be a perfect choice for supplying massive electricity to the electromagnets." They discussed more about generators, and eventually decided to use diesel-based generators for power supply, replacing the weak rechargeable batteries."

"But wait. Diesel? That too in the year 2162?" Peter interrupted. "Yeah! Isn't petroleum going to be finished in this century itself?" Rhea questioned. Aryan as well looked at William, waiting for an answer. "Well, looks like what I saw suggested that at least diesel was not completely depleted on earth, because they indeed used the diesel generators to generate electricity. And the reason for diesel surviving till that time- well I too don't have an answer for that." William replied. The NDJJC members nodded their heads, though partially satisfied with the answer. After a minute of unexpected silence, during which everyone looked towards each other, William asked- "Now shall I continue?" "Yeah! Of course. Go on please!" Aryan replied.

"Alright. So moving on, Gopiz and Alex discussed the diesel generators. They talked about how these kinds of generators can also be loud, noisy, and require regular refueling. But among all these facts, diesel generators felt like a perfect fit for the power supplying system in the giant Mepamas. "So, do we have the diesel generators here?" Alex asked. "Ummm. Yeah we do, but we don't have diesel here anymore." Gopiz replied. "Ugh! Why don't you have the fuel if you have the machines that need that fuel?!" Alex asked frustratingly. "That's because we don't use the diesel generators majorly anymore. All stuff these days happens on their hydrogen fuel or solar power." Gopiz replied, trying to justify. "Whatever. Now tell me where we can find the diesel fuel?" "I'm not very sure, but I think one of our warehouses, a bit far from here, might have it." Gopiz replied. "How far?" Alex demanded a distance or duration. "Maybe 30 minutes via Helicar? Yeah, approximately 28 minutes via helicar." Gopiz replied, confirming the duration of the trip. It was still afternoon, so Alex told Gopiz to take him to the warehouse, and prepare to bring at least some containers of diesel back, at least for basic testing. They both departed the ISROEM centre, went to their helicar which was recharged today's morning itself, and took off to the warehouse that Gopiz was taking Alex to. "This should work." Alex mumbled, during their flight. "What should work?" Gopiz asked. "This– this replacement of the power supply thing. I mean, I hope this is the only problem." Alex replied. Gopiz nodded in understanding. "Trust me, this would be the only problem. Remember, our diagnosis is never wrong." Gopiz said, giving more hope to Alex. This time, the helicar landed on a flat sandy surface, in an arid place, with little or no vegetation. After landing, Alex and Gopiz came out of the helicar, and Alex murmured- "What is this place? Seems like a desert to me." The desert-like place had nothing, except an old and rusty warehouse, without even a security gate or fencing. "No wonder diesel is found only here. This place looks so old." Alex mumbled. Gopiz chuckled nervously. They both walked inside the rusty warehouse, in search of diesel barrels.

"Did you find any?" Alex asked Gopiz, during their search for diesel barrels. "Not yet." replied Gopiz, from a distance. They checked every rack, every room, and even the attic of the warehouse. Gopiz found some old and rusty machines, while Alex found some old cartons with rusty tools like hammers, screwdrivers and what not. But no matter how much they searched, they did not find any diesel. "Literally, Gopiz... Where the hell is your Diesel?" Alex shouted at Gopiz, being angry at him for misleading him to the old and rusty warehouse. Frustrated, Alex turned back and walked towards the exit of the old warehouse. Suddenly, he tripped over something, and fell on his chin, once again. "Oww!" he groaned. Gopiz hovered quickly to him. "Are you okay bro?! Did you get hurt?" Gopiz asked hurriedly. Luckily, this time, the surface he fell on was smooth, with smooth tiling. So, this time Alex didn't get any wound. "I'm fine. But just tell me please, what the hell did I just trip over?" Alex asked, in slight pain due to the impact though. Gopiz turned behind, only to find a metal handle of a trapdoor on the floor. "We didn't notice this before, did we?" Gopiz mumbled. Alex got up and came to the same location. "This is a floor hatch, right? There might be something below it." Alex said. Gopiz pulled the metal handle, trying to pull up the trapdoor to open it. Alex helped him pull up the heavy metal trapdoor as well, and when they opened it, they saw a staircase going downstairs. "Whoa!" Alex got flabbergasted. "Shall we go downstairs?" Gopiz asked, hesitantly. "Obviously. We can't ignore a space literally below an old warehouse, especially when it might have what we need." Alex replied. Alex walked downstairs and Gopiz followed him. When Alex reached the bottom of the stairs, he noticed that it was completely dark downstairs, except for a blue glowing light, which seemed like a switch to turn on the lights. Alex pressed the glowing light button, and the lights of the large basement he was in, turned on one by one. And then he saw something he awaited- hundreds of large box-like storage appliances, looking like hybrids of washing machines and refrigerators, with all of them labelled as 'Diesel'. "I thought we'd find it in barrels." Alex said, turning to Gopiz. "Well, I think they stored the diesel in storage containers, especially designed for storing diesel for infinite time, keeping them fresh and not allowing them to expire. It's good for us only na." Gopiz replied. Alex realized that now the process became even more convenient for them, for they won't need to re-purify the diesel to use it, as it's already preserved and stored in a way that it won't expire. "It's great!" Alex mumbled. He then opened one of the large box-shaped storage appliances by its upper door, and saw glowing lights, and a smaller container- a barrel specifically, carefully kept inside the storage container. Gopiz hovered to the storage appliance, where Alex was also standing, and said- "Perfectly stored. The liquid diesel is inside this barrel. Now all we need is a smaller container to add this diesel in, and take back to ISROEM for testing the Mepama with a diesel generator." Gopiz stated. They both looked around, and Alex went to a corner and brought something. "Here, will this work?" Alex asked Gopiz, showing a small, 5-litre empty plastic can. "Definitely! I'll turn on the tap, you open the can and let it get filled with the diesel." Gopiz instructed. They both did so, and finally filled around 5 litres of diesel in the can. "Where did you find this can? Are there more so we could take more of them for testing?" Gopiz asked. Alex pointed to the corner, and when they went there, they didn't find any more cans. But when Alex looked at a rack near that corner, he shouted- "Gopiz! Look!" pointing towards the rack full of similar empty cans. Gopiz and Alex together filled 6-8 five-litre plastic cans, and still only used less than a half of the barrel in one of those hundreds of storage appliances. and finally came out of the basement with those cans of diesel, via the staircase. Gopiz closed the trapdoor, and they both left the old and rusty warehouse. "Let's go and test the Mepama with this diesel now." Alex mumbled, as they both sat back inside the helicar, after keeping the cans of diesel on the backseat of the helicar. Finally, they took off for ISROEM Centre, from the dry, arid and weird place, where there was not even a single drop of water.

Minutes later they reached the ISROEM facility. They went to their factory building along with the diesel cans, and Alex demanded Gopiz to now take him to the place where the diesel generators were kept. "The Archive Building." Gopiz replied. "Seriously? Why an Archive building?" Alex questioned. "I already told you bro, because diesel generators are something we no longer used for anything. So we put all the diesel generators in the large storage racks of the Archive building." Gopiz replied. "Are you sure that diesel generators would be compatible with our giant Mepamas? Also, do we have the large number of diesel generators for our 210 Mepamas?"

Alex asked further. "We have around 500. And yes, they're 101% compatible with our giant Mepamas." Gopiz replied. After some more discussion, they headed to the Archive Building, which was the only building not connected to other buildings of the facility through the Transpoloop system. So they had to walk till there. Once they reached there, Gopiz showed Alex the long and large racks in the much larger Archive building, having modern diesel generators in long rows. Alex and Gopiz lifted one of the modern diesel generators, which was of course heavy, but together they managed to lift it, hold it and take it to their factory building. It was almost 5 PM in the evening, and when they reached the factory building, they finally kept the heavy diesel generator on one of the tables. "The power supply wiring, will that be changed or something as well?" Alex asked Gopiz. "Nope. The wire which is for now connected to the batteries of the giant Mepama will just be disconnected from it and attached to the diesel electricity generator instead." Gopiz replied. "Alright, so let's replace it." Alex said, to which Gopiz agreed. They both spent thirty minutes working on the interiors of the giant Mepama, and finally unscrewed the previously attached rechargeable batteries from the Mepama, and detached it from the machine. Then they finally joined the bulky diesel generator to the giant Mepama and connected it to the rest of the Mepama through the power supply wire. After the entirely tiring and technical process, the giant Mepama was ready for the Round 2 of testing, with a new power supply. They carefully added diesel fuel to the generator's fuel tank, and then closed the tank's cover. Alex took a deep breath, while Gopiz said- "Ready? Testing in 3... 2... 1... Now!" And he tested the giant Mepama, switching it on. The utensil first stood normal, then it moved slightly, as if some forces were acting on it. Then it moved more vigorously, and then- 'Whoooooooptt' the utensil got attached to the magnetic base of the Mepama, which was the desired outcome! "YES! YES FREAKING YES! THAT'S WHAT WE'RE TALKING ABOUT!! WHO'S LAUGHING NOW? AWESOME, YES!" Alex exclaimed strongly, shrieking and shouting in joy. Gopiz shrieked too. They both were dancing like they broke a world record. But indeed, it was a marvelous achievement. They further increased the distance of the utensil from the Mepama and tested several more times, at last even keeping a distance of 50 metres- but the targeting system of the Mepama was so exceptional, that it still worked! This was a huge milestone for Alex's journey in bringing the IndWatch satellite down. Being super satisfied with solving the issue in the giant Mepamas, Alex and Gopiz went back to the Launch Base early today. Alex kept on thinking about the marvelous thing they just finished creating, and meanwhile they both reached their helicar and took off to the Launch Base.

The next day, when they came back to the ISROEM Centre, they also programmed the truck that Alex used for transporting ChefMate from Capitrolis to Launch Base, to come to the ISROEM Centre too. They then commanded that truck to follow them and reach the Archive building and park itself near the Archive Building so that they could load all the diesel generators in the truck and take it to different factory buildings for attaching them to all the other 209 Mepamas. They one by one kept all the diesel generators, and then took the driverless truck to different factory buildings, and unloaded a specific number of generators at different buildings, according to Mepamas situated in different buildings. Once they distributed all the diesel generators to all the factory buildings, which took hours by the way, both of them went to different factory buildings and this time commanded the automated robotic machines to replace the giant Mepama's rechargeable batteries with these diesel generators, in a similar way they did yesterday. The advanced AI-based machines understood, and began their task. By 2-3 hours, all the giant Mepamas' power supplies were replaced into diesel generators.

EIGHTEEN

THE PULLDOWN

Alex and Gopiz spent days testing all the giant Mepamas one by one, and managed to fix any major or minor issues along the way. Only some very insignificant issues were encountered while testing other giant Mepamas, and they were easily fixed after diagnosis, troubleshooting and rechecking for problems. Both of them, but especially Alex, was full of optimism and positivity almost everyday. They worked tirelessly and determinedly-transported all the giant Mepamas and by a hundred or more trucks form the ISROEM Centre to the Launch Base, attached and mounted those giant Mepamas on all those UAVs, set up the remote control and connection to UAVs systems, made ready the ground controllers and remotes for flying the UAVs and controlling the Mepamas, and at last, transported a lot of diesel from the same old rusty warehouse to the ISRO Launch base using the same fleet of trucks later, and filled all the Mepamas' generators with the diesel fuel. And finally, the evening of the day before the Pulldown of the IndWatch satellite came. With everything ready and set, they both sat on two chairs kept on the asphalt surface of the Launch Base Outdoors, where all the space planes and similar things were parked and present. Looking at the blue and purple-ish sky, and the sun setting behind a few hills, Gopiz reflected and said- "Really. An extremely important day tomorrow. When we'll bring that thing down and uncover the truth of people's disappearance!" "Yes. Our half mission will be completed when we find the truth! Then it would just be all about getting everyone back to this empty, silent world. I don't care if it's from hell or heaven. Tartarus or Elysium. Narak or Swarg. I'm gonna bring everyone BACK! No matter what!" Alex replied. "YES! That's the Alex I hoped for! We'll do it brother. Together!" Gopiz replied, and gave Alex a smile. Alex smiled back too, showing agreement. And finally, the sun had set below the horizon.

The calm winds blew, the new morning was calm and beautiful, all the fully-charged eleven UAVs– with so many Mepamas mounted on their sturdy surfaces– were parked near the runway. Alex and Gopiz commenced their Pulldown day with a quick coffee (of course only for Alex), and got ready. They went back into their Mission Control Room, but this time not for resting on mattresses there, but for using the room for the purpose for which it was built- managing the live missions and stuff. Gopiz turned on all the POV cameras of the UAVs, while Alex switched on the remote controller, which was connected to the signal receivers of all the 209 Mepamas, as well as the eleven UAVs. Gopiz opened the necessary softwares, turned on the large televisions displaying the live camera recordings of the UAVs, satellite's POV live recording, and the statistics of different aspects of the satellites. Gopiz then told Alex- "The IndWatch is currently just above the United Countries of Arabia, near the Red Sea. Just 6 more minutes till it reaches right above the Bay of Bengalia- when we can pull it down." "Roger that. So shall we take off now?" Alex asked. "Certainly, otherwise it would be too late! Let's go." Gopiz said. "Copy that." Alex replied, and pulled the small lever of the controller, which made all the UAVs take off one after another. "All UAVs in the air. Time to lower the altitude and orbit of the IndWatch satellite?" Alex asked. Gopiz sighed and replied- "Yes, definitely. Lowering the orbit right away." He then pulled a larger lever near the computer, which led the IndWatch satellite which was orbiting in the space, to decrease its speed, and fall into a lower altitude orbit, eventually lowering the height of its orbit. "IndWatch successfully lowered. ETA over Bay of Bengalia- 3 minutes 12 seconds." Gopiz informed. Meanwhile, Alex controlled and flew the UAVs just in the way Gopiz earlier taught him to. Despite just being a 13 year old 6th grader, he felt proud to handle and make a fleet of UAVs fly high in the year. As the large television screens showed the satellite's and UAVs' locations together on the same map, Alex and Gopiz saw that the UAVs' direction was towards the path of the satellite, and at the desired time, the UAVs with the giant Mepamas would be just below the satellite, and that would be the time when Alex would turn on all the giant Mepamas at their full capacities. Seconds elapsed, and finally it was time. "Anytime now. Alex! Get ready!" Gopiz said. Alex got all prepared to turn on the Mepamas right when Gopiz says, as the satellite approached the location of the UAVs. "And NOW!" Gopiz shouted in excitement, and Alex pushed the button, and the live camera recordings showed the giant Mepamas first slightly vibrated, as expected due to the large number of giant electromagnets- and then turned on powerfully. And everything went on as expected, and the satellite was just above the UAVs now, as anticipated– until, suddenly one of the UAV's live recording showed- the entire aircraft tilting and then immediately rolled onto another UAV, and the same happened with 3-4 more UAVs. "Boom!" "Bhaam!" "Bhaaash!" In the end, all the 11 UAVs collided with one another. Creating a massive explosion in the distant sky- above the clouds. Both- Alex and Gopiz desperately looked at the large television screens showing these live camera recordings, until all of them suddenly just turned into noise screens- showing no signal. "What. A. Fresh. Hell." Gopiz murmured- for the first time saying something similar to swearing. But nothing happened to the IndWatch satellite– it kept orbiting the planet. Alex simply removed the black ISRO cap he was wearing, and threw it down on the floor. He pushed his chair behind, stood up, and went to the table near his mattress where his backpack was kept. He kept back his Airtop into the bag, wore back his socks and shoes, picked up his phone and was about to leave the room. "Alex? Alex? ALEX! Where are you going?!" Gopiz shouted and asked him when he didn't respond. He turned to Gopiz, looked at him miserably, and without saying a word, left the room with his backpack. Now that the remote controller for the UAVs and Mepamas became frivolous, Gopiz just turned it off and switched off all the other Computers of the Mission Control Centre hall, and ran behind Alex. He flew and landed right in front of him, and kept stopping Alex- "Bro! Come on! It's just one setback! We'll figure out why this happened. We've come so far... Don't quit now! Come on! Listen to me–" But Alex didn't say a word, and didn't listen to Gopiz, just mindlessly kept walking towards the helicar parking lot. Once he got out, he went to the helicar they used generally, and despite Gopiz stopping him, he sat inside the Helicar, entered the destination as his Capitrolis home, and flew off, starting his journey back home.

He sniffled and wept all the way back– for more than an hour. "The last hope too– now destroyed..." he thought and sobbed. He couldn't believe that all the work he did for weeks, the frustration, great efforts, tough times, hard work and energy spent, turned out into this– this catastrophe. "I'm done living like this– I'm done surviving!" he mumbled to himself. He then wiped his tears, and just when the helicar was descending and about to land on his residential society's helipad in just a few minutes, he clicked on the helicar's computer screen, changed the destination's location from his residential society's helipad to an open green park, on a bank of the Yartrunas River, in

Capitrolis itself. Once the helicar reached and landed in the open and large park that was situated on one of the Yartrunas River's bank, Alex got out of the helicar, took a deep breath, "I love you- Mom, Dad, Jessica. If you're there, I am coming to you!" he murmured to himself, and suddenly ran towards the flowing Yartrunas river, and from the levee of the river bank, he dived directly into the massive flowing river- attempting to suicide. His body splashed and then sank into the deep waters of the massive river, his body struggling to get some breath- which is generally a natural instinct of a sinking human. Suddenly, there was an intense whooshed sound and movement, as if some claws snatched something from the water- just like a pelican would've caught a fish from the water. A flying robot took Alex out of the massive flowing Yartrunas River, and held him in his metal claw-like hands. And as it landed in the same green park, right in front of the helicar, he dropped Alex onto the ground. "Ughh! You were so heavy!" the robot said. "Come on! Yes we don't feel anything, but our hardware also has some limits and capacities!" shouted the robot. Alex opened his eyes, and his vision was slightly blurry for a while. "Who are you?!" Alex asked, groaning in frustration. "Relax! It's me. Gopiz." the robot replied, and then continued- "I kept following you using another helicar just behind you, and via the tracker I smartly threw and stuck on your pants in the Launch Base corridors when you were walking to leave." "Aaarghh! Why the hell did you have to stop me?! I was literally going to end all this! End my living! Everyone has already left, so what the frick I will do in this world, ALL ALONE??!!" Alex screamed at Gopiz. The tiny robot Gopiz, now got furious and shouted at Alex back– "ARE YOU A DUMBO ALEX??!! HAVE YOU LOST YOUR SENSES??!! YOU ARE KILLING YOURSELF DESPITE JUST ONE MISHAP??!! My god! What about those hundreds of hours? When we worked so so hard and tirelessly? Did we only do it TO SEE AN OBSTACLE IN OUR WAY AND THEN END IT ALL?! KILL OURSELVES?" Alex quietly listened to Gopiz, and was shocked to see Gopiz scream so violently as this was a side of Gopiz he saw for the first time. "And if you still are such a coward and selfish person that you'll kill yourself because otherwise you're feeling alone, that too which is temporary, then GO! JUMP INTO THE RIVER ONCE AGAIN, AND DIE. Good Luck." Gopiz continued in a stern and furious voice. Alex started weeping again, while Gopiz turned and went back to the elevated levee, and sat on the grass of the river bank, gazing at the afternoon blue and clear sky. Alex was in pain, because now he had no other idea, no other way, and no other approach to know where did everyone go or why. He lay down on his back, still crying uncontrollably. Minutes passed, but nothing happened. Gopiz kept sitting on the elevated river bank, watching the flowing, mighty Yartrunas river. Alex continued shedding tears, but suddenly stopped sobbing when Gopiz unexpectedly said- "I have another plan." And then he got up, and came back to Alex. "Perhaps, I know what happened and why." Gopiz said to Alex. "What– What do– do you actually mean?" Alex asked, in a broken voice, still fully drenched because of jumping into the river. "The UAVs we used could not handle the massive amount of vibrations of the Mepamas, which destabilised the UAVs and caused them to tilt, lose control and collide with each other." Gopiz told him. "Oh– Oh. Okay... And wha– what about your pl– pla– plan?" Alex asked Gopiz, with eyes that hoped for something. "The solution is three words– Moskva Air Base." Gopiz told him. "Yo– you mean the Moskva of Rus– Russia? Russia's capital city?" Alex asked, still in a slightly broken voice, but confused this time. "Yes. 30 years ago, Russia had built a massive military base near Moskva, so as to quickly respond to any potential attacks from its western side. But that's not important to us." "Then what i– is?" Alex asked. "That very military and air base, has around 80 advanced UAVs, the military ones. Probably the one ISRO had were basic UAVs, and their strength and stability systems were not like the military UAVs. That's why they were unable to withstand the extreme vibrations of the giant Mepamas. But the Russian Military UAVs will withstand such vibrations. There's no doubt about that. For they are the world's best, strongest, and most powerful UAVs." Gopiz replied. "So we would need to go to Russia? Another country? That's– that's–" Alex was trying to say something but Gopiz interrupted him– "Who's gonna stop us? Some people? Oh wait– they're the one who disappeared." Gopiz replied, sarcastically to Alex's late realization. "But literally we'll be travelling to another continent? Seriously?" Alex frustratingly asked. "Yes. Seriously. Otherwise, do you have any other solution? Except for attempting to suicide one more time?" Gopiz asked sarcastically, showing Alex a stern side of his, which Alex hadn't expected. Alex then started sneezing– "Aaaa... Chhhhii..." "Looks like someone caught a cold. Amazing!" Gopiz once again commented. "Come, get up. Let's go to your home. That's much nearer from here than the Launch Base." Gopiz suggested, gave Alex a hand, helped him to stand up, went to the helicar, and took off for Alex's house.

Once they reached Alex's apartment, Alex was not willing to come out of his blanket, because he actually caught a cold. He was sniffling and continuously sneezing. Gopiz made him the common cold healing soup– a special medicinal soup of those times, made from water and the soup mix. "Bro, try to understand. This is the journey of achieving anything." Gopiz told Alex, while handing him the soup mug. "In fact, it is the journey of life. You'll see obstacles, failures and what not– that will make you feel like THIS IS THE END. But it actually isn't. Real courage isn't the absence of fear. It means you'll do the shi– with or without fear! So gear up, and let's go to Moskva tomorrow in the early morning!" Gopiz preached, motivating Alex. "Can you add some sugar in it? I sipped the soup but it's quite weird without sugar." Alex demanded, completely out of the context of discussion. Gopiz sighed, and went to the kitchen, and brought him the soup with added sugar. Gopiz also tried finding some more medicines to cure the cold, from Alex's parents' bedroom drawers and boxes, and finally managed to get some good medicinal tablets. He gave them to Alex, to which Alex commented– "Waise toh you'll also be a good fit for a restaurant waiter or even a nurse in a hospital." Gopiz started at Alex because of the teasing comment to which Alex giggled, first hiding his laugh and then bursting into laughter. Gopiz laughed with him too, becoming happier because at least Alex's mind was letting go of those self-harm thoughts as his mind was now diverted. They spent the evening and early hours of the night laughing, talking to each other, and watching some funny videos on Alex's Airtop, eventually taking a break from the Mepama talks and discussions for today was a harsh day for both of them– but in the end, hopes still survived as they would retry!

NINETEEN
JOURNEY TO RUSSIA

This time before the sun rose the next day, they were packing their bags for Moskva. This time, Alex let Gopiz take the lead, for he was still mentally weak because of the incident that occurred yesterday. "Wait… WAIT! How are we going to Moskva without your charger pod? You didn't bring it, did you?" Alex asked anxiously. "Chillax! I knew we won't come back to the Launch Base so quickly. That's why when you suddenly left the Mission Control Room and were going to take off from the Launch Base, I hurriedly picked up my charging pod and took off just after you did, with it. It's in the helicar I came to Capitrolis in, and the same helicar we used yesterday to come back here, to your residential society." Gopiz explained. Alex understood, and continued his packing. "Bro, don't pack so much because we're just going there for 2 days max. We'll just tell and direct those Russian UAVs to fly and land at our ISRO Launch Base. In fact, it's just a one-day job. I'm just taking one additional day as a margin." Gopiz said to Alex, pointing to so many clothes that he was keeping in his luggage. Finally, they headed to the helipad building together. It was still the dark before the sunrise. The calm winds were blowing peacefully, and just after some minutes of walking, they reached the bottom of the building their helicar was parked on. They went to the top of the building using the elevator, got inside the helicar, and before taking off, Gopiz pointed at the helicar's computer screen, saying– "I thought we should just fully charge the helicar before directly going to Moskva for a nonstop journey. But this helicar is already 62% charged, so it won't take more than 10 or 15 minutes to charge it fully, i.e. till 100%." So both of them agreed to recharge the helicar till 100% to make it ready for the flight to another continent– Europe. The helicar first took off and then landed at the nearest Charging Station. There,

Alex and Gopiz waited for 15 minutes for the helicar to charge fully till 100%. "So why and how are these Russian UAVs better than ISRO's?" Alex inquired. "First of all, they're made for military purposes, hence they're much stronger. Secondly, they have many features of adapting to different situations, circumstances, including extreme vibrations– which meets our purpose." Gopiz replied. They both further discussed those UAVs, and their greater chances of pulling the IndWatch satellite to the ground using those UAVs. Finally, after fifteen minutes or so, Gopiz disconnected the charging cable, closed back the charging hatch, they both boarded the helicar and this time, took off for Moskva, Russia. The journey was of around 8 hours, and they bought some munchies from Alex's house– like some jalapeno-flavoured nachos, some chocolate bars, etc. They spent the first 2-3 hours sleeping, because they already woke up early in the morning, but Gopiz slept to save his battery just like he always did.

After they woke up, they spent some time scrolling Strings on the Mesocia app. It was also now that they began to see the rising sun, well above the horizon, a bright orange was captivating to see, for both of them. "Where are we, though?" Alex mumbled, and then opened his Maps and GPS app for checking their location. "Whoa! We're above Uzbekistan!" Alex said, after noticing their location. Gopiz smiled, but then also asked– "By the way, have you ever gone on a foreign trip before?" The question made Alex emotional, and reading his facial expressions, Gopiz regretted asking that. "Nevermind. Want some chocolate?" Gopiz asked, trying to divert Alex's mind. Alex agreed, and had some pieces of chocolate bar. "Thanks for taking the initiative to divert my attention, but we humans don't forget anything easily. But sure, I'll tell you about my foreign trips with my family in the past. We went to the Emirates, around 4 years ago, and stayed in two cities– Dubai and Emaria. Dubai was filled with coastal fun and luxury, while Emaria was beautiful because of its colorful city, beautiful and amazing canals, and gorgeous neon-lights falling on skyscrapers. This Emirates trip was fun because... Well I'll start from the beginning. One day me and Sierra returned from school and our parents surprised us with the Passports, Visas and tickets to the Emirates. Then the next day we took the earliest flight and reached the magnificent nation. Once we first reached our beach resort, me and Sierra got mad, funnily though. We made our own sandcastles on the beach and destroyed each other's sandcastles once we were finished. The game was so fun because it was like who made the most durable sandcastle and who destroyed the castles the best. Our parents watched and laughed while they lay down on a mat with cans of beer. And not only that! In the evening we went to the Dubai Underwater City– the small yet beautiful underwater city they've built– just like Akstonea has built one near their nation. Finally after Dubai, there was Emaria…" Alex narrated Gopiz his long story of his foreign trips in the past. He took almost an hour to finish with the entire story– but that was the purpose– they had to pass time. Gopiz, curious and enthusiastic to listen to Alex's full story too, heard the entire of it. When Alex finished, they both noticed that a total of 4 hours had already elapsed, and 4 more hours were remaining to reach Moskva. So Alex took out his Airtop and started a movie, and both of them saw it with interest.

The movie ended, but the journey didn't, still, an hour was left. "Disclaimer– You are currently flying in Russian Airspace. Make sure you have necessary permissions." their Helicar's automated voice alerted them. "Permissions? Pfttt!" Alex giggled. "I know right! As if anybody is gonna stop us." Gopiz added. And just as they were talking, two fighter jet planes whooshed from the front, and passed behind from both– the left and right sides of the helicar. Alex and Gopiz became stunned. "Wait! Does that mean… THERE ARE PEOPLE?!" Alex exclaimed, as he realized. But Gopiz had something else in his mind– "Oh no! I am thinking about that– I hope they are not the Go–" "THIS IS GORBA 712! I WARN YOU, TURN AROUND AS YOU OUTSIDERS ARE IN THE RUSSIAN NATIONAL AIRSPACE. I REPEAT– TURN AROUND IMMEDIATELY!" The fighter jet plane pilot spoke on the radio of the helicar, as he immediately brought the fighter jet on the left slide of the helicar, and flew it parallel to the helicar. The second fighter jet too came flying in the same manner, but on the right side of Alex and Gopiz's helicar. They both became scared now. Two military jets were intending to escort them outside the Russian airspace. "What do we do?!" Alex asked Gopiz, in a scared voice. "Lemme handle this. I know exactly what's happening." Gopiz replied, in a wise manner. He tapped on Helicar's screen, clicked on 'Disable Auto-Flying' option, and took charge of the controls of the helicar. "ARE YOU SURE?! DO YOU EVEN KNOW HOW TO MANUALLY FLY THE HELICAR?!" Alex started screaming at Gopiz, looking at him nervously and in a frightened manner. Gopiz immediately pushed the joystick of the control panel that came out of a compartment when he switched off the auto-flying command, forward attempting to descend the helicar extremely quickly. Their flying helicar immediately descended to a lower altitude in milliseconds, confusing the escort planes. "Bro they're fighter jets! THEY'LL REACH TO US IN NO TIME! AND OUR DEATH IS

JUST ONE MISSILE BUTTON AWAY!" Alex started panicking and shouting at Gopiz. Gopiz was still optimistic. He took an unplanned left turn, going off-route and in a direction different from their destination's. "BRO WHERE ARE YOU GOING? DO YOU EVEN KNOW?" Alex asked in a screaming manner. Gopiz remained quiet, as he focused on his navigating skills. The fighter jets immediately came just behind the helicar, and warned them once again. Gopiz took another left turn, but this time, making the helicar dive towards the ground, its nose vertically falling to the ground. Alex's heart skipped a few beats, and he was overcome with fear– the fear of dying. As the helicar was perpendicularly falling towards the ground, Alex started murmuring something like a prayer, and just when the helicar approached ground, Gopiz pulled the joystick backward and finally made the helicar fly horizontally again, and now just a few metres above the ground– which was covered with full of tall grass, looking like a grassland-like place. The fighter jets whooshed above and as they could not land just anywhere, they started dropping bombs on the ground, trying to hit the helicar. Gopiz immediately landed the helicar after in the grassland-like place, smashing and cutting through the tall grass, and the velocity of the helicar made the smashing grass cause cracks on the helicar's windshield as well. Subsequently the helicar slowed, and came to a halt. "Get out of the helicar immediately and do as I say!" Gopiz instructed. Alex opened the door, but as soon as he did, a large bomb exploded just 2-3 metres beside him. He started crying out of fear. "Stay with me Alex! Don't be scared. We'll get through this!" Gopiz shouted to Alex, and then gestured to him to kneel down and stay low in the tall grass to avoid being spotted by the fighter jets. The explosives continued to be dropped, often followed by a random firing of bullets. The fighter jets tried their best and did put all their efforts in finding and spotting the infiltrators hiding in the grassland, but eventually failed despite this all being in broad daylight, and finally just left with a message through the mega-speakers of the fighter jets– "You might've escaped from us right now! But we're alerting all the stations! And eventually, WE WILL FIND YOU!" And then they also gave a similar message in Russian. This made Alex super frightened. They kept crawling in the tall grass till they saw that the fighter jets were now gone. When they both slowly stood up, Alex started crying and saying– "It's all your fault! You only suggested coming to Russia! We can't even go back to India now! Flying has now become so risky THAT THEY'LL SIMPLY SHOOT US NOW! Hasn't this mass disappearance of people occurred worldwide? How did these people withstand that?! My god, I am so confused–" "They aren't People! They are the Gorbas! I literally forgot about them." Gopiz replied, realizing his mistake, and continued– "I should've remembered them. Being an Ultra Artificial Intelligence, HOW CAN I FORGET STUFF?! I hate these kinds of glitches!" "Who are GORBAS NOW?!" Alex frustratingly asked. "They are the guards. Robot guards, who were even about to be exported from here to India, because of strategic military alliances. They are used for wars, but Russia wasn't at war with anyone recently. Then, why?... I simply don't understand! Ugh!" Gopiz replied, but in the end being confused and perplexed. "So what now, huh? We can't fly. And only god knows where we are!" "We must sneakily and covertly reach Moskva Air Base, try directing the UAVs to India, and finally come back and leave Russia as soon as possible." Gopiz suggested. Alex started clapping slowly in a sarcastic manner, and then said– "Wow! Wow Gopiz, Wow! Go to a Military Base when these Gorgor– whatever armed robots are looking for us like hungry wolves!" "Bro we'll be able to do it. All we need to do is give the Military UAVs the command to fly to our ISRO Launch Base in India. And we don't even need to control them using a remote control or control panel or anything, unlike the UAVs we used earlier with remote controllers. Trust me, it'll be super easy." Gopiz assured. Alex was filled with fear as he didn't even have an idea how these devil-like Gorbas looked like. He thought, "Do they have horns? Do they have red eyes? Or do they look like aliens? Who– what are they?" But deep inside, he felt that there was nothing else to do except for what Gopiz was suggesting. "But hold on, if SateRadars are so common, and everyone but us are gone, won't they easily get our location using it?" Alex told Gopiz as he realized. "Oh my... SateRadars! I forgot there's a thing like that too! Ugh!" Gopiz said, realizing that the situation was more dangerous now. Alex looked here and there in desperation, at the open grassland landscape with distant hills. "So we must hurry up. Till the time they tell and share our information with other Gorbas and they prepare to catch us, we must quickly reach Moskva Air Base and initiate the process of Military UAVs' flights to India. At least a dozen of them." Gopiz said. Alex asked– "And what if we get caught or surrounded by them?" "Remember, I can fly? I can fly faster than the time they'll take to shoot us or aim weapons at us. So the last resort will be me picking you up and flying away. Now hurry up and get back in the helicar!" Gopiz instructed. "UHH... No! I won't fly again now! We were about to die!" Alex exclaimed. "Bro we'll drive to a nearby highway, but I'll drive manually so we can go at full speeds." Gopiz replied. This sounded better to Alex, so he got into the helicar, opened the GPS and Maps App on its computer screen and entered Location of Moskva Air Base. The nearest main road was 2 km away from their location, as the GPS and Navigation app showed. Gopiz drove through tall grasses of the rugged grassland terrain at the highest speed possible on such a surface. It took ten minutes to reach the main road, but finally they made it. Now Gopiz increased the speed to 150-170 km per hour. The ETA of reaching was 4 hours 30 minutes. But the main anxiety was about Gorbas looking for them, and was more intense in Alex– a 13 year-old boy trusting a tiny robot. They finally started driving on a highway, which was risky due to their 'Wanted' statuses. Time passed by, and the ETA was reduced to 2 hours 12 minutes. Fortunately for them, they saw no Gorbas yet, literally anywhere. "Are they gone?" Alex murmured. "Nah! Not so easily. To turn Gorbas on and off, a military commander's command– of a human commander of course– is needed. So it's pretty obvious that the human Military Commander did switch on these Gorbas. But for what... Well that's a mystery too! Plus, the fact that they can't switch off on their own pretty much gives us the conclusion that they're still active. It's just our luck that they didn't see us yet." Gopiz replied. This gave them, especially Alex, some confidence. They planned that they'll secretly enter the Air Base, stay out of Gorbas sights if they'll be there, and finally command and send the Military UAVs to their ISRO Launch Base. ETA became 45 minutes now. Gopiz's driving was superfast yet smooth, as if he's an expert driver. Alex was impressed at his manual driving and even flying skills, but he didn't say anything so as not to make Gopiz overconfident about itself. Suddenly, Gopiz applied brakes. "Don't do anything, don't even get out of the helicar." Gopiz commanded. "What?! Why?" Alex asked, anxiously. "Is there any Gorba?" he continued asking, and then looking at all sides. "Bro, not on the ground- in the sky. Look at that military helicars fleet." Gopiz directed Alex, pointing at the sky. Around 15-20 helicars in a proper formation flew across the bright blue sky with scattered clouds. Their formation looked magnificent, but it only made them more nervous, as it looked like so many Gorbas were heading somewhere. When all the helicars flew away and ceased to be visible, Gopiz slowly turned on the helicar and continued his drive. This time he tried driving off the highway, through some countryside roads. When Alex questioned him why he's taking the longer route, Gopiz gave the reason – "They'll most probably only check and patrol near main areas and roads like the highways, so there's risk in going via them." It took them around an hour, but finally they made it to the approach road of the Moskva Air

Base. However, Gopiz stopped the helicar right there, as he told Alex to cover the rest of a few hundred metres on foot, to avoid getting attention from any Gorbas nearby. They got off the road and walked parallel to it, but only behind the bushes on the roadside so that there was less chances of being visible to Gorbas if any. Finally as they reached the Air Base's large entry gate with the Russian Air Force beautiful emblem carved on the large sandstone building above the tunnel-like entryway, they saw and realized that there were no Gorbas near the entry gate. Gopiz gestured to Alex that they should move inside. But little did they know, Gorbas were a thousand steps ahead of them already. As Alex kept his first foot inside the tunnel-like entryway, with the gates already opened, he jumped in fear as he realized that some sensor detected him and suddenly triggered a ringing sound, and just then, hundreds of Gorbas came from inside and the outside of the Air Base at the entryway, surrounding Alex and Gopiz. "WE SURRENDER! WE'LL LEAVE BACK IMMEDIATELY! SORRY THAT WE ENTERED YOUR LAND WITHOUT PERMISSION!" Alex started crying to the Gorbas. "Kneel down and hands in the air!" one of the Gorbas shouted, with all the other Gorbas having their guns pointed right at Alex. Gopiz, according to their Plan B, intended to hover and get closer to Alex to pick him up and fly above. But before he tried doing anything like that, in milliseconds someone from behind tied their hands, and gave them a very minor yet effective electric shock, called a faint-shock, that temporarily made them unconscious as they fell onto the ground.

TWENTY

FROM PRISONERS TO GUESTS

It was the time after sunset when they woke up, and both of them were tied to their wooden chairs, in a dark room with only a weird hanging yellow light emitting some light on the old wooden table below it. And in front of them, a humanoid robot, with cyan glowing eyes on a LCD screen similar to that of Gopiz but body like a muscular human, and height of 6 feet easily. And it was not just a humanoid robot– it was one of the Gorba, who stared at them suspiciously. "Finally! You woke up! Slava Bogu!" Gorba exclaimed. Alex couldn't understand the language at first of all. But it was obvious that the Gorbas were waiting for hours for Alex and Gopiz to wake up again. Suddenly, the creaking room door opened, and another Gorba entered, but with additional armor and even a coat that looked like those that Military commanders wore. "SIR! GOOD TO SEE YOU! THESE INFILTRATORS JUST WOKE UP!" The Gorba who had been observing Alex and Gopiz informed his commander. "DISMISS!" the commander replied, instructing the other Gorba to leave the room. Alex looked at the commander in grief, still with tears in eyes. Alex tried explaining, "Sir could you please listen to us—" "FIRST TELL WHY YOU HOOLIGANS ENTERED OUR NATION WITHOUT PERMISSION!" the patriotic Gorba Commander asked violently. Gopiz replied, "We'll tell you everything but you must give us time to explain–" "NO TIME! NYET VREMENI! ANSWER QUICK!" the commander fiercely shouted. "DAVAYTE GOVORIT'!!!" Gopiz screamed at the commander frustratedly. "Psst... Translation?" Alex whispered, asking Gopiz what he meant. "I told him to shut up in Russian." Gopiz replied in a whispering manner too. Alex literally became astounded. Even the commander remained stunned, looking at Gopiz's audacity to scream at the person who had held them as prisoners. Then the Gorba commander sighed, and asked– "Okay. Who among you leader?" "He. He is the leader." Alex replied, pointing towards Gopiz. Gopiz looked back at him in confusion and perplexed manner. "Me? Leader? Huh." Gopiz murmured. "Okay, mini robot leader... Speak." The commander gave Gopiz the permission to speak up. So, Gopiz began speaking– "Okay, so look. Even I am an Ultra Artificial Intelligence-based robot, and he and I are trying to solve the mystery, we came here for some things we needed, like military UAVs–" "YOU CAME TO STEAL OUR MILITARY UAVs FROM US??!!" the Gorba became more hyper and aggressive. "NO SIR! NO! NO! We only came to borrow it, and then return them to you. We only need them to find the disappeared people–" Alex was speaking but the Gorba then interrupted him and asked– "Disappeared people? You mean all the human beings that disappeared but you?" "YES! Yes! Absolutely! We are doing some things by ourselves to find out what happened to them. And our mission requires the Military UAVs you have." Alex replied, in a hopeful tone as he noticed that the Gorba commander began taking interest in his explanation. "Hmmm... Tell me more!" the commander insisted. Alex took a sigh, and began the whole story of what he went through, how he tried finding answers, then how he went to Cheniaros, then finally to ISRO Launch Base, how he included Gopiz in his team, and all the remaining story till the event of coming to Russia. It took him 2 hours to tell the Gorba commander. But after hearing the story, the commander began to believe Alex and Gopiz, because the depth of details and the way of narrating the entire story was convincing. After listening to the entire story, the Gorba commander wore back his military cap, and rose up from his chair, and told them to wait for some time. And after saying that, the commander left the room, with no one else but only Alex and Gopiz. "Why'd you bother telling him the entire story bro? They ain't gonna help us anyway. Either they'll shoot us or deport us back outside Russia." Gopiz commented, and Alex looked at him in surprise, thinking about the 'shoot us' phrase. Suddenly, the door opened, with the Military Gorba coming back with two more Gorba robot commanders with one of them looking like the senior of the Gorba Commander they talked with too. So, in other words, the Gorba Commander was impressed by Alex and Gopiz's story and brought his senior and another commander to their interrogation room. It was now dark outside the grilled window near the ceiling. The senior commander said- "So, my junior says you are trying to find the missing human beings too." Alex replied– "Yes Sir! Absolutely, we just needed your Military UAVs for successfully bringing down the satellite we told sir about–" "Yes yes I know. He told me everything. IndWatch, we know about it, although it's surprising to see that you, a teenager and you, a mini robot, attempted so daringly the process of bringing the satellite down using your invention. That's why we've decided..." the Senior Gorba Commander paused, creating suspense and curiosity, while Alex and Gopiz looked in its eyes restlessly. "That we'll release and assist you." the Senior Commander announced. They both cheered with joy and thankfulness, and suddenly their techy handcuffs automatically opened and dropped on the floor, and their hands were free. "But we have a condition." the Senior commander continued– "I mean, we'll allow you to take some of our Military UAVs, and till the time you're in Russia, we'll ensure that you get your essential needs, like the boy gets food and the robot gets compatible charging pod, and all of such things will be taken care of by us. However, a team of Gorbas will go back to the ISRO Launch Base with you to ensure the safety of our UAVs and to confirm that you both are actually using them for what you stated. And if anything happens to them, we'll have no other choice but to end you. You'll be free anyways, the choices are however– Get the UAVs but with our Gorbas going with you and taking revenge if they're destroyed, or get deported empty-handed. We give you 60 minutes to think. Thank you."

Now this was something Gopiz and Alex remained stunned at. All the three Gorba commanders left the interrogation room. They stared at each other, miserably and wretchedly. Alex didn't speak anything, and so didn't Gopiz, and they both sat on their chairs, looking down at the wooden floor, thinking deeply. Then after some time Gopiz spoke up– "Alright then, let's tell them to deport us with our helicar so we can go back to our country." "Uh what?" Alex alertedly questioned and then continued– "No, not at all bro. We came this far for something, and won't go back empty handed." "Didn't you hear him? They'll kill us if we mess up." "Bro I was anyway trying to die when we first messed up. And this is the last hope, and I don't wanna lose this hope." Alex replied to Gopiz's statement. Gopiz thought for a minute, and then asked– "What if we find some other way? I mean, the Chinese UAVs aren't bad either. Although they're a bit less strong and stable, they're still far better than the ISRO UAVs we used–" Gopiz asked, trying to save both lives just in case. But Alex boldly replied- "CAN YOU STOP BEATING AROUND THE BUSH GOPIZ? LET'S JUST TAKE THIS STEP, and my decision is final!" Gopiz sighed, of course through a robotic sigh. And just seconds later, a Gorba Assistant knocked, came in and asked– "Have you made your decision? The Senior Commander is asking." "Tell him we choose to take help from him by taking the Military UAVs with the risk of dying in case we harm those." Alex confidently told the assistant. "Alrighty! If that's the case, you're no longer suspects, but our guests. And hence, the commander told me to ask you what you would like to eat." the Gorba asked, kindly with happy digital eyes. "I'll be fine with any Indian or General Cuisine Meal, if you could do that please." Alex replied. "Okay, great. Let me direct you to your dorm room. Follow me." the Gorba said. Alex and Gopiz got up from their chairs, and left the dark and weird interrogation room and entered the bright and calm corridors of the building, following the Gorba assistant. The Gorba eventually took them to a small but cozy dorm room, with lights, a cupboard, an attached bathroom, a small sofa and a chair. "We request you to freshen up and rest until we call you downstairs to the canteen for your dinner meal. Please feel like home!" the Gorba said, and left the room.

"Wow, I mean. Look at the contrast. A few minutes ago, they were treating us like prisoners, and now they're treating us like VIP guests." Alex said, giggling. "But bro what you still don't understand is that with all this comfort and good treatment comes the risk of getting killed. That's something you should be more concerned about!" Gopiz replied, still worried. "Look man, I almost died before as well. So if we mess up and get killed, I wouldn't mind." Alex replied. "But what if we succeed in bringing down the IndWatch satellite, but still harm the UAVs? This is the third possibility." Gopiz said, highlighting another case. "I don't wanna think so badly and intensely. I'm just going on with the flow." replied Alex who lay down on the bed, resting after the long day. "But Alex–" "NO MORE DISCUSSION ABOUT THIS NOW!" Alex shouted at Gopiz, being frustrated from his heavy burden of suggestions. But inside his mind, Alex had something else cooking up too, but he didn't share it with Gopiz, thinking that sharing it would only mean complicating things more.

An hour later, the Gorba Assistant came to the room and asked Alex to come downstairs for dinner. He and Gopiz went down, and entered a large canteen hall. So many Gorbas greeted and smiled at Alex and Gopiz as they walked further. Finally, they reached a canteen table with 3-4 plates, each containing a different dish– a butter and salsa sandwich, a curry with butter and garlic flatbreads, a biryani, and a side of chilli potato chips with mayonnaise. And the Senior Gorba Commander and the other two Commanders were sitting in front of these dishes, but on the opposite side of the table, waiting for Alex to take a seat. Alex did so, and soon he realized that in the entire canteen hall it is only going to be him who is going to eat. So hence, the presence of a canteen hall, dorm rooms, etc. along with Gorba robots who don't eat or sleep like humans, pretty much meant that not only this canteen hall but the entire building was originally built for human military soldiers or staff, but now they disappeared so Gorbas were in charge. Alex nervously smiled, and started having his dinner meal. He felt weird as all the Gorbas kept staring at him. It felt awkward, so he asked– "Sir, it's weird eating like this with everyone watching me. Can you–" "Absolutely, comrade! HEY ALL OF YOU! GO DO YOUR WORK! DISMISS!" the Senior Commander shouted to all other Gorbas, to which all of them immediately continued doing their own work, and stopped watching Alex. So now he continued having his dinner. Minutes elapsed and finally he was finished with his meal and burped satisfactorily. Gopiz watched him leaning back on his chair after being full. Then, the Senior Gorba Commander spoke– "So tomorrow morning, our A05 team will be helping you to program the UAVs to leave for your destination in India and land there, and then finally you'll go to the same destination with the team in our Military Passenger Aircraft. So tomorrow morning, we'll bid you farewell!" "Alright Sir! We appreciate the efforts. Thank you so much for your hospitality!" Alex replied, smiling at the Senior Commander. The Gorba commanders waved good night and left the canteen hall, just after which Alex and Gorba returned to their dorm room with the Gorba assistant guiding them. They reached the room, opened the door with the key card, and switched on the lights. "Ah yes! Gopiz, we got your Charging Pod machine from your Helicar, near the place where we um... Caught you. Anyways, I'll send someone to get it to you ASAP. Have a good night, both of you!" the Gorba Assistant said, went and closed the door. Alex went to the washroom for doing number one, and meanwhile, another Gorba knocked and entered the room, handing the large yet light Charging pod to Gopiz and pointing towards the socket in their room Gopiz could use for the charger. After this, that Gorba left the room too, and at the same time, Alex came out of the washroom. "You know I was thinking–" Alex was saying but then paused, and then asked– "Did anyone come while I was inside?" "Uh yeah! One of them came to give me my Charging Pod so I could charge myself tonight." Gopiz replied. "Oh. Okay. Well what I was saying is, that we just came to Russia this afternoon, and we're going back tomorrow morning. Isn't that too quick? I mean since childhood I always wished to visit this country, and now that I'm here, I'm being told to leave the next day. I wanna visit the main city, the main monuments, and the river!" Alex said, excitedly. Gopiz had a confused face, but he just asked- "Would they allow us to do so? I mean for them we were infiltrators." "Well, now we are their guests. And anyways, we have a deal with them– they'll help us with the Military UAVs and in return we'll give them back in perfect condition. I'm frankly surprised why they wish to help us. Maybe they too wish to find the missing or disappeared people and they see potential in us." Alex replied, and ended up murmuring to himself. So it was 10 PM now, local time, and Alex and Gopiz eventually decided to ask the commander if they could spend another day in Russia, visiting the central Moskva city. It was actually Alex's desire, for Gopiz was only worried about the choice they made. So finally, as they were super tired after all the exertion of the day, first travelling to Russia, then hiding from bombs and missiles, and whatnot, they decided to sleep– Alex went to his dorm room bed, and Gopiz went to and stood in his pod and began charging himself, eventually shutting down as he started to charge himself. Alex voice-commanded the lights to switch off, and slept calmly.

TWENTY-ONE
A TOUR OF MOSKVA

The next day's sun rose up, but this time in a new country, a new land. Russia, where our two heroes went and got captured and then also got converted into guests. Gopiz waited for Alex as his charging was finished before Alex woke up. Alex woke up, still with his eyes opening a bit only, and mumbled being all weary– "Whoa! You're already up?" "Uh yeah! My charging was fully completed hours ago." Gopiz replied. "Thanks for not making me wake up back then, because my sister always did it." Alex said, recalling his past while coming out of the blanket, still being a bit sleepy. "Hah! I see… Sierra, right?" Gopiz asked his sister's name. "How do you know the name?" Alex questioned. "You mentioned her, that too yesterday only, remember? Your trip to the Emirates?" Gopiz replied. "Oh yeah! I forgot. Anyways, did anyone come into the room before I woke up?" Alex inquired. "Uh nope! Not a single Gorba." Gopiz replied. "Alright. I'm going for number two, and a short shower. If anyone comes, knock at the washroom door and let me know." Alex told Gopiz, to which Gopiz agreed. Alex went to the washroom and took his clothes from his backpack that the Gorba assistant had already kept in the dorm room even before he guided them there last evening, and went to the washroom. Gopiz waited patiently for Alex, and when he came back, he was surprised to see that no Gorba came till now. It was 9:30 AM, yet no Gorba even knocked on their dorm room's door. After wearing his shoes, Alex got up and said– "I think they wouldn't call us again and again. We would need to go to them ourselves. And also, we have to ask the Senior Commander if we could stay in Russia one day, and I hope he does not get furious or something, and allows us to visit the main city and all. So let's go and find him." Gopiz agreed, and they both came out of their dorm room, only to see that the corridors were empty. They both went downstairs, and when they reached the lower floor, it was then that they saw so many Gorbas, walking, cleaning their guns and bodies with wet cloths, and chattering with each other. "Freshening time, I guess." Gopiz quietly mumbled, to which Alex giggled. And suddenly, the Gorba commander, not the Senior one, but the one they first talked to, came in front of them, and asked– "Good morning, druz'ya! How are you both? Looking for someone?" "Good morning! We were looking for the Senior Commander. We wanted to ask something to him." Alex replied. "Sure thing! He's probably cleaning himself right now, just like you can see others freshening themselves in your surroundings. Still, I'll let him know you guys want to talk. For the time being, you may consider sitting in the canteen hall." the Commander said. It felt a bit weird, but interesting too that robots were so concerned about keeping themselves cleaned. Alex then turned to Gopiz, smiled and teased him– "When was the last time you cleaned yourself?" Gopiz realized the taunt, and stared at Alex cutely. Alex bursted into laughter, and then Gopiz smiled and started laughing too. So for the time being, they both went to the Canteen hall and sat there. Alex asked for the Network Password from a Gorba, and he gave it to him after taking permission from the Commander. Alex then used the network to browse his Mesocia app feed. Minutes later, the Senior Commander approached them and sat on the chair opposite to them. "Good morning champs! You wanted to talk?" the Senior Commander asked. Alex replied, "Uh yes. Good Morning sir! Actually I had a request– Can we stay in Russia for one more day? We actually wanted to explore and visit the beautiful capital city of Moskva. It has been a travel dream of mine since childhood. So... If you could allow us–" "ABSOLUTELY! Now that you're our guests, it will be an honour to show you our magnificent capital of Moskva! The A05 team allotted to you, will take you to the city and show you the great landmarks. And why not? I'm glad that you wish to explore our beautiful country." the Senior Commander replied excitedly. Alex smiled as his request was accepted and the Senior Commander allowed them to stay in the country for another day. This one extra day wasn't related to their mission or goal, but it was like a refreshing trip and in fact, a good utilisation of opportunity to explore and travel as they came to a foreign country which is often not very easy.

Soon, after Alex had his breakfast in the canteen hall and Gopiz cleaned himself with a wet cloth he got from a Gorba, they met the A05 team– a group of 15 Gorbas headed by no one else but the junior Gorba Commander they talked with. "Oh! Sir you didn't tell us you are the leader of the A05 team. It's great to have someone we already know!" Gopiz said. Alex smiled, supporting the statement, to which the commander smiled himself. "Alright, so Gorba 1389, call Gorba 774 right now with the armoured military bus, so we can go to the main city." the commander ordered. "Roger that, sir!" Gorba 1389 replied, and used his inbuilt microphone to call the other Gorba who was the driver of the armoured military bus they were going in. The driver drove up the armoured bus to the main entrance, and everyone– the A05 team, Alex and Gopiz boarded the bus. Alex couldn't believe his eyes, as for the first time he was seeing a military armoured vehicle so closely. He felt privileged to be protected and guided by military robots, as if he and Gopiz were some VIPs. He smiled as he climbed into the bus and entered it, seeing the magnificent interiors with futuristic cyan ribbon lighting, dark walls with comfortable seating, and compartments and storage boxes for different military equipment. Finally after everyone boarded the bus, Alex looked outside through a very small window, and saw the Senior Gorba Commander waving goodbye to him, while standing on the stairs of the main entrance of the building. Alex waved back, though obviously his waving hand wasn't visible to the senior Commander as Alex's window was too small, only showing his upper face. And the military bus vroomed and departed from the Military base. Alex and Gopiz sat together, opposite to the A05 Team's Gorbas sitting, and looking at both of them with their robotic blue eyes. Some of them seemed a bit serious and strict, while others looked joyful and cheerful. "It's hilarious that even robots have different personalities. What an amazing invention of AI and robots." Alex thought.

It took them around 30 minutes to enter the main city. But finally when they reached, Alex peeked through the small window, and saw a beautiful fortified complex surrounded by reddish-brown coloured beautiful and massive walls with towers and angled wall Russian flags situated on the incredible wall's surfaces. As soon as the bus stopped and its doors opened, all the A05 team members got out and directed Alex and Gopiz to the massive entry of the fort-like complex. The junior Gorba Commanded, also the head of the A05 Team, welcomed Alex and Gopiz and announced– "Comrades, welcome, to the Honourable Kremlin!" "The Kremlin! I know about this! We were taught at school that it's a complex with many important buildings like the President's residence, the Red Square, St. Basil's Cathedral and whatnot!" Alex exclaimed, appreciating the beauty of the Kremlin, even though he was for now standing outside it, in front of its Main entrance– the Trinity Tower. They all proceeded into the Kremlin through the tunnel-like passage through the Trinity Tower, and got inside the complex. The Gorba Commander enthusiastically and proudly told Alex and Gopiz all about these important buildings and places in the Kremlin Complex. They were greeted by its majestic red-brick walls and sprawling courtyards. "Now comrades, we present you– the Cathedral Square! Now there are three cathedrals here as you can see." the commander showed around. "And that you see, is the Grand Kremlin Palace, where our President– Honourable Miss Anzhelika, used to live." Alex and Gopiz looked at the magnificent Kremlin Palace, and Alex thought– "Can someone be that powerful? That rich? That they get to live here?" Both Alex and Gopiz were in awe, looking at the extremely gorgeous mansion. They both explored and visited some more places around, like the Kremlin's New Tower, that was built to celebrate the 100 years of the country in 2091. Alex and Gopiz walked in the front with the Gorba Commander who showed them different places, just like a local guide would've done. Finally they got out of the Kremlin and went to the Red Square, and on their way, they also saw the beautifully and calmly flowing Moskva river, the river on which the capital city's name was changed from Moscow to Moskva. They spent hours visiting different places, like the St. Basil's Cathedral, the OneWorld tower– the headquarters of JARC (Japan, Akstonea, Russia and China) alliance, and even the Cosmonautics museum– the museum of Russian Space Agency– ROSCOSMOS, that interested Gopiz the most, for he too belonged to a space and universe-based context being a robot at ISRO. "This is amazing!" Gopiz exclaimed, after seeing so much advanced space and universe exploration technologies. In the late afternoon, after they visited all the main places in Moskva, they finally sat down on a few benches on a broad wooden promenade on the bank of the glittering Moskva river. Alex smiled now, satisfied with today's tour. "Sir, we both must thank you for all your efforts you made today." Alex thanked the Gorba commander. "Ah! You're welcome comrades! It's our pleasure to give you a tour of our beautiful country." the commander replied, smiling with his digital eyes on the LED display. Alex then turned to Gopiz, who was standing at the railing of the promenade, watching the flowing Moskva River. Alex saw him, went to him and asked– "So Gopiz! What are you thinking? Any prob?" "Oh! Hey! Not quite, just the same thing. We can soon become dead." Gopiz replied. "Or, we can succeed in bringing down the IndWatch, land the Russian UAVs safely, and find out what happened to everyone! Look brother, optimism is the key! And we won't just try... WE WILL MAKE SURE NOTHING HAPPENS TO THE UAVs!"

Alex replied, quite positively. Gopiz felt weird, as Alex was unusually positive and optimistic, while previously he was a paranoid boy. "But well, people can change. As things and people often change." Gopiz thought, not kind of thought, but processed, being a robot. Finally, when the sun started to go down, the Gorba Commander walked into the armoured bus, instructed the driver, climbed down and came out yelling– "Alright! All aboard!" Gopiz and Alex walked up to the bus, climbed into it, and sat on their seats, followed by the remaining A05 Team's Gorbas. When everyone got in, the driver started the military bus and headed back to the base. The journey back to the Military Base was however faster than the journey from the base to the Kremlin. When they all reached, the A05 Team Gorbas waved goodbye to Alex and Gopiz and headed to their storage and charging rooms, while Alex, Gopiz and Gorba commander came to the main corridor of the military building. They walked towards the canteen hall, and while they walked, the Gorba commander talked to Alex, explaining their tomorrow morning's plan for programming UAVs and leaving for India.

Today, the dinner was served to Alex earlier than yesterday, but with a slight variation in dishes, this time being– Potato & Paneer-Stuffed Kulchas with yogurt, Achaari-Cheese sandwich, and a side of fried fritters and tomato ketchup. Alex had his food passionately, and loved the dishes, happy with the quality as well as the quantity. This time the Senior Gorba Commander came to Alex and talked about their day-tour of Moskva and how Alex and Gopiz felt and what they liked. Alex talked and had his dinner simultaneously, and Gopiz sat beside him, smiling and nodding to whatever he said. As Alex finished his dinner, both of them said Goodnight to both the Senior and Junior Commanders and went back to their dorm room. As they entered their room, Alex collapsed in tiredness and fell onto his bed after the long day. He knew that it was his last night in Moskva, but now he started to become more serious about the second attempt of the Pulldown. He became stressed by the fact that they'd have to 3D print all the Mepama parts again, and get them assembled by making the automation machines collaborate and cooperate with each other and by managing them. But this time all this process didn't look so long or tiring– because this time there was no learning curve.

Yes, this time a few modifications were there, like this time they'd use vibration absorbers and stuff like that to decrease risk of failure further, but they both knew what they exactly had to do. Alex was lost in thinking all about this process, summarizing what they'll do and how they'll do it. But again, it was a relief that they managed and did the manufacturing process before, so they knew what they had to do. Gopiz looked at Alex, seeing him lost in his own deep thinking. He scanned that Alex was super engaged in his thoughts, and decided to keep quiet until Alex himself didn't say anything. So minutes later, around 9:45 PM, Alex asked Gopiz– "Alright, shall we sleep now? It's a big day tomorrow." "Hmmm... Sure! Good night Alex! I'll go charge myself too, although I still have a lot of battery, but still, just in case." Gopiz replied, and went to his charging pod. He switched it on, put both his legs into the pod space, and began to charge himself after shutting down. Alex now sighed, got up, went to the washroom for number 1. And finally, he came back, turned off the room's lights, and slept in the cozy dorm room.

TWENTY-TWO
BACK TO INDIA

The next morning was pretty hasty for both Alex and Gopiz. Alex forgot to set up an alarm for morning and it was not Gopiz this time, but the loud knocks on their dorm room's door that woke Alex up. Gopiz was fully charged, but he didn't turn on for now, nor came out of the charging pod. Alex woke up, in confusion, first opened the door because that irritatedly woke him, and said– "YES?! WHO IS THIS?!" "Ummm hi! It's me, Gorba 111. Your assistant whom you met the day before yesterday. I'm here to tell you that the A05 team is all ready to go to the UAVs hangar and Air Base division, and is waiting for you and the mini robot to come out." the Gorba assistant replied. "Uh... Alright! I'll reach there ASAP. Let them know I'm coming." Alex replied and closed the door. But then he turned to Gopiz, and murmured– "What's wrong with this guy now?" He looked at Gopiz's charging pod display which indicated– '100% Battery - Fully Charged' but didn't wake up Gopiz. Alex himself pulled and lifted Gopiz up, which immediately caused Gopiz to switch on, and then Alex kept him on the floor, making him stand and be all awake now. "Wait a minute– I didn't wake up by myself?" Gopiz immediately asked after waking up, being confused. "Nope." Alex replied. "Oh no... The problem I expected! It always happens, ALWAYS!" Gopiz exclaimed frustratingly. "What? What always happens?" Alex asked, curious to know about the problem. "You see, my Charging Pod is made in such a way that it is not flexible to different electrical sockets. It's only designed for the voltage supply sockets of the ISRO Launch Base, where I was expected to stay." Gopiz explained. "I– I didn't get it. You're saying that the Charging Pod is incompatible with the socket you used for its plug?" Alex asked. Gopiz replied– "Yes. You can say that. Basically whenever my Charging pod– the big pod-like charger in which I stand to charge myself–

is used in a socket that has more or lesser input voltage, such things happen and the Charging Pod malfunctions, leading to such issues like I not turning on by myself, unless someone takes me out of the Charging Pod themselves, like you did." "Oh... Well, don't worry. We're today anyway going back to India, to our Launch Base. So next time you charge, you'll charge there only. So the problem wouldn't persist." Alex said, pretty optimistically. He then told Gopiz that the A05 Team was waiting for them downstairs, at the main entrance. "Please do me a favour. I'll just be back from the washroom, and till then can you please pack all my belongings in my backpack and luggage bag? Thanks in advance!" Alex told Gopiz and rushed to the washroom for his number 2 business. Gopiz did as instructed. He packed the Airtop, the extra pairs of clothes, etc. back into Alex's luggage bag and made everything ready for departure. Alex came back, and was happy to see everything packed. He and Gopiz immediately left the room, walked downstairs with luggage, Gopiz's charging pod and bags, and finally reached the main entrance, where the A05 Team's head- the junior Gorba Commander was waiting for them. "What took you guys so long? We even have to program the UAVs and make them take off!" the commander said. "Sorry sir, we just woke up right now. But now we're all ready." Alex replied, nervously chuckling. The commander called the driver of the armoured bus, and the vehicle arrived at the spot. Suddenly, the Senior Gorba Commander came to the main entrance of the building too, where everyone was standing. All the Gorbas including the junior Commander greeted him 'Good Morning sir', so Alex and Gopiz did the same as they stood at the front. "So, kiddo? Leaving for your country?" the Senior Commander smiled and asked. "Yes sir. We thank you so much for your hospitality and support. Without your help, our mission would still have been incomplete and directionless. Now at least we will attempt it!" replied Alex. "You're welcome! It was also very nice to see a human after so many weeks after everyone else disappeared. But remember, not a single dent. Because you both are nice people- person, and robot. We also don't want to do any harm to you. So please do your mission in a way that nothing happens to our UAVs, so nothing happens to you." Senior Commander added. This made Alex a bit tense and nervous, but still he replied- "Definitely sir, we'll use and bring you back your UAVs safe and sound. It's our responsibility now!" The Senior Commander smiled, and then said- "I'm actually not kidding, but we really don't wish to kill you even if you fail, but that's what our protocol is when we lend someone something belonging to the Military. Da blagoslovit tebya Bog!" Alex raised an eyebrow and asked curiously– "Uh, what is that now?" "I said, May god bless you... All the best!" the Senior Gorba Commander replied, and waved his hand, and Alex and Gopiz saluted to him in return. He smiled even more at their gestures, and saluted them back. After saying goodbye Alex and Gopiz took their luggage bags, pod and backpack and boarded the armoured bus, followed by the remaining A05 Team's Gorbas boarding the same bus. "I'll order the Air Force comrades to bring you the Military Transport aircraft in which you can board and fly to India." the Senior Commander said to the A05 Team's leader, the junior Commander. They shaked hands and finally the junior Gorba Commander boarded the bus too. The doors shut and the armoured vehicle started moving. "Bro, wait! What about our helicar that we brought here?" Gopiz asked Alex worriedly, eager for an answer. "Ummmm..." Alex expressed, not sure what exactly to say while all Gorbas of the A05 Team looked at him, expecting an answer to be given to Gopiz. "We have a lot of helicars back there... Just, ditch this one." Alex replied, trying to act carefree while in reality he was just unsure what to say, and gave a random answer. Partially satisfied with his answer, Gopiz leaned back on his seat and sat comfortably.

Just within minutes, their armoured vehicle reached the centre of the Air Base over the concrete surface, where some military fighter jets and aircrafts were parked. And after a few subsequent seconds, the bus came to a halt, in front of an aircraft hangar that was more than twice as big as their ISRO Launch Base's UAVs hangar. Everyone stepped out of the bus, and stood on the paved concrete surface of the Air Base. "So, please specify the number of Military UAVs you'd require for your mission." the junior Gorba Commander asked Alex and Gopiz. "How many do you have?" Alex asked. "86, but only 81 of them are operational." the commander replied. Alex wasn't sure about the exact number of UAVs they needed this time. "If you could excuse us, we need a minute to discuss this amongst ourselves." Alex said. "Oh! No problem. Just try to make it fast." the Commander replied. While gesturing Gopiz to come closer to him, Alex walked a few steps away from other Gorbas. When Gopiz came to him, he asked– "What do you think? How many UAVs do we ask for this time?" "We used eleven UAVs last time. Just to make the chances of our success greater, we can consider doubling or even tripling the number." Gopiz replied. "Well, don't tell me what we CAN or CANNOT do. Tell me what is the best number of UAVs." Alex said, annoyed. "Alright. Tell them we want 25." Gopiz murmured. Alex confidently turned back to the Gorbas, walked to the commander and announced– "Sir, if you don't mind, we'd like to have 25 UAVs." "Uh… Let me confirm if we are allowed to give you that quantity." the Commander replied, and switched on his inbuilt microphone and called up the Senior Gorba Commander. The winds were blowing lightly as he talked and told the quantity to the Senior commander. Alex looked at Gopiz, and the atmosphere felt like slowing down, his heartbeats beating more loudly, because he felt that now they will deny lending this much quantity of Military UAVs. He smiled at Gopiz nervously, but suddenly heard the Senior Commander's voice– "Proceed!" from the inbuilt speaker of the junior Gorba commander who stood beside him. "Roger that sir!" the junior Commander replied, and commanded all the A05 Team's Gorbas to open up the UAVs hangar. The shutter gates of the modern and sleek hangar went up, and the lights turned on. Powerful and strong-looking Russian Military UAVs were parked in a proper arrangement in 5-7 rows. All the Gorbas immediately brought ladder-like elevating machines to each UAV, stood on them and reached the top of the wings of the aircrafts, and connected multiple charging cables to all the 25 UAVs, to ensure full batteries before letting them take off. All the processes and stuff took a while to complete, and Alex and Gopiz did nothing except staring at the Gorbas' hurried yet organized procedures of getting the UAVs ready for departure. When everything was ready, the Gorba commander approached Alex and asked– "Now, can you tell us the location of the airport or air base where you want the UAVs to land? We need to enter that location so the UAVs can automatically navigate to the destination." "Oh, right! Yeah, it's the ISRO Launch Base, near SpaceVillage, Northeastern Dravidia, India." Alex replied, and gave the location to the commander. "Copy that." the commander murmured and went back to the control panel in the UAVs hangar itself that controls all the UAVs and is used to enter the destination, program the UAVs, etc. Alex and Gopiz followed him and got closer to the control panel table too. "This control panel and stuff is more advanced than what we used in our Launch Base. Never thought I'd see such things in my lifespan!" Gopiz mumbled quietly, but Alex heard him and replied– "Same. And of course it's better than ISRO's technology. It doesn't matter even if India is the most richest and powerful country in the world, Russia has more advanced tech that they didn't expose to the world and kept it to themselves." And after a few minutes of electronic beeping, keyboards clacking, and machine processors whirring, the Gorbas operating the control panel turned to the commander, beside whom Alex and Gopiz were standing, and said– "Sir, destination and location successfully entered, and all systems are functioning as usual. Batteries are now fully charged of the 25 UAVs as well. We're ready for departure." "Alright, comrades!" the commander turned back to face Alex and Gopiz and exclaimed excitedly– "We're ready to fly the UAVs. Are you guys ready to watch them take off?" "Yes sir… Definitely!" Alex replied, enthusiastically. And subsequently, a Gorba sitting at the same control panel table immediately pressed a button, which started loud electronic whirring in a lot of UAVs, suddenly making the hangar too noisy to stay in. "You guys must go outside, the sound is often too loud inside the hangar due to the echo of electrical whirring of the aircrafts!" The Gorba commander instructed Alex and Gopiz by shouting loudly, to at least be heard by them. Alex gave a thumbs up and he and Gopiz got out of the hangar, and waited. One by one, the sleek, shiny, powerful-looking, and larger-than-ISRO's UAVs came out, took turns and taxied to the main runway of the Air Base. Finally, all the 25 UAVs lined up in the taxiway, one behind the other. As the Gorba commander came out of the hangar, he said– "So they're gonna take time to depart as the process will be one by one. Shall we get ready to depart on our own flight as well, using the other runway?" "Uh, okay! Let's do it." Alex agreed. The Gorba Commander once again used his inbuilt microphone and called up the Air Force pilots, ordering them to arrive with the Military Transport Aircraft at Camp 4, a specific place near another runway of the Air Base. "So, Sir, will all of us go now and the UAVs automatically take off on their own?" Alex asked, as he was still curious about the fully autonomous UAVs, while he and Gopiz had to manually control theirs. "Yes, of course! We have done all the setup and with no doubt these UAVs will now reach their destination, that is– Your Launch Base!" the commander replied. "That's kind of impossible, I mean, I never knew we could do so with such large aircrafts too!" Gopiz replied. "Well, if we can do it with cars, trains, helicars too, then why not large aircrafts like UAVs?" Alex replied, still in awe because of the advanced technology of Russian UAVs. They climbed back into their armoured bus, and when all the A05 Team's Gorbas boarded the bus after bringing the shutter gates of the UAVs hangar down, the driver closed the gates and started driving the bus. "Where to, Commander?" the driver asked. "Camp 4." replied the Gorba commander, and so the driver agreed and kept driving. "Alright, bud… Ready to go back to India? Your anxiety or whatever thing ends now?" Alex asked Gopiz, teasingly as Gopiz was quiet and worried all the time they both were in Russia, probably because of the risk Alex and he were undertaking. Gopiz smiled and nodded, still nervously. "We have arrived at Camp 4, sir!" the driver announced. "Thanks, comrade! After we deboard, you shall leave." the commander replied, and then gestured and called up all the entire team to stand up and get off the bus, after getting down himself. Alex and Gopiz too picked up their bags and luggage and got down the armoured bus, and while doing so, Alex saluted the bus driver Gorba, to which the Gorba smiled and saluted back, in respect. As Alex and Gopiz got down from the bus and put their feet on the asphalt-paved ground, they both got shocked to see the enormous, super-large, greyish-dark green coloured, and remarkable military transport plane, with its doors opened and a portable staircase placed to reach its doors which were at a height. "Beautiful!" Alex exclaimed. "Superb!" Gopiz murmured as well. "Presenting the Jumbo R78, an electric aircraft yet with capabilities which make it seem like a traditional jet engine aeroplane." The Gorba introduced the aircraft to them as they walked towards it with other Gorbas. The aircraft was parked and the Gorba pilots looked down through the cockpit windows and saluted the Gorba commander, and vice versa. Just as they were walking towards the staircase, Alex noticed behind and saw so many UAVs taking off into the sky one after another. "Hey look! The UAVs!" Alex pointed out to Gopiz. "Hmm. Wow." Gopiz replied, although not showing so much interest. Alex noticed Gopiz's this behaviour and felt that Gopiz's tenseness had to be ended one way or another. But for now, he continued walking with the A05 Team and the Gorba Commander.

"Hey, just give Gorba 166 and 187 your luggage and bags. They'll keep them in the cargo compartment, in the lower deck of the aircraft." the commander suggested Alex and Gopiz, before stepping up on the first stair of the portable staircase. Alex smiled and both of them handed over their bags, luggage and Gopiz's charging pod to the Gorbas, and they quickly ran to the lower deck opening, opened its hatch door, and kept the luggage inside the cargo compartment safely. After doing so, they closed the hatch, locked it and came back. And now, everyone began climbing up the staircase to the doors of the aircraft. Alex and Gopiz finally reached the end of the staircase after a minute or two, and because the door was at a height more than the height of usual planes' doors, climbing so many stairs made Alex pant and breathe heavily. When they entered the dimly lit yet beautiful interiors of the plane, one of the pilots came and handed two bottles of water to Alex. "Thank you so much sir! Really needed this. I really appreciate it." Alex thanked genuinely and heartfully. The plane's cabin looked quite like a business or first class cabin, and it was not at all how they showed in the movies– uncomfortable, filled with weapons and explosives and average seating and interiors. In fact, it really felt like it was some premium airline's aeroplane or something, rather than a military aircraft. The carpet flooring, leather seats with ACs, and square instead of circular windows– all this made Alex feel quite comfortable. Everyone had their seats and Gopiz of course sat beside Alex, giving Alex the window seat and he himself sitting in the aisle seat. Of course, being a military aircraft there were no announcements before the take off, but the flight began and the plane started moving, and taxied to the runway. Being the only operational aircraft in the entire Air Base, apart from the self-taking off UAVs on the other runway, Alex's flight didn't need a clearance to take off. So the plane reached the runway, took a 90-degree turn, and finally speeded up to take off. It was the first time Alex was sitting in a flight that was flown by robots or AI robots, as even in 2162, human pilots were used in flights for ensuring proper autopilot, operations and flight systems. But well, the Gorba pilots smoothly took off the plane, and soon the aircraft was high in the sky. Alex saw the tiny farms and buildings at the ground, and smiled– just like he always did while travelling in aeroplanes. Helicars although flew too, but didn't give the same feeling, as they didn't fly at altitudes as high as that of aeroplanes. "All good, comrades?" the Gorba Commander shouted from the front of the cabin, asking Alex and Gopiz. "Yes sir. Everything is pretty great!" Alex ensured. The flight took less time than the helicar did– 6 hours. Soon, when the plane started cruising high above the clouds, one of the Gorba robots of the A05 Team approached Alex and gave him a tray with food, having a proper meal like the ones Alex received in the military building's canteen hall. "Oh my– what is this, sir?" Alex asked, excitedly. "Our commander had brought you your breakfast for this morning. He told me to give it to you after we take off, since you didn't have your morning meal." the Gorba replied. This brought a smile on Alex's face. He thanked the Gorba, and the latter went back to his seat. Alex kept the tray on his lap and had his breakfast peacefully.

After he had his meal, he leaned back his seat a bit and slept, since there were hours remaining to reach India. He closed his eyes, and told Gopiz to wake him up if something happens or someone comes to their seat. But no one bothered both of them, and Alex woke up after 4 hours, somewhat covering up his last night's remaining sleep. He opened his eyes, noticed the time, and then saw the beautiful sky which had the sun going down towards the horizon. It was evening now and still around 2 hours were left. So he unlocked his phone and started watching Strings on Mesocia. Gopiz peeped into his smartphone, probably because he was trying to see the strings too. So Alex kept his phone in his right hand so both of them could see the strings comfortably. They did this for like more than 30 minutes, and laughed on funny strings, and watched other strings with curiosity. And while they were watching Alex's phone, the Gorba Commander came to their seats and stood in the aisle and said, "Hey comrades! Just 1 hour and some 20 minutes more for your ISRO Launch Base." Alex giggled excitedly and replied– "Haha... Yes sir." "Well I just came to ask you guys if you know the runway's length of that ISRO Launch Base because this plane takes a lot of it. So what's the length of the ISRO Launch Base runway?" the commander inquired. "It's around 14,500 metres." Gopiz replied. "Oh! That's more than double of what we need! Then it's definitely alright!" the commander exclaimed, and went back to his seat. "You're really kind of a knowledge bank!" Alex smiled and said to Gopiz. "Well... Not really a knowledge bank. I just know everything about ISRO and stuff related to it, but other things, I'm still exploring them and don't know everything so properly." replied Gopiz. "Still... And bro, promise me you'll be with me even after we find all the people. You'll be with me my entire life. Imagine, you're that important to me." Alex emotionally said. Gopiz wanted to say something but didn't, and just gave back a warm smile. Alex saw that too, and figured out that Gopiz's tenseness was still overcoming his normal self. So he decided to change the topic to something that's interesting and deep. "So, what do you think Gopiz? Is the universe everything? Or there's something beyond it?" Alex initiated a new conversation. "Um... Scientifically speaking, we have done wide research on neighbouring galaxies and their structures and features. But if you're talking about the entire universe, it's kind of hard to speak." Gopiz replied. "Yeah, but still... Don't think so scientifically, but explore hypothetical stuff and..." And Alex tried diverting Gopiz's attention from his own tenseness to the topic, by diving deep into it, and discussing every aspect that he could think of from the topic. Alex and Gopiz deliberated on this topic for all the remaining time that was remaining for the flight, and they finally put an end to that prolonged conversation just when they landed on the runway of their ISRO Launch Base. "Welcome back, bro!" Alex cheered to Gopiz as their plane landed and reduced its speed, while Gopiz just gave a faint smile. As the plane taxied towards the main complex buildings, the Gorba commander once again came to their seat. "Where do we park our aircraft?" he asked, hastily. "There is a section of open space especially for ultra-large aircrafts, just follow the red and green signs on the taxiway, they will direct you to that area." Gopiz replied to the commander. "Alright, I'll inform the pilots." the commander replied, and went. Through the windows of the plane, they also saw all the Russian UAVs parked in another open space of the Launch Base airport, in an organized manner. "They all have reached here too! Haha!" the Gorba commander said, happily. Finally after some more minutes of taxiing and taking a bunch of turns, the plane reached the wide and large space for ultra-large aircrafts with aircraft parking markings on its surface. It came to a stop after parking on one such marking, and then there was one issue– "How do we call up the portable staircase, for that someone had to be in the airport, but obviously there is no one here." the Gorba murmured, standing beside the seats of Alex and Gopiz. "I'll do it. I have flying capabilities, so you just open the plane door, and I'll bring one portable staircase to the aircraft." Gopiz replied, proudly. "You'll be able to do it? You sure?" the commander asked. "Definitely!" Gopiz replied. And so the commander told one of the Gorbas to open the aircraft's main front door, and Gopiz stood at the doorway's edge, and suddenly whooshed and flew straight to the area where there were aircraft ground-support vehicles, sat inside one of the self-propelled portable staircase vehicle, and brought the staircase to the aircraft, increased its height, and slowly attached it. "Yeah yeah yeah... That's it!" the commander yelled to Gopiz from the aircraft door, to tell him that the staircase was now attached to the plane's door. Everyone including the pilots finally got down the plane, and Gopiz came out of the cockpit of the portable staircase vehicle as well. He and Alex then directed everyone to the main complex building, which had their Mission Control Room. When they all finally reached and entered the main building, Alex proudly welcomed– "Alright Team A05! Gopiz and I, Alex, warmly welcome you to the beautiful ISRO Launch Base Complex. While we generally stay in the Mission Control Room and it is the room we generally plan our stuff in, you're free to set yourselves up, including setting up your chargers anywhere you feel like." The A05 Team of Gorbas was impressed with the hi-tech interiors of the ISRO building too, and looked everywhere in awe. "Pretty awesome, we must say!" the Gorba commander exclaimed and then continued– "We had no idea that even India had such an advanced complex just for space exploration and research! We'd like a place where there are a lot of sockets available, and a hall-like place for setting up our chargers and all. Do you have such a place?" "Yes, the Electrical Testing Hall. It's not literally a testing room for now, as it's newly built and set up, but it has plenty of open space and electrical sockets for your chargers and equipment." Gopiz replied. "Could you please guide us till there? We'll like to set up our chargers and equipment right away." the Gorba commander requested. Gopiz nodded yes, and took the entire team of Gorbas to the Electrical Testing Hall, which was just one corridor away from the Mission Control Room. Alex, who was now tired of travelling from one continent to another, went to the Mission Control Room, entered the hall through the stuck gates, and fell down on his mattress. It was 9 PM now, an additional 2 hours 30 minutes due to the time zone difference.

Minutes later, Gopiz came into the Mission Control Room too, took a chair and sat near Alex's mattress, facing him. "Everyone else is settled?" Alex asked Gopiz. "You can say that. I don't know why they've brought guns and weapons with their chargers to the same room they're settling in." Gopiz replied. "To kill us in case we fail. Lol!" Alex joked at the statement, and then also laughed and then said– "Just kidding, just kidding." "You shouldn't have struck the deal, brother." Gopiz expressed his thoughts, finally after days. "Why bro? What's the matter? Your face is showing that something's off, since days!" Alex also commented and asked. "We could have rejected their offer, gotten deported, and gone to China for Chinese UAVs, instead of risking getting killed." Gopiz said, clearly. "Well, Gopiz. I just did not want to make things more complicated and messy. So, I just saw the opportunity, and took it." Alex replied. "But didn't you notice that with this opportunity came the risk of dying? I mean, we could fail– there is that possibility!" Gopiz exclaimed, showing his anxiety. "Gopiz... IT'S SIMPLE. NO MATTER WHAT, WE'LL SUCCEED THIS TIME. I TRUST MYSELF, I TRUST YOU, I TRUST OUR SKILLS, I TRUST OUR DECISIONS. We'll succeed this time, and that's not something I hope, that's something I already KNOW." Alex replied, boldly and confidently. "Well, it's great. But also be realistic. You can die if we fail. And sure, if you think we will succeed, what if that 0.0001% becomes true and we fail?" Gopiz asked. "I was trying to die before as well, so I'd proudly die if that 0.0001% becomes true. I have no problem. And if it is about you, then you wouldn't have any use in an entirely empty world with just some military bots and no other humans. Plus you're recoverable as well, you have your memory, functions, and knowledge backed up in servers as well as your own chip. So you wouldn't TECHNICALLY die. And if we fail, I'd not be interested in living anymore anyway." Alex replied. "If that's the case, and you just want to surrender to our luck and results, then well, okay fine." Gopiz replied, agreeing to all that Alex said. "It's not just luck and results. It's also about the quality of our efforts and work and everything else we're going to put into making the Mepamas, testing them, and all other processes." Alex added. "Hmmm... Okay, I guess." Gopiz replied, now somewhat seeming more satisfied or calmer than before.

Suddenly, the Gorba Commander arrived and knocked on their non-operational sliding door (as it was stuck). "May I come in, comrades?" the commander asked. "Absolutely sir! You don't need to ask us for that." Alex replied, and the Gorba Commander entered the Mission Control Room, which was kind of a hall. "So look, I want to be honest with you both. Our Senior Commander has also given us additional instructions and now we will not only be ensuring the safety of our Military UAVs but also help you both in whatever your mission is, by helping you out in manufacturing, setting up, and whatever you need assistance in. So you know, it would be great if you could explain the entire objectives, mission and systems to the entire A05 Team together somewhere, so from tomorrow onwards we can help you both in your mission too." the Gorba Commander said. Alex turned happier to see that the A05 Team would help them in their manufacturing and setting up of the UAVs. It was indeed an extensive process, he knew that as he already did it all once. But seeing that now the entire Gorba squad would help them out, Alex felt even more relieved and motivated. "That's indeed wonderful, Sir! Even before we start the process, we'd like to thank you and Senior Gorba Commander wholeheartedly for your interest in helping us out! And yes, we both will explain everything to the entire A05 Team in the canteen hall, just a few steps away from here. Please bring everyone else to this room in 10 minutes, and then we'll go there." Alex thanked and told the Gorba Commander.

In those 10 minutes, Alex changed his clothes, went to the washroom, washed his face and tried to feel fresher. And then as he saw the Gorba Commander standing at the Mission Control Room's doors, he went along with Gopiz to them, greeted the Commander, and requested everyone to follow them both. They spent around 2 hours explaining each and every thing they have to do, including managing the 3D printing, assembly of giant Mepamas parts, integrating Circuit Boards, Microcontrollers and the power and signal systems, and even the mounting of Mepamas on the UAVs but this time with a twist– they discussed how they must minimize the impact of giant Mepamas vibrations or other effects on the UAVs, so they don't fail like last time. Many Gorbas came up with different ideas, each according to their own knowledge base based on their experiences and memories. And finally, they decided some great strategies to implement to reduce impact of Mepama Vibrations like Shock Absorption, More stabilized giant Mepama mounting structures, etc. And after a thorough discussion and deliberation, the entire A05 team returned to the hall they set up their chargers and equipment in and Alex and Gopiz went back to the Mission Control Room. After reaching there, Alex turned off the lights, got into his blanket and slept as it was around midnight, while Gopiz put his charging pod's plug into the socket in the same room, stepped into the pod, started charging himself and shutted down.

TWENTY-THREE
MANUFACTURING AGAIN!

It was not just the next morning that was busy, but all the subsequent mornings and entire days. Everyone, including the Gorbas of the A05 Team were working hard at the ISROEM Centre, using Transpoloop system for immediate transportation for themselves and even materials, and whatnot. Alex guided and sent a smaller group of 3-4 Gorbas to get diesel from the containers from that arid place Alex and Gopiz earlier went to, and a very robust manufacturing and assembly process went on for days, even more than a week. But obviously, no matter how advanced their planning and execution was, obstacles were inevitable. One such hindrance was when one day, one entire factory building's automated systems and robots stopped assembling the giant Mepamas' parts abruptly. "What's going on?!" Alex worriedly shouted and asked, entering the particular factory building after reaching there via the Transpoloop. "We're investigating the problem, Alex. But it seems that the automated systems have ceased working." one of the Gorba in charge of the factory monitoring replied. They brought the forklifts that had a ladder like equipment attached to it, and one of the Gorbas went high towards the ceiling using the forklift ladder. The reason he went to the ceiling was to investigate the robotic machines that stopped working and hung from the ceiling or roof. Gopiz watched all this, and then suddenly hovered and then flew to the ceiling too, assisting that Gorba robot. Gopiz flew and opened a large vent, and almost went inside it. "Gopiz! What are you doing?!" Alex screamed, confused as he saw Gopiz going into the duct. "I'm just going and checking the internal wiring issues. Lemme do it." Gopiz replied. "You sure that's safe?!" Alex asked, anxiously. "Yes, absolutely. The ducts are large and wide enough. I'll just see if there's a problem in the common internal circuitry or wiring of these automation machines." Gopiz replied, and went inside the ducts. For minutes, the Gorbas and Alex kept hearing voices of metal clanging as Gopiz walked and moved inside the metal ducts that included the wiring and circuitry. And finally, after minutes of clanging and moving inside the metal ducts, Gopiz came out of the vent, and flew down to where everyone was standing and waiting. "The Fuse. It's blown. Maybe unexpectedly too much current passed through the fuse wire, so it melted." Gopiz came back and reported. "UGH! Is there any solution? Maybe replace the Fuse wire or something?" Alex asked him. "Unfortunately, no. This fuse wire is imported as it is used for the circuitry of these automation robotic machines, and it's rarely found in India. Even if such a fuse might be in the country, we don't know where to find them." Gopiz replied. "FOR GOD'S SAKE! EVERYONE LEFT THE EARTH WITHOUT NOTICE AND NOW WE'RE FACING EVERY SINGLE FREAKING PROBLEM!!!" Alex shouted and expressed his frustration. "Calm down bro, it's not a big deal. The only solution is to abandon this factory building and shift all the Mepama parts and other important stuff to the adjacent factory building, and continue assembling and joining all that there." Gopiz replied. Alex sighed, because he had emotions of frustration, tiredness and anxiety. But the other Gorbas simply followed the instructions of Gopiz. Gopiz guided them all and helped them in taking the Mepamas parts to the other factory, and finally within an hour or two, they shifted all the things required for the assembling and remaining manufacturing to the other factory building. After everything happened, it was then that the Gorba Commander arrived, in the new building. "What's going on? I thought you comrades were in that factory building, but it's entirely empty!" the Commander asked. "Yeah sir. We had to shift everything to this building as the automation robotic machines and all that system stopped working." Gopiz replied, while Alex still sat on the chair, worried and sad despite the fact that the problem was now solved. "Oh well... I was monitoring other factory buildings, and I inspected each one of them. Everything else is good going!" the Commander replied.

After more days elapsed and the Mepamas were almost ready with all the power systems, signal receiving devices, microcontrollers, and diesel generators attached, it was Alex now who started to feel tense. He started feeling anxious. The progress was great, and the results of testing were amazing. The giant Mepamas were more powerful than before, with increased ranges as Gopiz and Gorbas took a lot of interest in testing the giant Mepamas from different distances, first 10 metres, then 20, 50, 100, 500 and even 1000 metres, that is a kilometre! And the Mepamas worked as expected, every time. When Alex should have been happy, he became more anxious day by day. It felt like a major dread had engulfed Alex entirely. Gopiz somewhat understood that the only thing that is to be worried about is the same thing he was worried about earlier, and hence, he also understood why Alex was tense. So one evening, after all the work for the day was done and the final giant Mepamas were transferred to the ISRO Launch Base via trucks, the Gorbas returned to their hall, while Alex and Gopiz returned to theirs. Alex was sitting on a chair, silently and deeply thinking about something. Alex was sitting beside a table, so he took a paper, wrote something on it, and kept the paper back on the table. "Pssst!" Gopiz heard a sound– it was Alex gesturing to him. He pointed towards the paper, and then gestured to him to read it. He then suddenly stood up, wore his shoes, and went to the washroom which was connected to the Mission Control Centre Hall– their hall itself. It was Alex's usual washroom, which he used everyday. Gopiz stood up from his chair, went to the table where the paper sheet was kept, and read– "I'm going to the washroom. Come inside the washroom to me."

"WHAT?!" Peter asked loudly, and Garima and Sandeep kept their hands on their lips, trying to hide their giggles and starting coughing, expressing disgust. "Uh, I think this is– Umm... A bit weird?" Rhea said. "William, we definitely don't record anything that is inappropriate because we're ourselves a junior journalism agency. You sure your story doesn't have anything inappropriate?" Aryan said , describing his agency's disclaimer. "GUYS! Come on! Why would I be so keen in telling you an inappropriate story?! Please, people! Stop judging the story before hearing it." William frustratingly replied. Aryan apologized, "We're sorry. Please continue!" "Thanks! So basically, Gopiz read Alex's message that he left on the table, and followed his instructions. He went inside the same washroom, and suddenly the door was shut and locked. "Bro. Why'd you call me in the washroom?!" Gopiz confusingly asked Alex. "Sshh!" Alex replied. "What?" Gopiz whispered and asked. "Look, even if we fail the day after tomorrow in our mission, I have a plan. Remember one extra giant Mepama we brought for final checks in our hall? In the Mission Control Centre room? We'll keep it there, aimed at the control panel only. So even if we fail, we can turn on the giant Mepama to activate its Magnetic Force, and pull all the Gorbas towards it and hold them together, not letting them go!" Alex slowly said, trying not to speak loudly so the voice didn't go outside the washroom. Gopiz looked in wonder at Alex's idea. "You're a genius!" Gopiz expressed, and continued– "Now you're thinking like the Alex I know! But wait, won't the Mepama's fuel get over in the end?" "What kind of Ultra Artificial Intelligence are you?!" Alex teasingly said and continued, "Bro logic! Mepama's diesel generator's fuel will run out, and so will the Gorbas' batteries! And they'll stop working after their batteries are over! And if the Mepama fuel gets over before their batteries, we'll refuel it! They'll be disarmed as we both have seen- they don't carry their guns or weapons regularly or usually. The last time they carried it was during our flight from Russia to here." "Wow! But did you plan this because you think we'll fail?" Gopiz replied. "No. I planned this because we are more likely to succeed in bringing IndWatch down this time, but less likely to keep the UAVs unharmed. According to my knowledge and prediction, most probably the after effects of Mepama Vibrations would be strong enough to destabilize the UAVs, but that would be much later after the satellite starts falling towards the ocean." Alex replied. "Alright, so you go outside first, otherwise if someone sees both of us coming outside of the washroom together, it can be suspicious. Just go outside, and cough once if there is no one nearby, so I can come out." Gopiz instructed. Alex agreed, got out of the washroom, went and sat back on his chair. He looked at the hall's door entrance, which also consisted of the partial view of the corridors too, and coughed once he confirmed that no Gorba was nearby. Gopiz came out of the washroom, went to his chair and sat on it. Now both Alex and Gopiz were relaxed, because they had planned and discussed an escape hatch just in case they harm the Russian Military UAVs.

TWENTY-FOUR
A Memorable Evening

The next morning came out, and today was the day of mounting the giant Mepamas on all UAVs. The process was even faster as now instead of just the automated robotic machines hanging from the ceiling, there were Gorbas that assisted in mounting the giant Mepamas correctly. They attached the Mepamas to the UAVs in the manner that they planned earlier, so as to keep the UAVs more stable and vibration-proof. They also used shock absorbers between the junction of the mounts and giant Mepamas, to further reduce vibrations. It took 8 hours, but after these hours of working so hard and quickly, everyone except Alex was tired, that is, their batteries became low. So after mounting the giant Mepamas on all the 25 Russian UAVs, all Gorbas headed back to their hall for charging, and even Gopiz required some charging. So for an additional 3 hours, there was no one Alex could talk to, as all the robots were charging. So Alex just sat on the asphalt surface of the runway of the Launch Base, and looked at the distant sea shore, and the tiny waves approaching, and then smashing against the beautiful beach sand. It was the time of sunset, and maybe the last evening of the Mystery of 'Where is Everyone', as tomorrow Alex just might find out where did everyone go. He had predictions already. He thought and reflected deeply– "It can't be that everyone just went to another place on earth. I am 90% sure that people have either escaped to outer space or something caused them to disappear. But I have had a strong intention since the beginning that whatever it is, it's related to space, because of those glowing lights above the clouds that I saw in the city CCTV cameras. And that's why I pursued the IndWatch Camera path, and not other ways of finding people. In fact, I don't know any other ways." He looked at the darkness spreading above the quiet distant ocean while thinking all this. The sun was setting behind the hilly mountains, on the opposite side of the ocean. "Without SpaceVillage, ISRO Launch Base, Gopiz, UAVs, Mepamas, Knowledge of Science and Engineering, etc. I wouldn't have come so far. But yes, all these were blessings. The blessing of the one above, the God, if they are present. God, what game are you playing? We all were your creations, and you disappeared your own creations? And if you did, why not me? You forgot me? Or you wanted to punish me? I think the latter is the correct one." Alex was thinking all this deeply. Suddenly, someone kept a hand on him, and he immediately looked behind and screamed. "Hey! Why are you doubting God? This is something you have to go through. It's the Path!" the soul-like, peaceful, smiling and transparent figure said. "Aaaaa! WHO ARE YOU?!" Alex shouted and asked. "Bro! It's me! Gopiz! I just came back after fully charging." Gopiz replied. "Oh frick! It was my imagination. What the heck?" Alex murmured. "Uh, what?" Gopiz asked. "Oh, well nothing! Where are the Gorbas?" "They're still charging... Their charging pods charge them more slowly." Gopiz replied. "Charging slowly... CHARGING SLOWLY?!" Alex exclaimed, and suddenly a malicious smile appeared on his face. "Gopiz, you can fly right? Can you fly very quickly?" Alex asked. "Uh... Yeah?" "Go and disconnect their charging pods from the power sockets. This way, they'll stop charging and lose battery! And they'll be discharged anyways! Mission Accomplished!" Alex excitedly said. "What kind of a logical human are you?" This time Gopiz said teasingly and then added— "Even if I disconnect their charging pods from the power sockets right now, won't they still have the remaining battery? Yes, they won't charge more, but their remaining battery would turn them on, and they would notice me disconnecting their charging pods, maybe kill me, and insert their plugs back into the sockets." "Good night!" Alex said, rolled his eyes funnily and turned his back towards Gopiz, after getting logically proven wrong. "LOL! Anyways, come on, our plan for tomorrow is anyway foolproof. So chill!" Gopiz tried cheering up Alex, and both of them were sitting on the paved surface of the Runway. Then they both turned and started looking at the whole fleet of Russian UAVs with strategically mounted giant Mepamas. "They look so beautiful!" Gopiz expressed. "They'll be proven beautiful if they bring the IndWatch down successfully tomorrow!" Alex said back. Gopiz's digital eyes looked into Alex's Eyes, and then Gopiz said by patting on Alex's back, "We'll succeed bro... Yes, our struggle will finally be over!" Alex smiled in return, and replied, "Hopefully yes!" And then continuing to sit on the asphalt surface of the runway, they watched the UAVs and the sun that had now set behind the mountains.

Gorbas were equally enthusiastic about tomorrow's Pulldown. After Alex and Gopiz returned to the main building, they met the A05 Team and the Gorba Commander suggested that we should have a barbeque party, even just for Alex as he is the only one who could eat. Alex tried turning down the offer but the Gorbas and even Gopiz insisted. It seemed like they wanted to make Alex more confident about tomorrow, and it was a wonder that even the Gorbas had the sense of feeling that someone is supposed to be cheered up to reduce their stress. Alex felt sad, that while he planned to deceive the Gorbas just in case the UAVs get harmed tomorrow, the Gorbas wished that he gets successful in the Pulldown and also tried to cheer him up by setting up a dinner for him. They went to the Canteen Kitchen, brought out some Paneer and Sweet Potatoes from the Refrigerator, applied some sauces on it that they found, and attached them to the barbeque grill sticks. "Where did you get this Barbeque Grill and Sticks from?" Alex asked. "One of us secretly went to the SpaceVillage and got this from a store. We all wanted to give you a nice and happening dinner before the day of your Mission." Gorba Commander replied, smiling. "And where did you get charcoal from?" Alex asked confusingly. "Uh… That too from SpaceVillage? Yes, the same shop." another Gorba replied. The commander kept ordering all the other Gorbas to make things ready for the barbeque dinner, and told Alex and Gopiz to wait outside for the surprise, in a green grass area surrounded by Launch Base Airport taxiways and runways. That grass area was a great location for a dinner because cool and pleasant winds blew there, the distant sea was visible, and the whole atmosphere and vibe was great. The grass area was a 5 minutes walk from their main building, so at first only Alex and Gopiz went there alone. "You know I don't feel so nice about it. They're doing so much for me, for us. And here we are planning ways to trap them and stuff." Alex said, with a disappointed face. "Bro, don't be so emotional. They are just robots, like me!" Gopiz replied, taking it easy. "Still, I really wish that the UAVs end up being safe, because I don't want to become the villain for these Gorbas." Alex said. "Alex, who's the villain actually? Them! They're the ones who threatened to kill us if we mess up." Gopiz gave a logical reply. "Yeah, but deep down, they don't want to kill us. I understand that they're robots, emotions are impossible. But whatever AI experiences they have with us, makes them want to help and assist us, not kill us. Look at them now, they're setting up an entire ambient dinner for us now!" Alex exclaimed, full of mixed emotions, and then added– "I just wish that God forbid, but even if we fail in bringing the IndWatch down tomorrow, the UAVs remain safe, so do we and so does their faith in us." Gopiz didn't say anything else after that, and then they finally reached the green grass space, after the 5-minute walk. They saw the beautiful full moon, and the dark clouds covering some parts of it. And just after some time, the full Gorbas A05 Team came out of the main building and Alex and Gopiz could see them coming towards both of them, with large containers, chairs, boxes, lamps, a packet of containers, and even a music speakers set! "Just look at their celebration... They're doing so much, just to make us motivated and confident about tomorrow's Pulldown. You'd want to break promises with such beautiful beings?" Alex murmured quietly to Gopiz, while they were still far away but approaching them. "Beings? They and even I are robots. Not living beings!" Gopiz replied. "Entities? That works?" Alex further replied, being annoyed.

Finally, the Gorbas reached the green grass area, set up the chairs, the barbeque grill, boxes, lamps and the music speakers, and finally the place was ready for a calm and great evening. Everyone took their seats, and two of the Gorbas opened the large containers that had the barbeque sticks with Paneer and Sweet Potatoes, lightened up the charcoal, and kept the barbeque sticks on the heated grill. "Alright, let's play a game, shall we comrades?" the Gorba Commander said. "Sure! I and Gopiz would love to!" Alex smiled and replied enthusiastically. "Well, then... It's called the RockThrow. While 2 of the Gorbas are busy handling the barbeque grill, the rest of us would make three groups of 5 each. And we have colored pebbles with us in one of our boxes. Each one would throw a pebble as far as we can, and the one whose pebble is the least far, will have to tell a story of their life experience, a memory, or anything like that. And then the next group does the same. It's a nice and active game to learn more about each other." the Gorba commander explained. "Sounds interesting!" Gopiz replied, interestedly. "Yeah, it is. But you all are robots, and of course you have greater strength than me!" Alex replied. "Hahaha... I can't argue with that! Yes, you're right. So what we need to do is reduce ourselves to be almost equal to your strength." the commander replied. "And how will you exactly do that?" Alex asked. "Pick up one of these pebbles, and throw as far as you can." the commander said. Alex picked up a green coloured pebble that fitted in his hand perfectly, lifted his hand backwards, and threw the pebble to a distance. "Done, I guess?" Alex said. "Gorba 556, go and measure the distance from the point he stood at." the commander told one of the Gorbas. "No worries! Leave it to me– I'll simply scan it!" Gopiz replied, flexing his technological advancements. Gopiz beeped for some seconds, and then informed– "That's 8.7 Metres." "Sweet! That was fast!" Gorba 556 exclaimed. "Yeah! This ability is amazing!" the commander agreed too. "Well, I use ISRO-manufactured technologies so yup!" Gopiz smiled and replied. Meanwhile Alex sat back down after throwing. "So, 8.7 metres... What's your age, height and weight, Alex?" the commander then asked. "13, and ummm... If you don't mind can I whisper it to you only?" Alex asked. "Why not! Tell it just to me then." the commander replied. Even though Alex was not overweight or underweight, for himself he was unfit, and of a lesser height too though he was fairly tall as well. So he went to the Gorba Commander, went close to his microphone ears, and whispered the details. "Alright! Listen up all Gorbas! Reduce your Ability Level to 7.561 arues and set the settings to reset the ability level to current one at midnight!" the commander ordered everyone. "Done!" "Donee..." "Ok sir!" "Copy that." "Done successfully!" all the Gorbas replied back after doing so. "What are arues?" Alex asked the Gorba Commander. "It's a measurement unit that we use for our ability levels. Now that we're reduced to 7.561 arues, we approximately match your levels of ability, in strength, thinking, everything!" the commander replied. "But there's one problem, Gopiz won't be able to do this... Can he?" the commander asked. "Well, he can't but it's alright. I anyways don't think he can do better than me. So I have no problem." Alex teasingly said. "Huh!" Gopiz replied. "Alright then, let's start the game!" The 2 Gorbas were managing the barbeque grill, and the others, along with the Commander, Alex and Gopiz, made three groups of five each. Light party music was being played in the background, and the first group, in which everyone were Gorbas, stood up, picked one pebble each of different colours, and started throwing their pebbles one by one. "Awww noo!" the Gorba whose pebble reached the least farthest exclaimed. "Alright Gorba 556, your turn. Tell all of us some experience or memory of yours." the commander said, gesturing all those Gorbas of the group to sit back down on their chairs. "Sure sir! Thank you for the opportunity. So I'm Gorba 556 and I currently serve in the Moskva Military Base. However, I was also sent for a special mission 3 years ago in Siberian forests. However sir, this is a classified experience according to our common network database. Shall I proceed or tell something else?" the Gorba asked. The commander hesitated, and then replied– "Just tell, it's okay. It's not like they'll spread the information. I trust them, and anyways, who else will they tell this to?!" "Okay sir. So we were sent by our Original Human Military

Commander, Sir Dimitri Antonov, to the Siberian Forests to track down and destroy a rebel camp in the forests. Those rebels were separatists that wanted to separate the whole of Siberia from Russia. It was a very important mission, and to prevent human soldiers from being harmed, we were sent as substitutes. So it was 4:00 AM in the morning, and I was in the armoured bus with my other Gorba teammates. We were discussing the strategy for the siege operation on their camp. We had taken rocket launchers and major weapons and guns for this mission too. We had clear orders to shoot at sight, because anyone in that camp was either a part of that separatist group, or associated with them, and both of these were our enemies. So coming back to the story, it was early morning and our armoured bus was heading to the region where the camp was situated. We couldn't see anything except the lights of our own armoured vehicles motorcade. Minutes later, our bus stopped, and on our built-in communication system, we heard some strict instructions from the Gorbas in the bus just ahead of us. They said– No matter what, don't step out of the VEHICLE! At first it was unclear to us what was wrong, but then, we saw a massive group of elephant-like creatures, or to be very clear... Mammoths– the extinct elephants, marching towards our armoured buses. Now no matter how bulletproof our armoured buses were, those giant Mammoths would've crushed us mercilessly!" the Gorba told a part of his story. "No way! Mammoths? I know a lot about them!" Alex exclaimed in surprise. "Wow! But it's strange, weren't they extinct? So how did they appear so suddenly?" Gopiz asked. The Gorba who was telling the story replied and continued– "Hahaha... You both are so deeply interested in the story! I appreciate your attention. But yes, how did Mammoths suddenly appear out of nowhere... Turned out, those were holographic projections, to scare us away. As we threw some grenades near those approaching Mammoths, nothing else happened except a digital distortion, and as soon as we looked closer, we realized that a remote controlled hologram projector was being used to scare us away. We immediately lifted it, and destroyed it, and continued with our journey! We reached the Separatists' main camp, blasted the hell out there, and forced everyone in it to surrender!" the Gorba finished with his story. "Aww man! I thought they were Mammoths for real!" Alex expressed his minor sadness. "But still, it's an interesting story because holographic projections are often super realistic, and it would've felt real anyway!" Gopiz replied. "Yes, it's indeed an interesting story, Gorba 556! Thank you for your narration." the Gorba Commander said. It was completely a night sky above now, with beautiful stars glittering and shining bright. The second group stood up, the Gorbas picked up one pebble beach, and began throwing them at great distances. "Yooo! Gorba 187! You're the person with the least distance! Alright, so tell us a story now." the Commander teasingly said. The second group's Gorbas came back and sat down, and meanwhile, the barbeque starters were ready for Alex. "Here you go, Alex!" one of the 2 Gorbas making the barbeque starters said while handing the plate with roasted paneer and sweet potatoes to Alex. "Thank you so much!" Alex smiled and replied. Gorba 187 came back to his chair and sat down. "Alright, so this is more of a funny story of me and my Gorba friends from my previous posting in Petersburg. We, together with our that group's commander, went to a pizza restaurant. Because our that group's commander was a human, he wanted a pizza from that restaurant. However, when we entered the restaurant and he was choosing the pizza from the menu, he pointed out and asked about a specific pizza, which had the heading– The Most Expensive Pizza in Russia. The person on the counter hesitated in answering and then called the restaurant owner. The owner was very boastful and offensive. He made a lot of derogatory comments to our Commander, mockingly calling him a Military Servant and a person who cannot even afford the expensive pizza in his thoughts or dreams. We all stormed out of the pizza restaurant, and our commander was filled with anger, seeking vengeance. We first went back to our armoured vehicle, but as we were about to sit inside the vehicle, our human commander, Ivan, who had been insulted by the pizza shop owner, ordered us to go and threaten the owner with guns to force him to make those most expensive pizzas in Russia, and that too not just two or three, but 100 of them, for completely free!" Gorba 187 told. "Whoa! Won't that be illegal?" Alex exclaimed. "Everything is fair in love and war, comrade!" the Commander said, teasingly. "That's a very very old statement, I think." Gopiz said. "Yeah, I heard of it in my history lectures, that people used to say this in the early years of the previous century..." Alex replied and then asked Gorba 187– "Anyways, what happened after that?" "Well, we took our Broa71 rifles, bursted into the pizza shop, and two-three people screamed seeing us aggressively bring guns into the public place. We went to the counter person, and pointed guns on his head, asking him to call the restaurant owner. This time, the restaurant owner acted like the kindest person on earth, and when we threatened him and told him to make 100 of those most expensive pizzas in Russia for free, he pleaded us to leave him otherwise he'd have to face major losses. We didn't compromise, and he spent like 4 hours making those most expensive pizzas of the country. When we finally brought them to our armoured vehicle, and finally the last pizza to our commander Ivan, he didn't like the weird sauces and taste of that so-called Most Expensive Pizza, and told the driver Gorba to take our vehicle to the Mir Refugee Camp– a camp with people with poor conditions and bad living standards. As our vehicle entered that densely populated Refugee Camp, those kids with ugly clothes but beautiful eyes stared at us confusingly, those people also watched our vehicle from a distance. Suddenly, Sir Ivan told the driver to stop the vehicle, and we stood in the middle of a narrow road, with refugee camp poorly constructed houses on both sides of the road, with children playing with wooden sticks and sand. Sir Ivan got out of the vehicle, opened up the storage trunk and one by one started giving out pizza boxes for free to all those refugee people. In fact, after everyone got a pizza box, still 9 boxes were remaining, and the commander gave away those pizza boxes too. So although we did something unlawful that day, even though we're Artificially built Intelligences, or just robots, I personally felt a sense of goodness that day!" Gorba finished with his story. And everyone listening clapped, including Alex and Gopiz. "Such a wonderful person." said Alex. "Yes, even I met him once. He is a pure gem!" the Gorba commander commented. Alex had finished his starters' first round so quickly while listening to the story, and he had no idea when the Gorbas who worked on the barbeque grill gave him another plate in his hands. "Wow, I– I literally finished it already and got another plate!" Alex exclaimed, giggling and laughing at the intensity of his attention he was actively listening to the story with. "Alright, so the final Round? Alex, keep the plate for a minute, let's just throw the pebbles and then you can continue eating." the commander suggested. "Sure!" Alex replied, stood up and kept the plate on his chair. All five of them threw the rocks one by one, and finally when it was Alex's chance, he lifted his hand backwards and threw the pebble with a force, but oops! The pebble instead of travelling forward, travelled upwards and fell down just in front of Alex, that too just half metre away. "LOL! Alex, remember you said that I couldn't do better than you? Who's laughing now?!" Gopiz shouted teasingly to Alex. Alex stared at Gopiz, and laughed at his own stupid throw. Everyone came back to their seats and sat comfortably. The barbeque stuff was over now and the 2 Gorbas now shut down the grill. "So, Alex! It's your turn now... What do you have for all of us?" the Gorba commander asked. Alex nervously smiled and thought for a while. And finally he got an idea, recalling an incident he went through in his past. "So, this is literally the story of the time I was just 7 years old, and my Mom took me to a mall. It might sound weird, but I was scared of AI and robots back then, despite the majority of the world being functional because of them. No offense, but they looked scary to me back then." Alex gave out the context. "No way! You mean if you were 7 years old and you would've met us, you would've freaked out?" Gopiz asked, being very astonished. "Uh, yes. Literally I would have screamed like I saw a dinosaur or something. But well, this story is about the turning point of my fear of robots and automated stuff. So my Mom bought me a cheesecake pastry and I was happily walking with her while eating it at the same time. However, as my Mom and I stepped inside an elevator, my Mom saw something that captivated her, probably some clothing store she was trying to find and stepped out thinking that I was still following her. And I realized seconds later, that my Mom remained out of the elevator, while I was inside the elevator, all alone except the fact that I was accompanied by a tall, muscular robot. The elevator's doors closed! And I shouted– Mommmm! And she must've realized that I got left inside the elevator, and the elevator started going upwards. Also unfortunately, the elevator stopped abruptly, as the power supply stopped due to unexpected reasons. And I looked up to my right side, and the muscular dark gray tall robot, who looked somewhat like you all my Gorba comrades, and that robot with large blue digital eyes on his LCD display, said to me in a robotic yet kind way with a smile– Hello, kid! And I shouted– Aaaaaaaaaaaaa! And my fear was so so strong that I hurt myself by running and bumping with the elevator metal walls, and the elevator was still stopped, with no lights. I panicked even more and so much that my pastry fell off my hands on the elevator's floor. 'Are you alright?' the robot asked me kindly, knowing that something was wrong, but its voice made me even more terrified. I banged the elevator's door rapidly and then I started crying as I saw blood coming out of my hands and my forehead, as I bumped these with elevator walls and doors. And I started crying so much that eventually, I fainted." Alex told. "Now that's some very abnormal behaviour, after all we're not some demons or ghosts– we're just robots!" one of the Gorba said. "Totally, bro who hurts their own hands?!" Gopiz exclaimed. "I know I know guys... It was stupid, but I don't know why I feared robots back then. But well, I am not finished! When I woke up, I noticed that the elevator was still stopped, with no lights. But strangely, there was bright light falling on me, which was not there before. I soon realized that the robot that scared the hell out of me, itself was working on me and treating my injuries on my hands and forehead, and put bandages on the respective wounds. That bright light was coming from nowhere else but the robot's built-in torchlight! So this made my fear of robots go away, and I quickly hugged that robot, feeling insecure of being stuck in the dark elevator for a long time. That robot all patted on my back, hugged and comforted me. 'It's going to be okay, kid! Don't you worry... You'll find your Mom!' the robot said to me. And these kind words were the turning point, transforming my fear of robots into a Love for Robots! He even gave me a packaged water bottle that he had in his mini-storage compartment. And finally after half an hour of being trapped in that small elevator, the power supply came back, the elevator went back to the ground floor and the doors opened, my Mom standing there with tears in her eyes because she left me alone. She hugged me as I came out, and asked me about those injuries and bandages. I told her that my extreme fear of robots got me wounded on my hands and forehead, but this kind robot helped me by putting bandages on these wounds and comforting me. My Mom genuinely thanked the robot, and others who helped her to get me out of the elevator after the power came back. One of the mall's managers came and apologized to my Mother for the power outage, and informed her that the robot I was trapped with was faulty and was malfunctioning. It was a nurse robot, which was generally used in Hospitals but as it was not working properly, he was sent to the mall robotics store. And that the manager himself was sorry in case of any inconvenience. And before we left for home, I shouted and asked the robot its name... He replied– Genesis! And to me, that robot was not faulty at all– he was a life changer for me!" Alex finished with his story, and a huge round of appreciation, clapping and hooting in approval was witnessed by Alex as all the Gorbas, including the commander and Gopiz loved the story. "Amazing story! I personally loved it." commented Gopiz. "Alright so it's almost 9 PM now... Let's head back to the main building, because tomorrow is a big day for all of us, we have to unveil the mystery!" the Gorba commander suggested. All the Gorbas started packing up all the stuff, and when Alex and Gopiz tried helping by picking up their chairs, speakers and other stuff, the commander ordered them– "NO! You will not do anything. This party was for you guys organised by us. So we'll be the one setting and wrapping it up." Alex and Gopiz smiled and left their chairs and other things they were trying to take back to the main building, and all the other Gorbas picked up the stuff and followed Alex and Gopiz back to the main building.

Finally, everyone settled for the night and Alex wore his night suit–comfortable and soft T-shirt and pyjamas. He said Good Night to the Gorbas and thanked them for a memorable evening, and came back to the Mission Control Centre Room. Gopiz was sitting there, reading a book titled– 'How to Become More Human - For Robots' Alex laughed at him and said, "Bro... Why become a human? If I were you, I'd be proud of myself." "I don't know, I don't like myself. My artificial soul, and weird limitations and stuff I don't even 'feel', because I can't feel; I can only detect!" Gopiz replied, with a sad face. "The fact that you realize your limitations and are 'irritated' by them itself is a feeling brother! Robots can feel, you just feel slightly differently!" Alex smiled and said. And Alex trying to prove his point, politely argued with Gopiz for quite some time, and when Gopiz actually realized or concluded that he too had 'feelings' due to his personal judgements and inferences leading his neural network software to behave a certain way, Gopiz finally agreed with Alex. It was around 11:30 PM at night, and both of them agreed to the urgency of sleeping now as tomorrow was a big day. Perhaps a day that could change the direction of their main mission- to find everyone, or maybe even reveal the truth about what happened to everyone. The crickets and different insects were chittering and making light sounds, and Alex felt the cool sea breeze's slight winds coming inside the Control Room–where they were getting ready to sleep– through the empty space of the window pane that Alex broke many days ago. Those winds were maybe signs of upcoming relaxation after a long journey and adventure they both experienced, or perhaps a symbol of reinforcement by calming them down– Alex thought. Whatever those calm, cool yet comfortable slight breezes meant, Alex was feeling an overall feeling of achievement. Not absent-mindedly, but as he reflected deeply, he took a chair from a table and put it right in front of that window pane-less opening through which winds were coming in. He then sat on that chair, with the cool air blowing against his slightly pink cheeks, and now he was feeling a sense of pride of the journey he had undertaken till now, the progress he made, and the 'Alex' he had become in the journey. He imagined– "If finally I find everyone and everyone comes back to this world due to my efforts, I'd be called a super expert– a thirteen year old boy who has worked so much on massive-scale manufacturing, physics, engineering, computer modelling and what not. All those calculations that my peers could not and will not be able to do, would be done by me alone! People would ask for mentorship from me, I'd be given the honour and fame no other kid would have ever gotten till this age. The President might even give me the Honour of Excellence or National Ratna Award! I'd not just be Alex, but Alex... The boy who brought everyone back to the world, went through so many diverse experiences, challenges, obstacles, went to foreign lands, yet he had the resilience to rise up back and accomplish his goal of finding everyone–" Suddenly Gopiz interrupted by throwing a pillow on Alex's head, standing behind him while he was facing the wind blowing past his face through the opening in the windows. "Oww! Gopiz is that you? How dare you?!" Alex screamed, though lightly and in a humorous way as he knew Gopiz's intention was similar. Gopiz laughed and replied, "Bro it's just a few minutes to midnight. Stop dreaming while you're awake and time to see dreams in your sleep!" Alex threw the pillow back at Gopiz just for fun, and they both started a funny and cute pillow fight against each other. Finally when the digital wall clock showed the time as 12:00 AM and beeped, Alex wished Gopiz good night and the latter went to his charging station and started charging himself, and the former switched off the lights, lay down on his comfortable thick mattress, got inside a blanket and slept after a thoughtful day.

TWENTY-FIVE
THE FINAL PULLDOWN

And finally, the sun of the day of the Pulldown that was awaited, rose above the sea, filling the entire sky with pink and mainly blue hues. Despite sleeping late, Alex woke up early, at 7:30 AM. He was out, on the asphalt aircraft parking, sipping a coffee he got from ChefMate. But this time Gopiz took long to charge himself up again too, and while he and other Gorbas were still charging, the Gorba Commander became awake, and came to Alex. Alex waved to the Commander as he was approaching Alex, but the Gorba Commander seemed unusually stressed. He came to Alex, put his mechanical hand on Alex's shoulder, and walked with him and said, "Comrade, at first Good Morning and may God bless you for your mission. However, as per our deal and our army protocols, we must remain in accordance with our demands as before. If any harm happens to our UAVs, especially crashing or total destruction, we'd have no option but to terminate you and your robot friend, Gopiz." Alex gulped, hesitated a bit, but knew that he was no less smart too, and had an escape hatch plan that he discussed with Gopiz, just in case. "Sir, we respect our commitment to the deal as well, and agree to follow the terms responsibly." Alex replied, obviously faking it but showing his assurance to the Commander. The Gorba Commander smiled and hugged Alex, as if the robot doesn't want to harm the kid, but has no other choice if he fails. Alex also remained stunned. He did not expect the Gorba Commander to act this way. He too realized that deep down the Commander wished that he succeeds in the Pulldown, so he and Gopiz aren't harmed. They both returned to the main building and the Gorba Team and Gopiz woke up now. It was just a matter of ten minutes of chaos, but all of them prepared themselves and got their respective seats in the Mission Control Centre Room. Once again, Gopiz turned on the

IndWatch Satellite statistics and information on the large computer screen, and extracted its location. "Currently over North Africa. Will take some time. Reducing Speed and Altitude now." Gopiz announced. "Copy that." one of the Gorba replied, who was assisting Alex in commanding the 25 Military UAVs with fully-fueled up Mepamas using the special Military Computer, that was used to give commands and instructions to the UAVs. That Gorba and Alex together worked out a predetermined route for the UAVs fleet to cover such that their trajectory intersects the line of IndWatch Satellite's orbit path. All the other Gorbas were standing behind the four chairs on which Alex, Gopiz and two Gorbas assisting both of them were sitting. Unaware of the extra giant Mepama kept behind them, the Gorbas looked at the large television-like screens in the front that showed the satellite and UAVs statistics and camera footage. The UAV fleet's route was set to intersect the satellite's path and then after taking a U-turn safely, land back on the ISRO Launch Base, one after another. After the UAV fleet's route was successfully planned, Alex looked at Gopiz, Gopiz started with hopeful digital eyes back at him, nodded and smiled, and Gopiz pulled the lever that reduced the speed and altitude of the IndWatch satellite. The satellite lowered into the orbit with the lowest altitude possible, still many kilometres high and very much above the clouds. Alex and the Gorba commanded the UAVs to take off, and one by one, the UAV fleet's cameras' live streaming showed each of the Military UAV taking off high in the sky, and within 3 minutes, all the 25 UAVs were flying high in the sky, in a more powerful formation.

Minutes passed by, and Gopiz instructed Alex to lower the speed of the UAV Fleet because the satellite was coming slowly and was taking more time to reach at the intersecting point. While the Gorba helped Alex in doing so, Gopiz announced the location of the satellite at that point of time– "Exactly above the Gulf of Gujeneras." Which was actually the Gulf of Gujarat, or what we call today– Gulf of Khambhat. Just after some 200 or 300 seconds, Gopiz immediately jumped out of his seat out of excitement and exclaimed– "Quick quick quick quick! Alright, only 80 seconds to reach the intersection point. Speed up the UAVs; switch on the Mepamas." Alex pulled another lever, which sent signals far away to the giant Mepamas on the UAVs and turned all those hundreds of Mepamas on. "Oh God... Please bless us!" Alex murmured as his lips started remembering god's and his parents' names. "30 seconds!" Gopiz shouted, ready to witness– either a miracle or a disaster. The large screen showed the satellite's and UAVs' camera live footage, and the satellite's camera showed the clouds deep down below over the ocean, while the same clouds were seen just immediately below the UAVs, through their own cameras. "Activate the Mepamas!" Gopiz shouted. "Doing it!" Alex replied in confidence, and pushed the Activating button. Once again, the massive vibrations started to be observed in cameras, but unlike the previous regular UAVs, these UAVs somewhat managed to overcome the forces of vibration of Mepamas. Now instead the aggression of vibration was seen on the IndWatch satellite. The satellite's camera displayed that the satellite felt slight shaking, and then immediately it felt like massive energy causing it to disrupt its smooth orbiting. "It's happening... IT'S HAPPENING!" Gopiz exclaimed, in laughter and awe. "Wait for it. Come on, it must happen!" the Gorba Commander mumbled, standing behind the chairs and staring at the large screen showing the camera footage. And 'Whrooommmshheeddd!' The Satellite immediately fell off its orbit, as if something made it forget its own role and pulled it as if through a magical giant hand, but it were the Giant Mepamas in action. The IndWatch's statistics screen showed a rapidly decreasing altitude display– "15 km... 12 km... 11 km... 8.7 km... 7.4 km...." "Alright, Alex, swap up quick!" Gopiz called him, gesturing him to transfer roles and let Gopiz do the hard part now– bring the UAVs back safe and sound. Alex reached out the Satellite control panel and Gopiz directed him– "As soon as the altitude reaches 1km, immediately open this cap cover and push this large blue button. This will deploy the parachutes and oceanic landing floatables." Alex said okay, and kept his eyes directly at the falling altitude numbers. Gopiz immediately opened the UAVs Control tab on the Military Computer, and checked the stats of the UAV fleet. He then immediately deactivated the giant Mepamas as their work was done now. But well... Nothing comes so easy... The thing that bothered Alex and Gopiz for long, happened– the Military UAVs came at stake! All the UAVs' camera footage suddenly turned into 'No Signal' screens with nothing but noise. Gopiz noticed the Gorba Commander making a frustrating face, and then gesturing to one of the Gorbas, and the Gorba about to leave the Control room– inferring that he is going to get firearms for their death penalty. "Hold on, sir! It's not over... IT'S NOT OVER... TRUST US!" Gopiz shouted to the Gorba Commander, trying to distract him and with that, the Gorba trying to get out of the room stopped too. Alex then said, diverting Commander's attention to the left side where Alex was, saying– "Yes sir! It's not known for sure whether the UAVs are harmed. Just wait and when you confirm, then you can go ahead and fulfil the terms of the deal." While Alex said this, Gopiz slowly and covertly reached the giant Mepama kept facing towards the backs of the Gorbas, and got it ready to turn on. But it wasn't needed! A MIRACLE– LITERALLY A MAGICAL PHENOMENON GOPIZ AND ALEX DIDN'T EXPECT– OCCURRED. The noisy 'No Signal' screens unexpectedly turned back into live streamings, and all the cameras of the UAVs were just perfectly fine, the only thing worth observing was that those UAV cameras showed that the fleet just came out of a dense cloud, as the last foggy traces of clouds were being seen. Gopiz ran to the UAVs Map tracking and confirmed the fact that there were no signals because the aircrafts went into a very dense and large cloud, and assured everyone that the UAVs are okay, even after the Mepamas' work was done! "WOOHOOOO!" the same Gorba Commander shouted in happiness and joy. The only thing left was the speedily falling IndWatch Satellite. "3.2 Km... 2.7 km... 2.1 km... 1.8... 1.7.... 1.6.... 1.5...." Gopiz kept murmuring the countdown. "1.2... 1.1!!! AND NOW! PUSH THE BUTTON!" Gopiz shouted in thrill. Alex tried opening the plastic cap cover of the button, but he took too many seconds... "WHAT THE HELL BRO???!!!" Gopiz screamed, pushed him away from the button violently and went, opened and unlocked the plastic cap cover of the button himself, and then pushed the button. The satellite's cameras showed some flaps immediately opening and balloon-like floatables and 4-5 parachutes unwrapping themselves and deploying in the open sky. The parachutes and floatables had to be deployed at 1000 metres or 1 Km, but they were deployed at 761 metres due to the slight delay. Gopiz was full of fear because of this. "Will it still work?" And yes, it did! The satellite's cameras showed the satellite smoothly and slowly splashing into the waters of Bay of Bengalia, and then both– the satellite, as well as the satellite's control panel in the Mission Control Centre hall– beeping in success. The satellite was now floating in the sea! On the other hand, all the 25 Russian Military UAVs landed safely back successfully on the runways of the ISRO Launch Base and got parked back in their respective markings on the asphalt paved ground where they were previously parked. Everyone was dancing and cheering like they had accomplished such a major mission– WHICH THEY ACTUALLY DID! Alex hugged the Gorba Commander and vice versa, but ignored Gopiz now. At first, seeing this behaviour of Alex confused him. But then he realized– the strong and violent push. "I am sorry bro! It's just that I was worried and super concerned for the IndWatch satellite, just like I was concerned for this mission and you! My push was more of a reflex action you can say."

Gopiz then apologized. "Huh! Reflex action? You're a robot. You could have controlled your actions!" Alex replied, still taunting Gopiz. "Well... Turns out we, this generation or version of AIs or Artificial Intelligences, have something inside us that helps us 'feel' something. Maybe it's just our digital limbic systems or some sort of neural system that allowed us to feel like you too. And perhaps my anxious feeling led me to act this way. Again, sorry brother!" Gopiz replied, kindly, cutely. Alex forgot his anger, and then hugged his closest robot friend, tightly, with tears of happiness dropping out of his eyes. Maybe it was the agony of weeks or even months that led to the level of happiness that was today on Alex's face. "Lessgo our Comrades! LESSGO OUR COMRADES!" The Gorba commander cheered and chanted along with all the other Gorbas, celebrating the BIG WIN!

They all headed to the Mini-Port of the same ISRO Launch Base, where Gopiz had guided them to. "Alright, so we're gonna tow and bring back the still floating IndWatch, and it'll take us around 2 hours for a round trip, 1 hour one-way." Gopiz told everybody. Finally, one of the Gorbas who went to check the condition of the Military UAVs came back to the group, and told the Commander– "Sir, these comrades are geniuses! Not even a single dent or scratch on our UAVs! The Mepamas' mounting was also done in such a way that they'll be easily demounted without much effort or any harm to the UAVs!" Alex and Gopiz smiled. The Gorba ordered everyone to give one more round of applause to both the heroes. And Alex and Gopiz looked at each other, proud of themselves and one another too! It was the time of 2:30 PM, and Alex, Gopiz and the entire A05 Team boarded a MarineJet, a kind of hyperfast jet-engine-based ship that was way faster than traditional ships that we know about today. That's why the journeys that were supposed to take 2-3 days would be over in just 60 minutes using the MarineJets! That was the level of speed of the MarineJets. Anyways, they all boarded one of the MarineJet with inbuilt capability of towing, loading or lifting using inbuilt cranes. Gopiz set the destination location to that of the IndWatch Satellite's location, everyone wore the seatbelts, the glass sliding roof closed and the vessel whooshed off. "We're just a pinch close to finding major clues about everyone's disappearance! Get ready everyone!" Gopiz motivated all the other Gorbas. Finally an hour later, they reached the location. They couldn't see any land or anything else but navy blue oceans with waves and oceanic hues with a contrasting large white-coloured satellite, with India's flag on it, floating on large orange-coloured balloon-like floatables. The label said– INDWATCH. Also, a blue light flickered slowly on it, and a small sound beeped. "Let's get to work, pirates!" Gopiz shouted. "Chill, we're not playing the Pirates of Laccadive game here..." Alex humorously answered Gopiz back. So everyone stood on the oceanic vessel's edge platform after opening the sliding glass roof. Gopiz used the crane-like machines to reach out to the IndWatch, connect it to the vessel's towing cranes, and finally the fallen, massive satellite was strongly connected with the MarineJet, and Gopiz instructed everyone to take back their seats as they'd head off back to the ISRO Launch Base. Once again, the futuristic-looking curved sliding glass roof closed, and the MarineJet proceeded back towards the mainland. On the way back while in the MarineJet, Alex raised a question that came to his mind– "Well, Gopiz... Can I ask something?" "Sure... Why not!" Gopiz replied. Just for context, Memobox was something like a computer drive that stored files and programs inside it, and it was the IndWatch satellite's Memobox that Alex wanted to access, to see the recordings of the earth of the day everyone disappeared. "Wasn't there a way that we could directly bring some Memobox-viewing computer to the IndWatch satellite in the middle of the sea, instead of towing back the entire satellite to the Base?" He asked. "There was, but if you were in charge of managing ISRO stuff, would you think it would be okay to just use and leave the billion-rupee satellite in the ocean only to sink? At least taking it back could open new doors like further research and stuff." Gopiz replied with logic. "But wait, who's gonna research? Other ISRO people are gone, for now..." Alex added. Gopiz didn't answer to this, as he realized this valid loophole in his plan. "Nevermind, just take it easy, lol!" Alex extended his statement.

It was finally 5 PM when they reached back. Everyone was eager to see the recordings of the IndWatch Satellite, but first they had to extract the Memobox from the satellite which was a complex dismantling process. So using a forklift, after they reached back their Mini-Port, Gopiz detached the massive satellite from the MarineJet, lifted it and loaded it onto an open truck, and drove that truck to one of the warehouses where there were automatic robotic machines for assembling and detailed work. Everyone else followed him, and he finally gave the commands to those automated robotic hand-like machines and finally after 1 hour and 30 minutes of intense dismantling of hard, strong and durable materials and components, the massive satellite's core object– the Memobox, was obtained! A book-sized golden and black flattened cuboid-like Memobox which looked small in size but was quite heavy, as bulky as an object of 5 kg! Gopiz took it in his robotic hands, and showed it to Alex. The latter's eyes glittered after seeing it, but little did he know that this was not an end of his mission, but the BEGINNING of a more Extreme, Intense and Adversity-filled journey! He was about to know something that if he knew what it was, would have never attempted to find out!

They all rushed to the Memobox-viewing hall, a super techy hall with many rectangular black shaped Memobox inserters, and they had a joint computer screen for display with them along a tiny touchpad for interacting with the screen. But it seemed like those Memobox Inserters were only for ordinary Memoboxes, because Gopiz took them to a special table, fully made of polished metallic gold-coloured zig-zag designs. "Wow! Is this real gold?" Alex asked in curiosity. "Yes. We got this from mining on the sun..." Gopiz replied. Alex stared at him in disbelief. So Gopiz completed- "Of course it's not real! We hardly get money only for our Space Missions, forget interior decoration." Gopiz made a funnily frowny face while saying this. "Anyways, get this inside and read it!" Alex told Gopiz, as he was eager to know the clues. Alex opened the luxurious-looking special Memobox Inserter by putting his finger on a touch switch, as Gopiz told him to, and the computer screen turned on. A tray-like drawer came out of the Memobox Inserter machine, with lights in it slowly glowing bright and dim, prompting to keep the Memobox inside the tray-drawer. Gopiz kept the delicate heart of the IndWatch... More of a brain with memories, inside the tray-like drawer, and the Memobox went inside. Suddenly, an icon appeared smoothly on the computer screen, with the label– 'IndWatch Satellite'. Everyone was looking at the large computer screen, Gopiz, Alex, the Gorba Commander as well as all the other Gorbas. Gopiz clicked the icon to open a list of folders, with different labels. He found the folders containing the past video recordings, and opened the folder. A software opened, and Gopiz navigated to the date Alex told, of the early morning when it was dark and everyone disappeared. What everyone saw was unexpected. A massive wave of horror impacted everyone looking into those screens. Alex's jaw remained open for minutes, for the whole time he looked into the computer display. Massively continent-sized dark spaceships, around 5 or 6 of them, surrounded the massive yet comparatively weak earth and displayed rotating patterns of maroon and bright purple lights in all the places of the earth. Alex started trembling and shaking with fear– this was something he saw in the CCTV recordings of his city of Capitrolis too. The IndWatch satellite was orbiting the earth during this point of time, but this view of the earth only felt that it was from a science fiction movie. Alex went to a nearby table, found a packaged water bottle there, had a few sips and came back. The lights continued to be rotated. "What the heck is this–" Gopiz said but suddenly, such a bright flash appeared on the screen that the screen showed nothing except massively bright white light that was tough to look at even through a computer screen. Alex and all the robots had to cover their eyes during the flash, and then after the flash... There was this weird combination of sounds- a deep roaring, along with electrical whirring and mechanical clanging and whooshing sound, and the spaceships began to slowly turn and go away, as if leaving the planet. "THEY'VE KI– KIDD– THEY– THEY'VE KIDNAPPED EVERYONE BUT ME!" Alex screamed and exclaimed in horror. And what a timing the Universe has for people, but immediately after Alex said this, there was this intensely massive earthquake and the Gorbas opened up their inbuilt shields to protect themselves, Alex and Gopiz. And suddenly, the entire massive structure of the entire building, including 4-5 floors above and the ceiling, roof and all the structure above of the room they were standing in, was thrown away like a football by a large mechanical entity. Six humanoids dropped down from above, with weird black shaped blades, gun and laser all combined in one weapon. "Mi Jecokrazitomre! Ewamspokerazi!" those beings spoke through their ugly space-suit masks. "Do you understand Gopiz? Can you translate?" Alex quietly said to Gopiz, with hands in the air, indicating surrender. "Negative. This language doesn't match any of the languages in my knowledge." Gopiz quietly replied. "MI BELONVIZSHI!" one of the guys violently spoke. "UH! UH! WE CAN'T– CAN'T UNDERS– WE CAN'T UNDERSTAND YOUR LANGUAGE!" Alex told them, clearly. "Tyaornmisto... Glem chauristo!" one of those aliens commanded his assistant, and that ugly alien, with weird mask just like all the other humanoids, threw something directly at Alex's head and even though he tried to dodge, he couldn't escape it. The thing wrapped around his years and head like a snake that wanted to hold his head tightly, but do nothing more. There was a weird smell too, and Suddenly the Gorba Commander ordered his team, "EMERGENCY GRENADES!" And a huge wave of grenade bombs were dropped near those alien-like beings. "Mi torenjha! Hahahaha!" they discussed and laughed, at least it seemed like. Suddenly one of them took out a container with a gas, released it just above those dropped grenades, and the grenades melted as if they were immediately melted by molten lava! The Gorbas didn't have firearms with them because they were in the Electrical Testing Hall, another hall or room. But Alex realized something... He could understand… He could understand what those aliens were saying… "Huh?! You guys can talk in English?" Alex asked those aliens. "You slave, we aren't talking in English, you're talking in our language, but you think you're still talking English– Hahahaha!" one of the alien-like masked beings replied. "You have to come with us, we're taking you to the place where we took everyone else!" another humanoid said, that one seemed like a more senior person. "ALEX! WHAT'S HAPPENING TO YOU??!!" Gopiz shouted violently. Alex replied, "WHAT? WHAT'S HAPPENING TO ME– AAAAAAAA!!!" He noticed that he was simply fading into thin air and his legs were disappearing, followed by his lower body, stomach, first getting converted into a white bright light, then flashing out and vanishing. And this all kept happening until Alex within seconds was completely gone from the Memobox-viewing hall, and found himself in a very uncomfortable and dusty room of something that looked like a spaceship from the interiors. And then suddenly it felt like the whole structure, or spaceship started moving and speeding up. "WHE-WHER– WHERE ARE YOU TAKING ME??!!" Alex cried. "In just a few hours… We'll be greeting you– WELCOME! TO THE ULZELEKAN EMPIRE!" the senior alien said."

"That. Is. Crazy!" Aryan exclaimed, full of thrill and excitement after hearing the story. "No way this will be real, but if this will happen, NDJJC will be the first one to predict that this might happen!" Rhea replied. "Yeah, only because I told you guys first! Hahaha!" William replied, jokingly, and then continued– "Anyways, it's night time guys, Mom's gonna call me for dinner, and she might get upset if I reach home late. Greater Kailash is quite far away from here… I might use the metro! Thank you for being wonderful listeners and for the tasty treat this evening of snacks and stuff!" "Wait! What about the next thing you just mentioned? Ulzekekan Empire? What is that?!" Peter eagerly asked. "Come on! Save something for the next time! Goodnight!" William replied, stood up and left the cabin.

Outro

So finally, everyone were kidnapped by those Ulzelekan Aliens, who later also took Alex with them, and who they are, why they did this, and where they took all and were taking Alex now, the answer to all these questions, lie in the next book- ME 2: The Empire. The Ulzelekan Empire, what it is, why it is taking away people- only the sequel can tell it all! So, the two things you can do now, is either make presumptions, or wait for the sequel!

Stay Tuned! ;)

About The Author

Akhil S. Vernas, whose official name is Akhil Sharma for now, is a young author who at an early age, have crazy and huge-level dreams. He for now is a visionary entrepreneur with bold, world-changing dreams. His small ventures, are just either started or growing- like Journeo, GraphiBro and KidsCast, but come under the larger group or collective entity of what he calls the Aks Corporation, though unofficial for now. While his crazy dreams like building his own country- Akstonea, are a separate topic, his stories and writing mostly contains works that are easy to understand and interpret. He believes in simplicity rather than so-called 'Expensive English' or 'Posh English'. Hence, though he writes very seldomly, his stories have the essence of easy to understand words and language.

If we talk about writing, Akhil loves writing since he was a kid. He once wrote a series of 13 short stories, called 'Peter Heffley Series', of a teenage boy living in the United States. He took the inspiration for that informal series of short stories from his own memories of living in the US, when he was very small. But unfortunately for him, those stories were stored in a smartphone that was later reset and all its data and notes (in which Akhil wrote those short stories) were deleted permanently. Now the Peter Heffley Series exists, but only in his own memories. Those stories had the experiences of the boy named Peter, who lived with his parents, and encountered weird cases, like an Underground World, going on a Vacation but with twists, etc.

In the end, Akhil wishes not to be passive in his life, but bring groundbreaking changes to the world by actively contributing to the human civilization and society, be it through his storytelling, his actions, his ventures or businesses, or anything else.

*Author's Instagram Account: **@akhilsharmavernas***
*Author's Email ID: **akhilsharmavernas@gmail.com***